SECOND BEST

by the same author
(Published by Secker & Warburg)

ALBERT'S MEMORIAL
HAPPY ENDINGS
WALTER
WINTER DOVES
SUNRISING
MISSING PERSONS
CRYING OUT LOUD

DAVID COOK

Second Best

faber and faber

LONDON · BOSTON

First published in 1991
by Faber and Faber Limited
3 Queen Square London WC1N 3AU

Phototypeset by Wilmaset Birkenhead Wirral
Printed by Clays Ltd St Ives plc

A CIP record for this book is
available from the British Library

ISBN 0–571–16484–6

For John Bowen with thanks

Lists

'My name is Graham John Holt. I am a single man aged thirty-six attempting to adopt a ten-year-old boy. And to this end I have been asked to write about myself as honestly as I can.'

I never cease to be amazed at the way in which words, which group themselves without any difficulty into sentences inside my head, sometimes emerging as conversation, sometimes remaining where they are as thoughts, become clumsy and disobedient the moment I try to write them down and cannot be made to express either feelings or information in any easy or elegant way.

'I am the only child of Edward and Enid Holt, who for forty years were Postmaster and Mistress at this sub-post office here in the village of Readby, south Warwickshire, where I live and have lived all my life. Since my mother's death from cancer eighteen months ago, I have been Postmaster. My father has had a severe stroke, and might as well be dead, but of course I do my best to keep him going and see he has everything he wants.'

The image of a helicopter hovering over the waterlogged fields of Northern Ireland remained momentarily after I had switched the television off.

I sat again, adjusted my position to avoid confronting my own reflection in the now dark screen, placed the tray containing what was left of my supper back on my lap, picked up the cutlery and stared down at the Lean Cuisine haddock and cauliflower, wondering if the two-thirds left on my plate could be safely frozen for another day.

I had put on weight. Short men should watch their weight. And the pear-shaped man I used to catch sight of in the wardrobe mirror could no longer change from pear to carrot for a few seconds by simply forgoing oxygen. Would it be better to freeze the haddock or to throw it away?

About nine fifteen of an October evening: I have the date ringed on the kitchen calendar – 21 October. Another hour and I would be in bed. I carried the tray to the kitchen, and on a list headed 'To Do' added the words, 'Decide about haddock'. Lists were my addiction, my way of moving forward, lists about laundry, dry-cleaning, housework, groceries, unanswered correspondence. By placing ticks or crosses beside items required, ordered, secured, by striking bold lines through tasks fulfilled, until the next time, next month, next week, next year, next reincarnation, my life progressed.

All my lists had headings – 'Wanted', 'To Do', 'Med' (for Medical, not Mediterranean), 'Stock Replacement: Shop', 'To Phone' (seldom anything on this one), 'Household', 'Cupboard Under Sink'. There was frequent overlapping between lists. I imagine that this is bound to happen.

The 'Wanted' list lay on the kitchen table next to 'To Do'. I picked it up to check the items. Tucked between 'bread', 'milk', 'tea-bags', 'something for lunch (ham or pork pie)', 'sugar', 'Chinese cabbage', I had absent-mindedly written two other words, 'a son'.

As I considered the list, pacing the room and chuckling silently to myself, it appeared to me that my desire for a son had come before that for Chinese cabbage, sugar, or even pork pie, but must somehow have seemed less urgent than the staples of bread, milk, etc. Was there, I wondered, a row of shelves at Safeway on which sat boys, school-uniformly dressed, priced by size, colouring and age, and with sell-by-dates stamped to the soles of their shoes?

The joke over, I screwed up the spoiled shopping list and sat down to begin a new one, but found myself unable to write anything on it. Even bread and milk seemed less necessary than they had.

I sat in the kitchen, engulfed in what those not raised in the country would consider silence, but which is not silence, for within the quietness of the room in which I sat I could hear the slow persistent ticking of the clock, the drone of an aeroplane many miles away, the scratching of a twig against the next-door neighbour's kitchen window and, far more importantly, the creaking of my father's bed as the old man turned in his sleep.

I already had one son upstairs. A seventy-seven-year-old backwards-forwards-out-at-ends-every-which-way father, who needed constant attention. No room! No room! One handicapped geriatric child was enough.

'Having spent all my life in this small, but now growing village, I am in a position to know and be known by almost everyone in it. I do not think the people of the village wonder why I have never married, because they are used to me not being married. I never have been married, and have always lived with my parents, and now have the responsibility of looking after my sick father. That kind of thing is common in villages.'

I remained sitting, telling myself that in a moment or two I would prepare a hot drink and take it to bed. I was a bit depressed, no more: I knew the signs, a little under the weather. (An expression I've always liked. What, I have often wondered, might it feel like to be a little on top of the weather?) I needed my health and couldn't afford to succumb to fantods and broodiness. Perhaps I should do what I very occasionally did, and take half of one of my father's tranquil-lizers.

'A son'! The idea persisted and with it other less pleasant ideas. 'They' would never allow it. I would be laughed at. The very idea was insane. Neurotic. Unhealthy. I knew nothing about real children. The village would be a May Day procession of snide looks from end to end. From Lower Readby through Middle to Upper Readby and on beyond as far as Shenington sniggers would be passed from hand to mouth.

Customers would either boycott my shop or arrive in buses to peer and point at the tubby little bachelor sub-postmaster who had tried to adopt himself a son.

By the time the church clock's version of 'All Things Bright and Beautiful' had given way to eleven sonorous strokes, I admitted to myself that the idea I'd tucked in between the tea-bags and something for lunch was not a new idea. A feeling of injustice, a sense of things being the wrong way round had sometimes swept over me as I prepared for my father food which I knew would not be eaten. Just as when young I had been told about the starving children of Africa who would appreciate the milk puddings I had found hard to stomach, so now I had begun to be convinced that some child, some parentless boy, would appreciate a fraction of the attention I gave to my father's welfare.

'My own childhood was one in which I was made to feel extremely secure and safe. I had all that a child can need in every respect. For, as well as all the material advantages an only child gets, my parents were a happy, well-balanced, affectionate couple, who had thought long and hard before embarking on a family.'

I had always watched them together, my own parents, studied their actions, movements, expressions, couldn't help myself. And they were so busy accommodating each other that they had often forgotten I was there, so that this watching was all the more easy. I can't now remember when it was I first began to notice the looks they exchanged, the glances full of a private meaning, and my father forever touching her or she him. They would place the backs of their hands together as they stood side by side over the washing up. Father's fingertips would tap lightly on the back of mother's neck as they sat at table. Her fingers would be tucked into the waistband of his trousers as they walked around the garden. 'This is all ours, yours and mine. Here is safety.' Everything achieved with one hand. Eating food, weeding, massacring greenfly, scraping the grease from plates.

It had all seemed very natural when I was six and they in

4

their forties, but at seventeen with my parents into their fifties and old for their years either the touching and stroking had become more urgent, more obsessive, or I had simply begun to observe them even more closely – searching perhaps for some guidance as to how I myself might be expected to respond to women. 'Graham John Holt has always felt the need for guidance in everything. Very little has ever come naturally to him', school report, circa 1972. My thirty-six years of watching, first as a child from beneath the table, and later from the shadows by the cupboard under the stairs, have done nothing to build initiative or confidence.

Of course they had touched me too. I've nothing to measure it by, but I don't think I lacked physical contact with either parent. Yet at mother's funeral, as I stared across the open grave at father's trouser legs and the large ungainly hands dangling beside them, and imagined those hands moving through the house like injured birds looking for a safe place on which to roost for the night, I remember thinking, 'It won't be on me those heavy fluttering fingers come to rest.'

Later his hands had fulfilled my imagined prophecy, had flopped without conviction on the backs of upright chairs, had clasped and unclasped themselves on the tablecloth as though attempting to relieve cramp, had hidden in trouser pockets, jangling keys and small change so loudly that the sound could be heard two rooms away. Those hands had built yet another bird table, the fourth, fashioned a new box for shoe-cleaning materials, mended one fence and erected another. They had assembled six model aeroplanes from kits taken from the shop, having first rearranged the entire stock, with the result that nothing could then be found and several customers complained that a bus ride into town would have taken half the time and been twice as cheap, had cleaned the house from top to bottom, built shelves where none was needed, scribbled endless notes to a dead wife, and posted them in cracks in walls, cemetery urns and even in the hollow trunks of trees. Finally they had removed the Cellophane wrapping from twelve ounces of double knit wool, rewound it, leafed through a pattern for a fisherman's jersey and had commenced knitting. Needles held close to his face, elbows tucked into his ribs, in imitation of the person whose presence he sought, my father knitted, though no self-respecting fisherman could ever have been expected to cast off in such a jersey created with such anger at such speed, and in wool of my mother's favourite colour, haze pink.

Grown up, already running (since he had given up) our sub-post-office-cum-shop, I had watched all this, not from beneath the table any more but from its other side, where she had always sat. Every room in this house is a small room, almost miniature, yet somehow my parents had achieved the knack of never seeming to be separated from each other by furniture.

A week after the funeral, I stepped back to assess the first vase of flowers I'd ever arranged, and realized what I was doing. I was rehearsing the art of moving fluidly around mother's furniture. Like a dancer given new choreography minutes before curtain up, I was concentrating on staying close to my new partner, always remembering to be one jump ahead, always expecting the unexpected, working hard to circumvent mother's tables and chairs smoothly and yet appear as normal as possible.

I would be standing where she had often stood, beside father at the sink, making small talk to disguise my sideways glances, waiting, watching a pulse ticking away in his neck, the sharpness of his clenched jawbone, the worrying brightness of his eyes, expecting that at any moment a cup or a glass would land on the floor causing an explosion followed by the collapse of stout parent. I held myself balanced and taut as a mainspring, ready to catch my father and give support. I had begun congratulating myself on how naturally I fitted my mother's metaphorical shoes. Even my flower arrangements were beginning to look more like hers. But when the moment finally came, it was as though I had executed the highest, most elaborate, most perfectly artistic leap, only to land face down in the third row of the stalls.

I was caught wrong-footed, out of step, by no means prepared. Every move I had rehearsed proved to have been wrong, particularly the final one of reaching across the breakfast table and clasping father's hand in my own in an attempt to stop his lower lip from trembling.

His collapse was total, more frightening than anything I had ever experienced as a child. Later, with father undressed and in bed and the noise of his wailing and keening from above still audible, I stood in my favourite shadow by the cupboard under the stairs, holding the cupboard door behind me half open for reassurance and staring blankly into the empty living room, while the doctor explained to me about the heart pills, the anti-depressants, the tranquillizers I was to give father, and how I must be careful that he did not become addicted to them. And those legs, which only recently had sashayed and side-stepped so expertly, had begun to shake, until finally, without warning or apology, I vomited on to the rug.

It had taken mother three weeks to decide on that particular rug and she had purchased it on the day before her final visit to hospital. Taken to the bottom of the garden, it refused to burn, merely smouldering and giving off an acrid smell which hung around the village for a week causing customers at the shop to ask whether my drains were blocked.

'What some of the people who know me do wonder is why I suddenly want to adopt a child and am I sure I know what taking on the responsibility of a young person entails.'

In fact the question most asked has been, 'Are you sure you really like children?' Usually, after replying in the affirmative, I add, 'But I'm not sure that I could eat a whole one.'

My regular customers have never been backward when it comes to giving advice. 'You should get married. Take a week off and have a look round Birmingham or Leamington. Find yourself a woman with a ready-made family if you don't fancy the idea of all that messing about between the sheets. And don't think standing there behind those bars in a clean shirt every day fools anyone. You need company and comforting; it's only natural.' I haven't stood behind bars or a grille for over ten years. Ever since decimalization, it's been reinforced transparent plastic, with a slot for letters, money, and bad breath to be exchanged, but Madge Brayshaw rejects all modernization.

If I still don't know what the responsibility of a young person entails, it is not for want of telling.

When I remember that first moment of discovery over the Lean Cuisine, it is almost as a moment of comedy, with myself pacing the kitchen and laughing to myself over the little addition I had made to my shopping list, because that's my way, to try to diminish what is painful by making a joke of it. But when I think about what I had done I know that I must have been a little mad, or at least desperate. Yet I did nothing more immediately about the discovery, and might never have done anything at all, if I had not seen a two-column-inch announcement in the local paper to the effect that foster parents were desperately needed in the area, and there was to be an open meeting to tell people what was involved. So I went.

Very few besides myself attended, and those who did all wore the expressions of people who had wandered in by mistake, and were really expecting a game of whist or a beetle drive. I took a notebook, indicating the seriousness of my interest: I still have the notes. The two social workers who conducted the meeting did tell us pretty honestly what would be involved.

There would be medical examinations, checks with the police and with Social Security records. There would be something called 'preparation' and something called 'home study'; the first seemed to mean filling out forms, the second was reading books and pamphlets. There would be group meetings to attend and at least six visits from a social worker whose object would be to get to know us – at this point a duffel-coated woman sitting next to me began to hum under her breath, 'Getting to know me, getting to know all about me. Getting to like me, getting to hope he likes me,' and shortly afterwards left the meeting. There would be letters to write – to the PPIAS if we were interested in adoption (I have it written out in full in my notebook, 'Parent to Parent Information on Adoption Service'), and to various Local Authorities.

I took some of the forms away from the meeting and also some of the pamphlets, and read them. The forms required truthful answers, which would assist in evaluating my suitability. Some were factual. Had I helped or thought seriously of helping with the local Scouts or Cubs? It wasn't clear whether I was to consider this as an alternative to adopting a child, or simply as a means of gaining Brownie points. Some were matters of opinion. Would I describe myself as a mature, stable, patient and persistent person. I could safely assume that the answer 'No' would disqualify me from any further form-filling. Which would get my goat most – lies? wetting the bed? stealing? carelessness? indifference? cheating? I was at first so bemused by the cosy middle-classness of the expression 'get your goat' that I was tempted to write 'coming home pissed and glue-sniffing on a Sunday'. Would I prefer the kind of child who yells, kicks and has temper tantrums or one who silently sulks when upset. I plumped for the first, since I have always been rather good at sulking myself. What did I most look forward to about having a child in my home? I wrote 'Companionship', and immediately considered that I had made an error, the first of many.

My life has always been one of routine, and it now began to seem that even the process of attempting that most extraordinary thing, the adoption of a son, would be reduced to routine also, with one plodding step after another along a course already laid down until I reached the point of success or failure, and that either would come as an anti-climax.

I was warned from the beginning that I would be required to write about myself in order to assist the Social Services in their evaluation of me as a prospective parent. It is what I have found most difficult. If there were any way in which they could bypass the distorting process by which thought is turned into writing by plugging straight into my brain, that might be more embarrassing, but easier for me, and it would tell them what they want to know.

Was I a mature, stable, patient, and persistent person? I considered that this was for me to know and for them to find out. I suppose, if you think about it, that I must have been at least some of those things. Certainly the whole process, from the moment I saw, looking out at me from the pages of the *Guardian*, the boy I knew I wanted for my son, to the first time we met as prospective parent and child, seemed to take for ever.

Outing

They had been told that they were to be exposed to nature, that they would experience the countryside at first hand. The parks and gardens of the towns and cities where they'd spent the best part of their lives up to then, not always constructively, were all very well, but were no substitute, the committee had decided, for the real thing. Self-sufficiency had also been considered important. Cooking their own food over a camp-fire would enrich their self-worth. The words 'tooth and claw' had been used several times by a plump and plummy lady who had once spent half a day in Epping Forest. 'A hill, a wood, birdsong, fresh air, fields in which cattle chomp the grass.' A small balding man in bi-focals said he had heard that these days the bulls run with the cows quite often. 'So what?' the Epping Forest lady had retorted, looking directly into the eyes of everyone around the table in turn. No one observed that October and November would not be the best months of the year to see cattle in the fields, either chomping or bonking.

They had driven for two and a half hours, singing along to pop music from a transistor radio, telling jokes, eating the crisps, chocolate and pork pies they had bought with the money given to them for their lunches. Now they were walking. They had left the warm mini-bus with the steamed-up windows, loose exhaust pipe and faulty brakes, and walked up a cart track leading to woods. At the end of the track, they found what remained of an asphalt runway left over from the last war. It ended in a turning circle through which a large blackberry bush had sprouted. A woman's shoe, three beer cans, two used condoms, and the discarded remains of a pornographic magazine had attached themselves to the thorns of the bush.

Already they were experiencing the countryside in both tooth and claw. Leggo grabbed the magazine and with the speed of one practised in such matters inserted it between his anorak and shirt before anyone except Pimple, walking behind him, was any the wiser. Forty-nine-year-old Eric, whose job it was to bring up the rear, to make sure that no one made a dash back to the unlockable mini-bus, and who was bent double under the weight of a double burden – his own rucksack and the fact that his wife had given him a rollicking in public before they left – saw nothing but the mud beneath him and his own hands, which he held out ahead of him inches from the ground in case he fell forwards. And tall muscular Ron from Australia, whose idea this 'outing' had been, strode on at the front in his bush hat and long baggy shorts, waving his arms, giggling to himself, and exclaiming 'maaarvellous' to every conifer he passed, as though he had never seen a man-made wood look quite so welcoming before.

Leggo, Rusty, Jed, Fang, Vernon, Pimple, Chris and James, they marched along a narrow bridle path from which the woods fell away downhill, further and further from the comforts of the mini-bus, a crocodile of eight boys and two men, no longer singing, hardly speaking, each of them carrying a rucksack the size of a Robin Reliant, staggering and slithering to keep their balance, as they collected thicker and thicker layers of Warwickshire clay on their shoes and icy cold rain dripped from their collars and ran down their spines to warm itself between their legs.

They were to camp here ten days, pitching their tents in a field next to the wood for safety. No fires were to be lighted in the wood itself, and any boy discovered attacking the young trees with some sharp implement would be returned promptly to the children's home and docked any privileges he might not have had docked already. Fang had asked publicly four times that he and Vernon be allowed to sleep in the mini-bus, but Fang had a police record for arson and the mini-bus, which stank of petrol, was considered to be more flammable than a young wood of spruce and pine in the wettest October for a decade.

The field in which they were to camp was below the woods on the same hill. In fact it was all hill, and a very steep one, so how were they to pitch their tents? They looked down into the valley below, where nestled the comfortable village through which they had been recently driven, looked back at the woods through which they had scrambled and slithered to reach this field, looked over their shoulders to the barbed-wire fence and the ploughed field beyond their own field.

'It's not flat, sir.'

'Well done, Chris.'

'How we gonna pitch tents, sir?'

'Some of us could sleep in the mini-bus, sir. I get dizzy spells looking down that far.'

Ron and Eric took themselves off a few yards further down the hill to discuss the forty-five degree lie of the land, and to look for possible flat bits. The only area within sight resembling flatness was back on the bridle path.

Eric said, 'I suppose we can't camp on a bridle path?'

'Not wide enough. Ramblers wouldn't be able to pass. We'd never hear the end of it.'

'What ramblers? It's raining.'

'I'd visualized enough room to have the tents in a circle. Better sense of togetherness. Easier to keep an eye on them.'

'This can't be the right field.'

'It's the one they've marked.'

'Who marked it?'

'God knows.'

'Perhaps a prayer then? To ask directions. Preferably before the light starts to go.'

'Don't get tetchy, Eric. You're here to enjoy yourself. It's all part of the great adventure.' Ron folded the rain-soaked map energetically, and began climbing back up the hill towards the boys, who had sat themselves down on the damp ground to wait for someone's inspiration.

'Up, up! You'll get piles. Right! Remember that picturesque little spot we passed at the end of the old runway? The one where Leggo picked up the filthy porno mag when he thought I wasn't looking?'

'That's where we pitch tonight.'

'It's all tarmac, sir!'

'True, Chris. And here was I thinking you were sleep-walking.'

'How do we bang the poles in, sir? And the pegs?'

Leggo suggested Fang's head.

'Only if the more traditional method fails.'

James, who had neither removed the rucksack from his shoulders nor sat on the ground, turned on his heels and began retracing his steps.

'You, boy!' James stood still where he was. 'You boy' never referred to anyone but himself. 'Wait for the others, and don't be so bloody long-suffering. This is a holiday. An adventure. Enjoy it.'

There had been another time, another wood. Not a thirty-year-old man-made one with the trees all in straight lines, but a natural one with ancient trees, gnarled and decaying. No tent then, just a double sleeping bag. Damp ground. And they had lived in a hole in that ground, a hole they had dug out themselves and covered in leaves. He remembered his father's unshaven face, listening and waiting for the dawn. Not a make-believe adventure that time, but a real one. Then, they had been close enough to the sea to hear it. Autumn, almost wintertime, not unlike now.

The pocket transistor radio, given to him by his father, had forecast snow and blizzards, and a man's voice reading the news had mentioned both their names. 'John Lennards and his six-year-old son, James, are still missing. The public are advised not to approach Mr Lennards. Instead, anyone seeing this man and his small son should contact the police.'

He had not understood why people should be told not to approach his father, had imagined measles or the flu, and had watched his father's eyes watching him. He had seen them fill with water and had decided on flu. Certainly both Jimmy and his father had shivered a good deal, until the warmth within the sleeping bag had soaked into them, and his father had fallen into sleep. He himself had not slept, not at first, but had lain listening to his father's breathing. Not snores, just loud heavy breathing, which had moved his father's stomach and chest up and down rhythmically. And with that stomach and chest, Jimmy's head had also moved.

What he remembered most were the looks. Very few words, for there had been very few. And the moment outside the school when his father had grabbed him with both arms and thrown him on to the back seat of the waiting car. His forehead had made violent contact with the door handle and he had screamed out in pain. Then he had seen his father's expression, the one that warned him of the dangers of screaming out loud, the expression which instructed him always to scream inwardly and never again to let anyone know that he had been hurt. And he had worked hard ever since at obeying that instruction given in one very brief glance.

Now it had been decided that he should be put forward for adoption. They had asked him what he felt about that, but he had not felt anything. So they had agreed to go ahead anyway, before he became too old, since, unless he was found a family before too long, he would spend the whole of his childhood in Care.

Before that, long before, he had made his own decision. Not whether to be nice enough to persuade a strange family to adopt him; that would be up to them. This decision had been about who he was, and had been made the moment he realized the advantages of being two people instead of one. It was not a decision to be made public. It would be a secret which only he would know. Unless of course he was ever allowed to see his father again. Then they would either share it, or he would go back to being the person he had been before his father was taken away, and he had come into Care.

Since then his mind had been over and over those last few days he had spent with his father. The old car being driven fast. Its shaking and rattling and threatening to fall to pieces. Its being driven through red lights, over zebra crossings on which people were about to step, on to roundabouts without stopping and around bends on two wheels. And the way he had sat, feeling the pain close to his left eye, and then later the warm dampness between his legs turning cold as he realized that he had wet both himself and the seat to which he clung.

For over an hour they had driven at high speed and he had kept himself clenched up tight, hoping the heat from the car would dry him before his father noticed, until finally the car had pulled into a lay-by where his father passed water into a ditch before taking a bag from the boot of the car and unpacking it, ripping open neatly wrapped brown paper parcels and Cellophane packets, removing pins and handing him new clothes to put on, new clothes with their labels still attached.

Long trousers, the first he had ever worn, so long that they had to be rolled up many times causing a heavy bulkiness around his ankles. An adult's trousers, stiff and thorn-proof in camouflage colours, Army trousers for the smallest soldier in a regiment of two. And a khaki shirt and tie, V-neck pullover, clean underwear and a pair of tiny boots which made sparks fly as he marched along the road.

He had stood in that lay-by on that country lane removing his school clothes while his father watched the road. And he had screwed up his damp trousers and underpants and wrapped them in the rest of his school clothes, and his father had taken them from him without comment, soaked them in petrol from a can, placed them in the ditch and set fire to them.

Then he remembered standing to attention for what had

16

seemed a very long time, his heels together and his arms straight at his sides, while his father bent down and looked closely at the place where the door-knob of the car had struck his forehead. He had begun to ache from standing so stiff and straight, but his father's face had remained close to his; his father's eyes had remained looking at his eyes and at the bruise. Then his father had moved even closer, had placed his lips against the bruise, gently at first, then with more force, so that it hurt, and had remained in that position for a long time, as though trying to think of something to say, touching the bruise with his lips and pressing hard. Until words were finally whispered, secret sad words from the warm lips of an unhappy man. 'Who do you love most, Jimmy?' 'You, Dad.' 'Always, Jimmy? Promise always.' And a promise had been given, never to be broken, never ever, on pain of death.

It was the second time his father had come for him, but on that earlier occasion, when Jimmy had just turned five, there had been no fast car, no hole in the ground, no long trousers. His father had appeared suddenly from the bushes at the edge of the playing field and had called his name, had been simply a white face among green leaves, calling 'Jimmy!', and Jimmy had turned, and had run towards the man in camouflage gear, and they had gone off together, but only for two weeks. 'It's only tempr'y, Jimmy,' his father had told him, 'This time it's only tempr'y.' His father had already written a letter to the home, which he posted from the railway station, a letter saying, 'I have taken Jimmy with me for a bit. I am his dad. I will bring him back,' and he had been brought back, as promised, after two weeks, and left in the playground from which he had been taken. Their adventures during that fortnight had been mainly make-believe. They had stayed in his father's attic room, with the toilet down the hall, and hardly gone out.

Every wall and flat surface in that room had been covered with some object which played a part in those make-believe adventures. Maps. Charts. Army kit. A wall chart with diagrams of knots was pinned to the wall: Jimmy had been instructed in the uses of a bowline when he had only recently learned how to tie the laces of his shoes. There had also been ornaments, brass Gurkha knives crossed on a plinth, dead bullets forming the handles of the two blades, and a Boer War officer's helmet in miniature, also made of brass. Even a primus stove had been stored beneath the bed, together with a first-aid kit, bandages and a home-made splint. This splint had been used to set a broken leg during their ascent of Everest. Jimmy had slipped from a glacier, forty thousand feet, and had landed badly. While the splint was being assembled and placed on his leg he had been given a lecture on the importance of remembering the correct way to land. The accident had happened on day seven of their imaginary expedition. On day eleven he had been lifted from the glacier by helicopter when they were a mere two thousand feet off reaching the summit. 'Just like life,' his father had explained, 'lets you get within reach of something important, and then dashes you down.' His father had even known who the men in the helicopter were, their names, ages and their hobbies. The whole make-believe adventure had been packed with tiny details such as these, all written down in beautiful slanting joined-up writing in a stiff bound home-made diary called the log book to be kept, his father said, for his old age.

But on their real adventure he had not kept a log book or a diary. They had abandoned the car and had started to walk, taking with them a large kit-bag and a small sharp spade. They had walked for miles, keeping to country lanes and bridle paths. His father had said they would catch rabbits for food, but they had failed to catch any rabbits and had lived on damp biscuits and glucose tablets, drinking tea without milk, made from spring water. They had dug a hole in the clearing of a wood close to the sea, had intertwined branches to cover the hole, and had lain in the hole inside a large sleeping bag for six days, coming out only at night to stretch their legs, to spend a penny, and to boil the water for tea on the small primus stove which had once lived under his father's attic bed.

No helicopter had arrived to rescue them and his father hadn't talked much about adventures then, hadn't talked much at all. The pocket transistor radio could not be heard inside the hole which had been their home. Only after darkness as they sat on logs waiting for water to boil, Jimmy could hear faint voices and faint music by pressing the radio close to his ear. Many times he had been about to ask his father what they were going to do, and each time had stopped himself. Traps for rabbits were set and reset, but nothing was ever caught. The tea and the biscuits ran out, later the glucose tablets. Leaves were collected and boiled, berries picked and eaten. Spending a penny became more frequent and more urgent, which seemed odd when they were eating much less. His stomach had hurt and he had cried inwardly with the pain, but still could not bring himself to ask his father what they were going to do.

On windy days they hardly felt the wind, but could tell the force of it by the rapid movement of clouds and the fact that they could smell the sea. On those days Jimmy had thought of fish and chips with thick slices of bread and butter, hot sweet tea and chocolate ice-cream to follow, had imagined round-abouts, swings and a big dipper, candy floss, and sticky pink rock with the name of a town written all the way through it. Where were they? All his father would say was that it was not that kind of seaside town. No entertainments, just a few boats and an ever-growing estate of retirement homes.

At dusk on the ninth day his father had left him, had been gone all night, and had only returned in the early morning, even more silent than before. With him he had brought a woman's leather shopping bag filled with parts of things. Part of a sliced loaf, part of a cooked chicken wrapped in clingfilm, half a pot of jam and a piece of very smelly cheese. There were also potatoes, which they had baked in their jackets in a small fire, an expensive looking tea caddy with some tea in it, a

19

bottle of milk and half a bottle of whisky, which his father had drunk slowly over the next four days.

All this food had not lasted them long. Being so hungry, they had eaten most of it that very morning, and their stomachs, which had pained them with hunger, now pained them because they were bloated. But that day and the few that followed, the days of lying in the hole beside his father while his father slept, were the best times he could remember.

His father never asked him to promise love again, not even on the last day of their adventure, when they left the wood as they had found it, Jimmy dowsing the ashes of the little fire and spreading them, while his father filled in the hole, placing a mat of dead branches over the whole area which had been their home.

They had walked to the nearest road and then along it, trying to hitch a lift. His father's only words to him then had been muffled and unclear. They had come finally, after a long silence, and were not in answer to anything since James had asked nothing. Only four of the words had he understood. These were 'Let down . . . no boat.'

Much later they sat in a transport café, waiting for the police to come and collect his father, holding hands in silence and watching the road, the traffic, the lorry drivers, who looked at them but pretended lack of interest. Jimmy and his father had watched everything there was to watch, so as to stop themselves from looking at each other. Then two police cars had driven on to the forecourt, and his father had said the fifth word, which was, 'Sorry.'

To have his father holding his hand, gripping it tightly like that, and in public, was unusual, and had frightened him. There had been no promises, made or asked for, no goodbyes, no more words other than that whispered 'Sorry'. And whether the apology was because he had realized that he was hurting Jimmy's hand, crushing it inside his own, or because he was about to be taken away, James would never know.

On the following day he had woken in a proper bed in a

dormitory of eleven other proper beds. The posters on the walls had been of snow-covered mountains, of the sea lapping against rocks, and of a fun fair at evening, with the lights of the big dipper and the big wheel reflected on the faces of children eating candy floss.

It was in that dormitory – others similar would follow – that he had first betrayed his father, had momentarily forgotten that special expression his father's face had taken on, the expression which had warned him not to let anyone know when he was hurt. It was there with the posters, and the eleven other proper faces watching him from the eleven other proper beds, that he had screamed and shouted and had wept as he tore at his proper bedding and the proper pyjamas they had given him, had shredded everything to the size of bandages, while the eleven other faces watched from their pillows, many of them alight with pleasure and interest as though they too were at a fun fair eating candy floss.

It was in that dormitory that he had first been told he had emotional problems and must be given pills. And after two days there, when the pocket-sized transistor radio he had brought with him from the wood had been stolen and he had not screamed, but had slowly and deliberately smashed the screen of a television set with a billiard cue, he had been given other, stronger pills, and been locked in that dormitory all day 'to bring him to his senses'.

One of the senses he had been brought to was that he no longer wished to be known as Jimmy, except by his father when he next saw him. From then on his name would be James. Another sense to which James had been brought was that for his own safety he would become two people. One of those two people, James, was the one who was trying to hammer steel tent pegs into crumbling asphalt with a stone, bringing the stone down deliberately on to the back of his hand, making it bleed and swell but causing no pain. The other was the one who had shared a hole in the ground with his father.

Abscess

'It's your own view of yourself we most want.'

The woman tilted her head slightly to the left. Throughout the interview she kept her head tilted to one side or the other unless it was in movement between them. Her chair was higher than mine, so that she had to look down on me, a half-smile teasing the left corner of her mouth.

PPIAS had advised me to write to more Local Authorities than my own. There are six Local Authorities within two hours' driving distance from our village and I had already been refused, sight unseen, by four of them. Post offices are required by law to be open except on Saturday afternoons, Sundays and public holidays – when of course all other public offices are also closed – so that for me to attend an interview it was necessary to arrange for a deputy, in this case Lynn, one of the ladies who come in on a part-time basis to assist me. So far I had kept my intention secret from the village, but it would not be a secret much longer if I had to take many of these mysterious afternoons off.

The County Council offices were built on the principle of a fortress, in which the basic construction of concrete and plate glass was surrounded by a six-lane dual carriageway in place of a moat. The car park was reserved for Council officers only, so I parked in a multi-storey car park half a mile away, crossed the dual carriageway with some difficulty, and made my way through computerized glass doors into an open-plan harem, with Muzak, huge palms, staircases of imitation marble and illuminated fountains of recycled water, in the basins of which goldfish swam. At the reception desk, a sophisticated

22

young woman wearing flyaway glasses and a wish-I'd-stayed-at-home expression directed me to Child Care on the other side of the dual carriageway. 'It's behind a derelict public house. Cross the temporary car park, go over what looks like a building site, and you'll see some Portakabins.' As I worked my way back across the ring road, dodging a couple of Ford Granadas which seemed to regard me as a target, I wondered what, if not children, could be cared for in the architect's wet dream she and the goldfish inhabited.

Her instructions were exact. There, in her high chair in the Portakabin, looking like Miss Havisham, with the dust from the building site drifting in through the ill-fitting windows, I found the lady with the perpetually tilted head, who informed me that, among all the other tasks I should be required to perform to demonstrate my suitability to adopt, I would have to write about myself.

'I usually suggest two possible ways of getting started. One is to imagine that you are someone else, a close friend, say, writing down their thoughts about you.' It seemed unwise to tell her that I had no close friends; they would find that out soon enough. 'The other is to begin by giving a run-down of how you spend your average day, a kind of diary. It's your own view of yourself we most want, as I said, but it's amazing how when you start with something as simple as "Seven thirty. The alarm rang and I got out of bed," you very quickly add quite personal thoughts.'

I had stopped counting the number of times the woman tilted her head from side to side. Instead I concentrated on keeping my own head still and wondered how one's thoughts could be anything other than personal.

'It's not an advertisement or a job application; you don't have to sell yourself. Something about your home and your surroundings certainly. Your own childhood and parents. How you see yourself. What you believe in, what you're hoping for.'

I had been conscious, over conscious that whatever else I

did or said in order to impress, my first priority must be to look whoever interviewed me straight in the eye. This is not easy when those eyes are contained in a head constantly in movement. I was, after all, an oddity, a single man in search of a child, and by now a single man watching himself so closely that even the simple act of crossing my legs seemed to have taken on some form of significance.

'Do your neighbours know about this ambition of yours?'

'Not yet.' If I could get through this interview and others, and reach a stage in which I was being taken seriously, that would be the time to let the village know, if it hadn't found out already.

'Does it matter to you what they might think?'

'They'll have to know. If I'm successful, they'll be his neighbours too.'

'Good! Good thinking! But what if the child you adopted was caught stealing or cheating?'

I said that children did steal and cheat sometimes. Not many in our village, but it had been known. The pub window had been broken, and bottles taken from the bar. The Canadian maple in front of the chapel had been vandalized. Other parents had to manage this sort of thing, and I supposed that I would.

The inquisition went on. How would I cope with sex education? How would I handle a child who masturbated in public? Or one who was verbally sexual? Did I like lots of physical contact? Was I a cuddler or a touch-me-not? What, on a scale of one to ten, did I estimate as my degree of security with my masculine role?

The lopsided smile twisted its way slowly across her mouth from one corner to the other, without ever covering the complete width of her lips. She was laughing at me as she watched me crossing and uncrossing my legs, watched me watching myself. I was a grubby little man attempting to procure himself a ten-year-old boy. How funny! I had always assumed that social work, with the bad press it invariably

24

gets, was the pits as far as job satisfaction went. Who could have guessed it would turn out to be such a hoot? She would enjoy the situation for as long as she could prolong it, and then reject me.

Did I consider that I had an open mind? Was I, did I think, capable of changing it? How sensitive was I to the feelings of others? Did I consider myself to be really in touch with my own feelings, and was I able to communicate them well? Note after note made on a yellow pad of recycled paper, while the woman's almost uncontrollable amusement was held down by these mocking movements of her head from side to side and the half-smile at the side of her mouth! How did I usually cope with rows? Did I remember ever having thrown things? What about religion?

How did I spend my free time, doing what, and with whom? Would I be able to spare time to answer a child's questions, encourage its interests, attend its school events? What could I remember about my own childhood? What did I suppose 'good parents' were like? The woman mimed quotation marks by lifting both arms into the air and twiddling her fingers. This was something I would later notice social workers doing frequently. Had I any useful experience in looking after the children of neighbours or relations? Did any of the children of my village have problems or disabilities? Could I imagine what it would be like living with a child who is slow on the uptake? 'What exactly are you hoping for out of this relationship?'

I had decided it was important for me to relate to another human being, fully and properly, before I forgot how – assuming, that is, that I had ever known how. That was what one was meant to do, what we were put on this earth for, what life was about, surely. But the answer I gave was that I was hoping to be of use to a child who needed a parent.

Time passed. Had I ever experienced my valuables or property being damaged? How did I think I would react if they were? Had I ever considered adopting a black or mixed-

25

race child? How would I attempt to help a black child who tried to wash itself white?

At the very end of the interview the woman took a bottle of pills from her handbag, popped two into her mouth, and announced apologetically that they were to relieve the pain of a tooth abscess.

Smiling her lopsided smile, she said that she would not be conducting my assessment, but that the department would be allotting another social worker to me, and that she hoped we would get to know and like each other and together form an ongoing and positive relationship, and enjoy our meetings as much as she had enjoyed the last hour or so. Meanwhile perhaps I would like to make a start on my written assignment.

'At six ten a.m. I am woken by the voices on Radio Four. By six fourteen I'm usually in the kitchen, filling the kettle. Or rather half filling it, since the plumbing system is old and noisy and would wake my father, but half a kettle of water doesn't empty the pipes sufficiently to start the tank refilling.

While waiting for the kettle to boil, I return the crockery I have washed and left to drain the night before to its proper place. My mother used to say, "Everything in its rightful place, and a time and place for everything." She was a stickler for order and tidiness, particularly here in her kitchen. In that respect me and dad were spoiled I'm afraid.'

Everything in my dead mother's domain, her centre of operations, in which she slaved to prepare nourishment for her 'two boys', is blue and white, even the air freshener. Her extra large blue and white striped teacup has been taken from its special hook, wrapped in newspaper, and is now hidden at the back of a cupboard. Photographs of her have been removed to a locked trunk in the attic, her clothes and make-up given or thrown away, yet still the whole house reeks of her not having gone very far. Could it be that, after a lifetime of order and tidiness, she has just popped around the corner

26

and is being made to wait in some celestial antechamber, before being called to her rightful place?

'By seven o'clock I'm sweeping out the shop. As well as being a sub-post office, we sell a variety of things – stationery, a little haberdashery, small toys, even pot plants in the season. We also act as agents, supplying school uniforms for the children at the local primary school and the comprehensive seven miles away.

'At approximately seven fifteen the post arrives, and I sort it ready for delivery. This can be quite interesting, since one seems to develop an instinct for which letters contain good news and which bad. Bills, of course, stand out a mile. But it's against the law to delay them or interfere with the mail in any way.

'Dad's usually awake when I present him with a mug of sweet tea and his first pills of the day, round about eight o'clock. The stroke he suffered has been made more complicated by depression and anxiety following my mother's death. They were a devoted couple, who had hardly spent a night away from each other since their marriage. And me being a late-born only child, I suppose it would be fair to say that I was a little over-protected. We were a very close family. What's left of it is still close.'

Sitting by the window of father's room, once my parents' room, with my own mug of sugarless tea, I will engage in a brief one-way conversation, since Edward's vocabulary now is no more extensive than the two words needed to name his dead wife's perfume. 'Blue Grass.' If there is someone in the phone box across the road, I will name the person and speculate on whom the call might be to. If there has been a frost overnight, I will inform my father of this. If there is fog enough to hide the hill opposite, I will relay this item of information also. While he, the man who taught me how to tie my shoelaces and comb my hair, leans with his back to the light, noisily blowing at the tea (the temperature of which I will have already tested on my way upstairs) before slurping it.

The weather conditions beyond the double-glazed windows are only subjects for conversation; they do not greatly affect either of us. Neither will be taking the car out, or attempting a long journey. But maybe soon, just maybe, I could well be making many journeys.

'You need company and comforting, it's only natural,' Madge Brayshaw was to say. Were company and comforting given and gained by those fully rounded persons I had read so much about in all the many pamphlets on adoption? Up until eighteen months previously I'd had both, after a fashion. I'd had a father and a mother, and stretching back before that I'd had a spotlessly sanitized childhood, with a change of Aertex support systems every other day. I'd had Sunday afternoon outings in the car, singing along to 'Sing Something Simple' from the car radio; as a family, we had harmonized with the Cliff Adams Singers. I had been a wanted, planned for, waited for, only child, a fully rounded 'gooseberry' to a devoted couple. In those days I'd had plans as well, not large plans, but attainable ones. One of these plans was to extend that safe sanitized childhood indefinitely.

On those Sunday afternoon rides I always had the back seat to myself, and with it the decision whether to sit behind father or mother, the middle of the seat being a no-go area. Once a choice had been made, I was not allowed to move. Nothing annoyed the family chauffeur more than an ambulant back-seat passenger obscuring his rear view.

The parched and cracked lime-green leatherette of the Morris Minor's back seat hissed with satisfaction when sat on. I had been convinced that this seat possessed unnatural urges, and when left in the garage too long, pined for the warmth of my bare flesh to be pressed against it. Icy cold at first touch, within minutes it became disgustingly hot and sticky, so that to disengage the back of one thigh from its surface while rounding a corner was to cause a sound similar to that of a fly zip being lowered, and this sound was invariably followed by a sympathetic enquiring glance from mother, and a request for a boiled sweet from father.

When finally, aged twelve years and ten months, I was

presented with the long trousers I'd given up all hope of ever possessing in this life, the by then deep and sharp fissures in the stained lime-green leatherette, into which I had many times sunk my exploring fingers, had reacted like a lover about to be abandoned, attempting to tear the 40 per cent Terylene/60 per cent wool mixture away from my bottom.

'Does he know where he is?' This social worker stood at the foot of Edward's bed watching him pluck at the bedclothes, his attention seemingly taken up by the window and the top of the hill beyond the playing field. Her name was Debbie, and she was a different and much younger social worker than the lady of the Portakabin.

I explained that I had no idea whether father knew where he was or not, or of anything which went on in the old man's mind.

'Would I be right in saying that there's a fair amount of bitterness between you two?' She moved round to the side of the bed, sitting on the edge of it, and took Edward's right hand into her own. I told her that it would depend on what she thought constituted a fair amount, and that I didn't consider myself crippled by it.

'Perhaps it's just your literary style, then. Every solution to a problem brings with it another problem in my view. I like what you've written so far. I'm just more practised at making allowances for people's lack of experience with a pen. The few who find they have a literary bent distort the picture in a more complicated way.'

I replied by saying 'I see', but I didn't see. Did she mean that I had a literary bent, or was she being sarcastic? This social worker wore large tortoiseshell ear-rings, a head band studded with diamanté, a denim jacket over many jumpers with a brief bottom-hugging skirt revealing woolly tights. Her make-up was outrageous – a pancake foundation the colour of blue milk, jet-black mascara, lip gloss of pillar-box red (which she may have thought appropriate for visiting a sub-postmaster), aubergine eye shadow, cinammon blusher. Her mini-ringlets were secured with coloured chiffon bows, her round spectacle frames were almost big enough to cover her cheek-bones, and she wore ugly heavy thick-soled Doc Marten boots. At what age are social workers recruited? How long do they train? This one appeared to be no more than an infant of the species, a teenager who had been at the dressing-up box.

The Infant Social Worker was trying to attract Edward's attention. 'Hello, Edward. How are you today? Are you all right? Is there anything we can do to make you more comfortable?'

The old man's head moved slowly from side to side, just as it had while watching his dead wife's clothes being removed from her side of their wardrobe. Since no one had asked him a by-your-leave, he'd protested in the only way he could.

Thinking him asleep, I had recruited the help of one of the women from the shop. We had just grabbed at the silk-padded hangers mother had made, and shuffled them out, drifting past the foot of his bed, with mother's dresses and slips wafting out behind us in a breeze of Old English Lavender and mothballs. I suppose we may have looked to him a little like those overpainted Barbie Dolls on 'Come Dancing'.

When we realized he was awake, Mrs Fenshaw had congealed into a statue by the chest of drawers, and I had joined her there, looking towards him and wondering whether to continue as though we hadn't noticed his concern, or to drop everything and run. In fact we didn't have the choice. A lady from Help the Aged was sitting expectantly in her van outside, having already made room for mother's things between a stuffed stag's head and a tea-chest of secondhand thrillers. By then dad probably thought we were standing there to judge the military two-step and wondered why we didn't hold up score cards. So he had lain there, moving his head slowly, as he was doing now, and later, when I'd gone back to remove mother's shoes from under the bed I found his eyes closed and there were what may have been tears on his cheek. I say 'may have been' because dad's eyes did often water as part of his condition.

Since my father was proving to be no more responsive to the Infant Social Worker than he usually was to me, and their conversation did not progress, I took her to the kitchen, where I had set out mother's blue and white china on the Formica-topped table.

We sat on chairs with seats covered in plastic of gentian blue sipping tea. 'I hope the house isn't always as clean as this. It must have taken you three days to prepare for my first visit. Can I see it a bit more rough and ready next time? I'm not from the Health and Safety Inspectorate, you know, and it is a ten-year-old boy you're hoping to have living here.' I had decided that ten would be the right age, neither too old to control nor so young as to require mothering and, in so far as she had been prepared to express an opinion, the Portakabin Social Worker had seemed to agree.

After tea we inspected the living room where the Infant Social Worker asked if I had my own memorabilia and, if so, might she see them? I don't keep such things as a rule, but managed to find several school photographs, identifying the protagonists for her, and she commented approvingly on the muscular thighs of the boy who had fielded at silly mid-on in the cricket team. I explained coolly that the boy, now a man, was unemployed and lived on the council house estate.

The money box in the form of a Negro's head, which I had used as a child, caused her to purse her lips and tut-tut, but she soon became engrossed in the mechanism by which the Negro's arm and hand, holding a coin, could be lifted to his open mouth and the coin inserted. 'All these should have been melted down years ago by rights,' she said.

I replied stiffly that the thing was an antique and that my mother had told me it was worth money.

'Do you really suppose they were intended to be a reminder of the poor and starving Third World?' I had, of course, never suggested any such thing. 'More likely that head is telling the thrifty British middle-class child it was given to what a drain the Third World is to the rest of us with our contraception and our so-called planned economy.'

Reluctant to get trapped into a political argument, I handed her my photographs of school drama productions. The ones she seemed most interested in were those of boys in wool wigs and grass skirts. 'Where are you on this one?' I pointed to a palm tree. Though mine had not been a speaking part, there had been a great deal of comedy business with Robinson Crusoe's dog.

'What are these boys you were at school with doing now?' I recited the names of three farm labourers, two bricklayers, a motor mechanic, and the school success, who had left the village and opened a theme park in South Shields.

'How many still live in this village?' I plucked a number out of the air. 'How many do you still see of those who are married?' I explained that, standing behind the post office counter as I did, I saw almost everyone who lived hereabouts at some time or other.

'You know very well what I mean. We've still got to establish if being a middle-aged single man sitting here in the midst of all this rural fertility isolates you, or if you have the kind of support system the adoption panel will consider viable. In other words, Graham old chum – ' She stopped in mid-sentence, noticing the expression on my face, then smiled and continued. 'Cheer up! It gets far worse than this. Think of it as a period of psychological pregnancy. You're being given time to fantasize about what it will be like to be a parent in a variety of situations. Said to be very good for you, unless of course it goes on too long.'

Though I can follow the jargon well enough now, at this stage I understood very little of what she was saying, but it didn't seem worth telling her so, and the Infant Social Worker rattled on happily as, I was to discover, she liked to do. 'No, what I was going to do was say the magic words, "Support, support, support, friends, friends, and more friends." And if you haven't got any, then get some, and fast. Start cultivating people. If I took your papers to a panel right now, what with your old dad up there half comatose and you and your lofty attitude to the world in general, we'd both be laughed out of the County Council offices. 'Cept that you wouldn't be there to hear the hooting and guffaws. It would be me who'd be losing any street credibility I had, and you'd just shed a few soppy ones and go on trying again somewhere else. Complete perfection isn't necessarily a good thing to present a disturbed child with, but we're a long way from that, aren't we, Gray?' (Nobody else has ever called me 'Gray', even at school.) 'Oh, and I'm not as young as you think, by the way. Nobody's allowed to do this job until their balls have dropped.'

I had quite forgotten that standing on top of mother's china cabinet there was a bronze figure, six inches high, of a naked pre-pubescent boy, holding above his head a tray on which mother had once placed her hairpins. The not-so-infant Social Worker spotted it.

'Well,' she said, with an emphasis suggesting that the moment should be cherished, 'what have we here?' I sensed that the question was rhetorical. Transparent as a breeze, she went on to express her interest in bronzes and admiration for this one. Statues of children, whether sculpted or cast, always fetched high prices at auction. Did I have any others? She would love to see them. Anything at all depicting children? It was just amazing, she explained, how animals and children were always in demand.

'No, I don't have anything else like that. It was my mother's.'

'Tell me about your mum. She must have been getting on a bit when she had you. Bit of an afterthought, were you?'

'My parents waited fourteen years before having a child. Me. Their only child.'

It was true that for five of those years Edward had been in the army and the army had been at war, yet other women had conceived while their husbands were on leave. And when the war ended, giving birth had become a national pastime.

My parents had apparently spent the mid- to late 1940s watching this epidemic of fertility with interest, had smiled knowing smiles at the sight of heavily pregnant women ascending or descending from the once-a-day village bus, until finally, nine years after the war ended, Enid herself had found it necessary to avoid the seat over the wheel lest the pot-holes in the road between Pencilwood and Bishops Itchington should shuffle her insides like a pack of cards, leaving her minus the knave.

Mother was thirty-five by then, father thirty-nine, old by local standards to begin a family. When, later, I had asked them about those nine years between the end of the war and my birth, my parents had smiled their secretive excluding smile. They had a routine, my parents, Edward and Enid Holt, of over-rehearsed speeches and tired family jokes, in which the dates of national and international events were dotted like currants. It was as though a loop of newsreel had become stuck in a home-movie projector.

'If we'd had you sooner, you'd be over the hill by now.'

'Nineteen forty-five. Mussolini killed.'

'Wasn't he thought to have called in at The Bell once for a drink?'

'No, that was Frank Turnstall in a bad temper and a pair of his wife's riding boots. Hush up! I'm giving the lad a history lesson. What year were we on?'

'Nineteen forty-five.'

'Correct. Hitler's suicide. Ran up too large a bill at Fenshaw's the Butcher. Then Hirosheema and Nagiwhatsit got themselves bombed just in time to save our bacon. Then we had VE Day and I returned home to a hero's welcome and your mother, who by selling her favours nightly up and down the Fairmile, had managed to save forty-six pounds and threepence ha'penny at her local post office, and make them a take-over bid.'

On and on it went. A wartime radio double act, with no new material and no laughter from a studio audience to allow them a pause for breath.

'Where'd I got to?'

'Still in nineteen forty-five. At this rate we'll be up all night before you've reached the contraceptive pill being produced the year before Graham was.'

This had been mother's way of reminding me that they could, had they so wished, have avoided giving birth to me altogether. It had seemed to me then that the contraceptive pill was neither here nor there, since they had managed perfectly well to delay my arrival for nine years without it.

'That's right. We waited. And when we didn't wait, we were careful. You were planned for, expected and thoroughly prepared for. And I hope you remember and appreciate the welcome you got. Everything decent and above board and no slip-ups.'

In fact my mother's memory was faulty, but this particular fault had embedded itself so deeply in family folklore it was never exhumed. True, the pill had been discovered the year before my birth, but it hadn't been generally available until I was almost six years old. A little late for prudence.

'Time to move on.'

'Nineteen forty-six. National Health Service Act, and not a moment too soon. Meg Thomas played Lady Godiva in our pageant and had a cold for the rest of the year.'

'She'd a temperature before she mounted the horse. Sweated right through her body-stocking in all the wrong places.'

'The horse went by the name of "Smiley" after that. Your mother was second in line for the part.'

'Understudy. I got all the goose pimples, and none of the glory.'

'Nineteen forty-seven, school-leaving age put up to fifteen. Coal nationalized. Wedding of Princess Lillibet to a Greek chap with a plummy voice acquired by constantly putting his foot in his mouth. Nineteen forty-eight, Gandhi murdered. More nationalization, this time Railways and Electric. Nineteen forty-nine, end of clothes rationing.'

'Nineteen fifty, Labour back with a reduced majority. Iron and Steel nationalized. And Gas.'

Gas. Much later, mother had lain on the sofa in front of the fire, draped in her pink nylon housecoat, sleeping away hours, weeks, months, between endless bouts of loud pro-longed burping, as the thing inside her sapped her energy, turning it into the gastric wind she had spent a lifetime suppressing.

'Nineteen fifty-two, George the vee one dies and your mother cries on and off for a week. Nineteen fifty-three. Trumpets sounded. Best year of our lives and me a mere slip of a thing at thirty-nine. Everest was conquered. Elizabeth became the second, and we all watched it on a thing called the telly down at the school. Stalin died. Sugar rationing ended. Piltdown Hoax was discovered, and an even bigger hoax, Graham John Holt, seven pounds four ounces, with a shiny blue scalp and a willy the size of an acorn, took twelve hours of agony to make it to his own coming-out party. The rest is history.'

'Whose agony?'

'History, all that pain is now mere history.'

She had wanted flames, 'It's tidier, Eddy. No slow decay-ing, shut in a box down in the wet clay. Just a little sprinkling of ash for the wind to play with, that's how I'd like to trip off back from whence I came.' Much nearer to the tripping off, she had changed her mind, and had been assisted in the change by my father's saying he needed something more substantial than a puff of wind to mourn. Good Old Steady Eddy, always handy with a chivalrous remark. And she had smiled and shrugged her shoulders at him, mere bones they had been by then. 'The plot by the lilac then, that dark red one by the vestry door. And no grand box please, it's such a waste.' Lilac, honeysuckle, any bush which smelt sweet, posted on sentry duty at the doors of all the outside privies of her youth.

'Don't worry!' they had said at the Cottage Hospital. Starched white faces above white collars. Unhealthy, blood-less faces to be tending the sick. What did they do with all that

36

blood they took from people? At every visit, while my father sat by the bed and held her hand, I had searched out a different face and they had all said the same. Later they had changed the message, still all in agreement but what they had said this last time was not 'Don't worry' but 'We're sorry'. Over and over again, 'We're so sorry about your mother.' I had never realized there were so many sorry people under one roof, all working for the nation's health.

This mass sorrow was in some way supposed to make me feel better about the pastel-coloured line drawing who was fading into the whiteness of the pillow. Nothing was visible of my mother in those last days but the deep lines of her face, its contours seeming to have melted, the skin translucent, the eyes so pale, only their quick frightened and furtive movement giving away their location. The flaky scalp showed through her thin white hair, which had once been wiry, strong and black. Her neck had disappeared into the narrow rounded shoulders, the body's reflex against too much pain. And the mouth, always thin, but expressive in mockery, had now become a quivering pencil line curving downwards at each corner.

I had remembered mimicking her grimaces, clownish expressions intended to punctuate her parochial humour, expressions of disbelief, surprise, pain, disgust, had remembered echoing her own warning to me that a bolt of lightning would strike, freezing the grotesque expression for ever on the face of the mocker. The only inaccuracy in this forecast had been that sudden bolt of lightning. My mother's permanent expression as she lay there dying, had been of disbelief, pain and disgust all combined, but it had not been placed there by any meteorological force in a split second. It had grown steadily, as steadily and surely as its cause had grown.

Life Story

In order to help people willing to adopt older children to come to a decision – 'older children' meaning those who are no longer babies – the older children being put forward for adoption would sometimes be asked to write about themselves. Any child unable to write would be sympathetically questioned by a Care Worker, who would then do the writing for him.

Most of the older children put forward were able to write, but they still required guidance, which would usually be provided in the form of a list of questions. Such a list was presented to James. He was instructed to think carefully about the questions, before writing the answers neatly on the paper placed before him. It was explained to him that his future happiness, or lack of it, might depend on the answers he gave.

What kind of new parents was he looking for? What were his hopes for the future? His expectations? When he thought about himself what sort of person did he think he was? Which did he consider to be his good points, which his bad? Most important, in what way was he going to make efforts to be liked, since only by being liked did he stand any chance of being chosen?

These questions were already familiar to James, since often the children were given such questions to answer in class as preparation: it was also – though this was never stated – to try to find out what made them tick. The stated reason for the preparation exercises was that the children should always be ready to give people who might consider adopting them a clear and truthful picture of what they were like. So they were not to write rude things or anything which might scare these people off. They were to concentrate on soppy things, like saying they liked dogs or horses or watching football, or that they disliked semolina pudding. Sometimes during these preparation classes the older children swapped their likes and dislikes. 'I want scuba-diving this time. You can have stamp collecting.'

No one told the truth and no one told everything. The fact and severity of their emotional problems would be added later by someone else, couched in language which would make these problems seem less frightening and more like a challenge to any prospective adopters. *'Needs resourceful energetic and patient parenting'* usually meant that a straitjacket would be required for Henry. *'A lively, robust boy with a cheeky smile, who would do best as the youngest member of the family'* meant 'Leonard is a bully who enjoys torturing smaller children.' *'Sometimes naughty when frustrated, but enjoys rough and tumble games with all the laughter and tears that go with them'* meant 'Rodney is an uncontrollable nasty piece of work who will tear your home apart the first time you cross him.'

It was called the Bungalow. You went there with your 'special person', your Key Worker, to draw, paint, make models, play with toys, bake cakes, or simply to lie on the floor staring up at the ceiling. You were supposed to say anything which came into your head; that was the point of it. The Bungalow was supposed to be like home, like a real home, except that although there was a kitchen and a bedroom with a single bed, nobody lived there and all the rooms were very small and filled mostly with kids' things.

You were supposed to talk freely to your special person, to express yourself; you had an hour to do that. Away from other children and other staff, you were free to concentrate on yourself. 'Free expression' it was sometimes called, but James knew that what things were sometimes called and what they

39

were often differed. An important element of these hour-long sessions would be your Life Story Book. You didn't have to work on it. It could be left unopened if you chose, but then leaving it unopened would be commented on and you would be asked why. 'Didn't you feel up to thinking about the past, James?' That was why you went to the Bungalow, to find out about what had happened to you and why, so that everyone could begin to feel better about it.

'Do you want to talk about your Life Story Book?' Bernard was James's special person at the moment. They knew better now than to assign him a woman. Bernard never needed quick replies to his questions and that was in his favour. He was about twenty-seven, with bleary sad eyes which made him look permanently hung-over, and still wore what used to be called tank tops and are now exclusive to Oxfam shops.

'Why?'

'Just thought that now you're taking this adoption business seriously, we should do some work on your past.'

'Who said I was taking it seriously?'

'I do have a small bit of news. If you're interested.'

Whenever the word 'news' was mentioned to James, another word came into his mind. This word was 'parole' and was really a word of Jimmy's. It was a word confined to Jimmy's mind only, and would never be uttered by James, who yawned, stretched himself, turned to face Bernie the Tank Top, and, in order to indicate the amount of interest he felt, placed his elbow on the floor and leaned his chin on the palm of his hand.

'Don't start frothing at the mouth, will you? I did say a small piece of news.'

'Bit. You said "bit". It goes in a horse's mouth.'

'Is that a fact? Well now, this information did in a sense come straight from the horse's gob, so shall we open the book at the "My Third Year" page, then?'

It was like one of those children's programmes on the television, with rituals and set rules. At each of these sessions it must always be James who opened the book, because it was his book about his life. The fiction was that it was James himself who wanted to re-examine what had happened to him. Otherwise the session would do no lasting good.

James got to his feet wearily, crossed the room to where the Life Story Book was and fingered the corners of the pages to count them so that when he opened the book it would be at the relevant page and no other. There would be no unnecessary trips down memory lane, no sudden flashes of anger or fear, no catatonic starings at out-of-focus snapshots, no jumping from James to Jimmy and back again. There would be no loss of control, just a weary, uninterested ten-year-old playing out the Bungalow game with a camphor-scented tank top standing too close behind him.

'Look at the page, and tell me in your own time what you remember.'

'Tell me the news first.'

'Then will you talk to me about this page?'

'Thought you didn't approve of bribery.'

'God, you're a bloody difficult sod to help, do you know that?'

James said, 'That's more like "free expression". You're getting the hang of it now. And yes I do know, as a matter of fact.'

'This page. You looking at it?'

'I'm looking.'

'Heavens for small mercies.'

'Well?'

'Well, we think we might know the name of your maternal grandparents. That's your born-to mother's parents.'

'I do know what "maternal" means, strange as it may seem. Can I close the book now?'

'No. You haven't said anything yet about that page.'

'What's to say? You could write their name down if you like and I could add some question marks after it. That suit you?'

'Read me what's written on the page.'

'You're joking!' James slammed the book shut and moved to the other side of the room, picking up a toy car from the floor as he did so.

Whenever they moved him, wherever he went, there was one question he would always be asked sooner or later. Sometimes the question would be asked in the form of a statement of disbelief. 'But you must have a photograph of her.' Enquiries would follow, letters would be written, phone calls made, and he would listen to the calls or be shown the letters. 'We have a very distressed young boy here, who has no photograph of his born-to mother. I wonder if you can help at all?' On and on it went. Those of whom the enquiries were made never could help, because there *was* no photograph of James's born-to mother, whose name and whereabouts were unknown to any of the authorities.

'You're nowhere near ready to start a new life with a new family, are you?'

'Who's going to stop me?'

'You are. You're going to stop yourself. No one is going to agree to your moving in with a new father when they realize you haven't said your goodbyes to the old one. I'm supposed to help you get in touch with deep-rooted feelings, help you take them out, look at them, and pack them away again. I have to know what stage you're at, or at the very least give a fair impression of knowing. I have to represent you and to tell them honestly if I think you're ready. I know all this seems to you like an exercise designed to upset you, but believe me, it's for your own good.'

'Gobbledygook!'

'You know what I'm talking about. You don't want to deal with the past because that would mean admitting what happened. Well, what I see standing right there where you are is not the ten-year-old, highly articulate and almost adult James Lennards, but a six-year-old who's just wet his pants and is about to burst into tears to get his own way. A little boy playing at Cowboys and Indians, and waiting for the cavalry to come and rescue him. You're too full of shit for your own good, Jimbo. Too full of those tuppeny ha'penny adventure stories.'

In the past James – then being Jimmy – would at this moment have experienced what one of his previous carers would have described as a rush of blood to the head. Instead what James now felt was a sudden tightening of his throat and stomach muscles. And whereas Jimmy would have physically attacked the person who had caused the blood to be so redistributed, would have thrown things, smashed things and would at some point during these activities have injured himself in order to impress on such a person the degree of anger and fear he felt, James remained still, clutching the toy car he had in his hands and looking towards the window, outside which real cars moved and real people went to buy food, exchange library books, have their shoes repaired, collect dry-cleaning.

There had been a blue dress. His fingers had gripped the hem of it. And sometimes his fingers would be removed by other larger fingers, the nails of which resembled large drops of shiny blood.

Her legs in black stockings had always accompanied the blue dress and had moved beside him, indicating the direction in which he should trot to keep up with her. At other times these legs were still, and he would watch them, waiting for any sudden movement which meant he must move also, must change direction to keep up with the legs. He could not grasp these as he did the dress, his fingers gained no purchase, and so he had patted them with the palm of his free hand and held firmly to the hem of her dress.

When he was not standing or walking beside her, holding the blue dress and patting gently at her legs to remind her that he was there, then he would be sleeping in her lap or bouncing on her knee.

She had said, 'Love me,' and had shown him how to place

43

his arm around her neck and to press the side of his face against hers. James could remember that these things had happened, but no more of what the experience was actually like than the smell of the make-up on her face, the smell of her legs standing or moving beside him and the fact that she had long dark hair. Not its exact colour, and nothing, nothing at all about the shape of his mother's features, or the colour of her eyes. He guessed that those eyes had been blue, since his father's were brown and his own eyes were blue. But knowing what their colour must have been had not helped him whenever he tried to reconstruct her face, nor had he been able to remember the sound of her voice when she laughed or spoke the only words he could remember her ever saying.

The words 'Love me' changed in his memory over the years. Sometimes he remembered 'Love Mummy', once or twice 'Love Mary', but at most times simply 'Love me'. Had she ever called him by his name? She must have. Why would she not have used the name she'd given him? Yet he could not remember with absolute certainty that she had ever spoken it. Which name would she have used anyway? Jimmy or James?

There had been times later, many times, when he had invented things for her to say to him, things he would like to have remembered hearing from her, but although the woman he talked to inside his head talked back to him, used his name (always Jimmy), gave advice, praised him, shared his unhappiness, she had remained a young woman in a blue dress whose long hair hid her face.

James no longer sought out this faceless woman who play-acted being his mother, no longer lay awake winding and unwinding a sample of blue wool and nylon fabric around his fingers or holding it over his nose and mouth, had not done any of those things for some time. Now, if he needed to talk privately to someone inside his head, he invented conversations with his father, whom he had no difficulty in remembering. And if those smells he remembered, of his mother's

44

stockings or the make-up on her face, came back because another young woman happened to stand close to him, he moved away from this real young woman in the here-and-now, or he held his nose and breathed through his mouth, until the real young woman moved from the here-and-now into the there-and-then.

That was the articulate and almost adult James; that would be *his* behaviour. If Jimmy had been subjected to the cocktail of memories aroused by such an encounter, he would have had one of his rushes of blood to the head, would have felt high, would have wanted to vomit, would have imagined himself shattering into small fragments. And as the rush of blood subsided, often while Jimmy was curled up in a ball on the floor, imprisoned by the large buttocks of an overweight member of staff, he would have seen himself free-falling through space. The words 'He's coming down now' had been used at just such moments, and these words may well have triggered this particular image.

The mere tightening of James's stomach and throat muscles could in no way be compared with the strength and variety of the emotions Jimmy had felt, but then it was Jimmy who had slept in a hole in the ground with his father and not James, and it was James who was to be prepared for adoption.

Nothing ever happened. The woman in the blue dress, whose name might have been Mary, was never found in order to have her photograph taken for her distressed son to pin on his portion of wall. 'Camera-shy', James would say, shrugging his shoulders and smiling apologetically at the people who had gone to trouble for nothing, and who were now making noises to prove how sympathetic they were. If he told them, as he did, that he had no wish for a picture of his born-to mother, they replied with even greater sympathy, saying that they knew how angry he must feel inside, and that they understood that too.

His anger, they had explained to him many times, would become dangerous if bottled up, and they would suggest he went for long runs or worked out in the gym, threw all his energy into a pastime, found something he could excel at. 'What are you really good at, James?' they would ask him and he would tease them, saying, 'There was something I used to do well. I was really good at it. It was a pastime, in a way. But I don't do that any more.' And he would rub his right thumb and forefinger together as though feeling a length of blue fabric, then cup that hand over his nose to retain an imaginary scent and, as he removed the hand from his nose and spread the fingers wide in the air to release the imaginary scent, James would smile his most charming smile. The smile of a conjuror.

In the street outside a large black poodle held one of its legs in the air and limped along on the remaining three.

'You said it came directly from the horse's mouth.'

'Did I say directly? I'd meant by way of a letter from a new prison social worker who has got your father to acknowledge that, if he's now willing to give his blessing to your being adopted, he can't reasonably object any longer to your knowing your born-to mother's name. Which was Connolly, Mary Connolly.'

'Maiden name.'

'Isn't that what I said?'

'No. You said "name". Mary Lennards is her name now. Maiden name's the name you have before you marry.'

'Once again I stand corrected. Perhaps it's all the window-gazing you're indulging yourself in that's making me forget-ful. Would it be possible for you to bring those expressive eyes of yours round this way so that I get the pleasure of them for a minute?' James turned to face the man who not only usually waited for replies, but was usually indifferent to having eye-to-eye contact. 'What I'm about to tell you is important, James. I want to know that you've heard me and understand. It seems that your father never met your mother's parents, and only knew that she came from a middle-class suburb of Bristol, not which one. This new broom of a prison social worker tried to get him to talk about what happened to your mother when you were three, but on that subject his lips have remained sealed. Now, I know he's never replied to any of your letters, but I'm about to write to him again and I'd like to enclose a note from you. I'm not going to tell you what to say, I wouldn't dare, but if your note contained a question about your mother, it's just possible your father might tell us a little more. So would you like to come over here, please, and write your mother's name in your Life Story Book? If you prefer we can do what we always do, and start by writing it in pencil.'

James began slowly to cross the room towards the man in the tank top, who usually waited for answers. As he moved, he started to recite what he knew to be written on the 'My Third Year' page of his Life Story Book. He did this in the manner of a six-year-old boy seeing the words for the first time.

'This is a drawing I did from memory of the house where my parents lived when I was born. It has a gate that won't shut and a chimney with smoke coming out. It has five windows at the front and five more at the back. The front door is painted red, but might have been a different colour when I lived there. I left there when I was three, and don't remember . . .'

Preparation

I saw the picture of Jamie in the *Guardian* on a page of photographs of older children hoping for adoption. He was the right age, and not mentally handicapped (which I might have found difficult to deal with) or black (which the village would certainly have found difficult to deal with), and he had a way of looking, a kind of reserved expression, a holding back from any sort of immediate commitment, which appealed to something in my own temperament. Or at least I thought so.

Another hastily written letter, another visit to a Local Authority. This time the bit of child care I needed was situated in a shop on the High Street between a butcher's and a newsagent's, its windows full of photographs of children, glossy ten-by-eights of Lisa, Sean, Jane, Emma, Paul and Christopher and many, many more, a whole cast of smiling faces staring out through the shop window at passers-by, like members of a repertory company advertising their talents and reminding the public that the show at the end of the pier changed twice weekly.

More questions. Had I been processed and assessed by any other Local Authority? Yes, I was just starting the process of being processed. Was I now applying, or had I ever applied, to adopt any other child? No, James Lennards was the first child I had enquired about. To my surprise, the fact that I was new to the game appeared to be a bonus. 'Sadly, it's often the most unsuitable people who persist, you see.' Would I turn out to be one of those unsuitably persistent persons?

*

'Something must have happened to you.' This was the Infant
Social Worker on her second visit, stretched out on the sofa
with her boots off. 'Something you've successfully blocked,
hidden away in your subconscious. Look, you're thirty-six
and claim only to have had one minor romance and no sexual
experience. That's highly suspect, verging on the psychotic.
Yet you appear to be reasonably well adjusted. How come,
when you've had so little experience of life? Now my rule of
thumb is to take more notice of what the client has done and is
doing than what they say. So I'm asking what happened to
you to send you scuttling inside your shell. It doesn't have to
have been something sexual, though that is the most likely. I
mean, for God's sake, what have you been doing with
yourself sexually since you were fifteen?'

I wanted to reply, 'Masturbating,' and now I would, but at
that time, my experience of the Social Services still being
slight, I was embarrassed and evasive. 'No more than what's
usual, I suppose, for someone of my age and background.'

'DIY?'

'If that's what you want to call it.'

'Hell's bells, Gray, masturbation's so unfriendly! I've
managed to fit at least one good screw a fortnight into my
busy schedule every year since I was sixteen, and you're an
attractive man. Why haven't you been more generous with
and to yourself?'

'This is a village where everyone knows who's doing what
to whom. I'm not saying we don't have the occasional scandal
when somebody's husband or wife asks for their letters to be
redirected three doors down the street. But even if that sort of
thing, with all its complications, interested me, which it
doesn't, I'd still have to be standing behind the post office
counter smiling every day, and that might prove a little
difficult if I'd been bed-hopping my way around the village
the night before. I really don't think I've experienced any
sexual or emotional traumas in my life so far, I really don't,
and I refuse to let you talk me into one.'

'Not even when you were an adolescent?'

'I can't remember any.'

'You must have been the only adolescent in Britain who didn't.'

She had mentioned sixteen as the age at which she had begun her own fortnightly encounters. I remembered myself at that age, a delayed adolescent, part-child, part-teenager, washing and bathing obsessively, squeezing spots and applying vile-smelling after-shave lotions and foot powders, saving secretly for a chest expander and sleeping with a handkerchief stuffed into my underpants to avoid the tell-tale stains of wet dreams on the sheets. There had been nothing any more traumatic than my embarrassment at my own sexuality and my lack of control over it. No shadowy older figure, either male or female, had seduced me in some dark corner of the churchyard or the playing field. I had attended socials, and had shuffled round the floor holding various partners, some of whom had been generous enough to refer to what we were doing as dancing, but none of them had invited me to place the uncontrollable bit of my body into theirs, and I'd been far too well brought up to attempt to gate-crash.

The silence was heavy between us, and was probably affecting my assessment adversely. The Infant Social Worker sighed. 'All right, so you have a very low sex drive. That's not as uncommon as the advertisers would have us believe. But what about emotions? What have you been doing with those? How am I supposed to convince my elders and betters that you're not the Abominable Ice Man?'

'By convincing them how sincerely I want to adopt a child.'

'And kill your chances by admitting that you're only capable of feelings when a ten-year-old boy is involved? Come on, Gray! What happened to you while you were growing up?'

'Nothing.'

'You really mean that?'

'Yes. Nothing important. Nothing I can remember.'

'You haven't grown up at all really, have you?'

'If you say so.'

'Haven't grown up or grown away. You're still back there in your infancy, trying to negotiate some sort of contract with your mum and dad. And what that means is that you are the world's worst bet to be an adoptive father. You know something? If I hadn't met you and begun to like you, I wouldn't even consider you as a candidate to baby-sit my stick insect. On paper you're a non-starter, a walking disaster area. On paper you have more minuses than the stock market crash of whenever it was. I'm not joking, Gray; I mean it. You won't get even close to a child at this rate. And I happen to think that's very sad, because my lower abdomen tells me you've saved everything up for your dad, and now that's no longer an option you could just be ready to give and give to a child until it hurts. For Christ's sake, Gray, give me something I can work with!'

The Infant Social Worker was a creature of the cities. She had grown up in Manchester and been to college in Nottingham. It is hard for people of her background to understand the life of a village or even a small market town.

The market towns of Banbury and Leamington Spa had not been at their zenith for the entertainment of young persons in the mid-1970s. Pubs there were, and discos too, and the music played in these was not that dissimilar, I suppose, to that of the northern cities, nor were the coloured lights which winked and blinked and pulsated in time to the music's heavy beat in any way inferior. What both towns lacked, when on Friday and Saturday evenings the older burghers had counted their takings and shut up shop, was any feeling of youthful excitement. Instead there was a studied, conscious and watchful air of merry-making, as if the young people of these towns had a fair idea of what they ought to be doing in the way of enjoyment, but could never feel certain that they were getting it right. The extravagantly made-up eyes of the brightly dressed and heavily perfumed young females betrayed a certain desperation. Tiddly born-again Teddy boys were too deliberate in their half-hearted anarchy as they threw beer cans at each other, urinated into the petrol tanks of parked cars or vomited against the windows of the new Marks & Spencer. Perhaps the relish and abandon said to be natural to the young were to be found at Oxford, where town and gown took their pleasures separately, but Oxford was too far away.

It seemed to me on those Saturday nights that one was either half of a couple or part of a small group of the same sex. How one single unit of a male or female group got itself promoted to being one half of a couple was a mystery to me and remains so, since conversation, even if one had been any good at it, was made impossible by the amplified heavy beat of the music.

I used to stand alone in some shadowy corner I had paid five pounds to occupy, guarding the pint of shandy I had timidly ordered and would nurse for at least two hours, and try to make out the words of the songs. This was not only my defence against boredom; it also allowed me to appear preoccupied and therefore not self-conscious. As the lights invaded my shadowy corner, turning me red, green, orange, blue, I would strain my ears, first to guess the titles of the songs and then to understand as many of the lyrics as I could. I never bought records or tapes of these songs, to play over and over in the privacy of my room in order to learn what Blondie, Silvester, High Tension, Police or Status Quo had to say to me, since I considered them a waste of money. The songs were mostly about love or the loss of it. They were about getting on down or getting right up, which I'd assumed in my innocence to be instructions as to how one should dance, if one cared to dance, which I did not.

Sometimes I saw people of my own age whom I had known at school; sometimes they were in groups, sometimes in couples. I never made any approach to join any of the male groups, far less the couples, and was not asked to do so, though I suppose some of them must have seen me, but I had not belonged to any such groups at school either so it would have been late to start.

More even than the Saturday nights I dreaded the Saturday afternoons which preceded them. From teatime onwards, father and mother would make remarks, intended to be humorous, about my appearance or the change in it which was about to take place. The moment I approached the cupboard in which shoe-cleaning materials were stored, the words 'brothel creepers' would be heard from the living room as invariably as cold ham salad was served for Saturday tea and its consumption followed by the checking of football pools. The atmosphere of irritable disappointment which followed the checking of the pools' results was what my parents' jokes were intended to lift, but they did not lift it for me.

Since public transport ignored the village after nine o'clock, I would drive my father's car to town on those Saturday nights. During the winter of my twenty-sixth year, I became convinced that my father and mother were following me into town by bus and spending money they could not afford on taxis to get home before I did, simply in order to see for themselves what I got up to while I was supposed to be enjoying myself. The discomfort and self-consciousness I already felt were made worse as I looked constantly over my shoulder and round corners, expecting to see them, dressed as though for a village social, attempting to camouflage themselves among the young, who seemed to be getting younger by the week.

My only excuse for this paranoia is that my parents' interest in what I had done and where I had been had become heightened. Had I spoken to anyone? 'Anyone' of course meant any woman. Had I enjoyed myself? I should certainly try my best to do so, since I was only going to be young once. (My parents were not so cruel as to suggest that the once had

53

already passed and that I had wasted it, though that was my own belief.) They had not expected me back so early. Should I perhaps try Warwick next week for a change? Had I thought of Stratford-upon-Avon? It was not as cosmopolitan, of course, except in the summer, but a better class of person was to be found there. And what about the Young Farmers? I wasn't myself a young farmer, true, but they must allow a few select outsiders in to their dances, and they did seem to be a jolly lot if the manner they got themselves dressed up for Lammas Fair was anything to go by. My mother once spent an entire month singing the praises of the nursing profession and left casually on my bed the local paper with an announcement of a forthcoming grand ball in aid of the Red Cross marked with a red star.

I did not join the Young Conservatives, the Young Farmers and their jollities, nor did I become a stretcher case for the Red Cross. For a while, I continued to arrive alternately in Banbury or Leamington Spa at seven thirty prompt of a Saturday evening, but now spent longer and longer sitting in father's car doing crossword puzzles and watching young people troop grimly from pub to disco and back again. Finally, aged twenty-eight, I was no longer required to endure my parents' jovial remarks about my preparations for Saturday evenings. I simply stopped making any.

The preparation classes were held in the community centre of a housing estate. There were to be six altogether, once a fortnight on Tuesday evenings; if we missed any, we might be required to re-take the course. The Infant Social Worker had warned me that the experience would be similar to a crash course in Car Maintenance, except that our subject was Child Development.

There were twelve of us, five married couples and two singles, seven units, removed as far from each other as possible on chairs arranged around the walls of a large under-heated room with bad acoustics. We waited in silence like children attending school for the first time; the palms of some of us were sweaty, the knees of others trembling; we all seemed to have lost the ability to smile without appearing imbecilic. Some of us had dressed down, others had dressed up, each of us with a different idea of what the ideal parent would be wearing this winter. The man nearest to me, who was talking a little too loud and too much, had already confided that it had taken three stiff whiskies to get him through the door and that he would gladly exchange all his management skills and his BMW for a higher sperm count.

Our instructor was Margery. The Infant Social Worker had told me I'd enjoy Margery: I had wondered why she used the word 'enjoy' instead of the word 'like', but wondered no longer when the instruction began.

Margery had brought with her from the back seat of her Fiat Uno a tiny cushion of amber velvet on to which a large 'M' had been embroidered. Holding the cushion in one hand, she stood, plucked an imaginary thread from the sleeve of her cardigan, and commanded us supplicants to form a circle in the centre of the room, which she then joined. As we stood there, shifting our weight uneasily from foot to foot and smiling our imbecilic smiles, she suddenly hurled the cushion across the circle and smote the four walls of the room with her name, 'MARGERY!', as if imitating a car-bomb explosion in a busy shopping precinct. Arms went out every which way to catch the cushion, all missing, and the woman at whom it had been aimed retrieved it from the dusty floor, told everyone shyly that her name was Anthea and threw the cushion back to Margery. Anthea, we discovered later, had some experience of encounter groups and knew the ropes.

When we had all revealed our names, growing more expert at catching the cushion as we grew more used to what was happening and Margery's aim grew less wild, she announced that we were the wettest, most constipated group she had met for a long time and that, unless we all stopped feeling sorry for ourselves and produced a great deal more energy and enthusiasm within the next forty minutes, she would either cancel the course altogether or change its subject and teach needlepoint. It was clear to all of us that this was what Margery said to every group at the beginning of the course, and I realize now that her intention was to bring us together, because the dislike which we all by now felt for her was almost palpable and made a bond between us.

None of us, she said, glaring round the circle, should run away with the idea that being given the child of our choice was in the bag. We were going to have to earn parenthood. Adopting was more about giving than taking and her job was not only to make sure that each and every one of us was capable of giving enough, but that what we were offering was worth the accepting.

'Droopy wallflowers are a waste of my time. I can tell by just looking that at least eight of you are still skulking inside your cosy little shells, and we've already been going ten minutes. You're praying I won't victimize or scapegoat you. Well, I will. You're hoping I'll sit down and shut up and show you some nice reassuring statistics, or better still play a video of *The Sound of Music*. Well, I won't. Any children who might – I say might – come into your lives, will almost certainly have been picked on. And before these evening sessions are through, every one of you will have been given the opportunity to know just what that feels like. Now, if there are any husbands and wives standing next to each other, they shouldn't be, so move. We have two singles and equal M and Fs, so find a member of the opposite sex you've never set eyes on before as a partner, and sit down on the floor in couples.'

The other single and I chose each other, and the married couples moved on the principle of a whist drive, the husbands going left, the wives right. My partner wore a kind of turban as a hat, and kept dabbing at her neck with a scented handkerchief. Margery looked at the six couples with obvious dissatisfaction. 'Very unimaginative grouping,' she said. 'Now, when I say the magic word "Give", choose quickly

56

who talks and who listens, and the talker do just that – talk – not about the weather, not about your favourite food or your political leanings. About childhood. Your own. Everything you can remember, from cutting your baby teeth to the sighting of your very own first pubic hair. You have three minutes. The listeners will then have three minutes each to enthral us all with what they've learned about you. I for one can't wait. So GIVE!'

'You'll have to do the talking,' my partner said. 'If I'm put into an embarrassing position of any sort, I freeze up.' Margery was already shouting, 'Come on! You've had long enough to decide. Let's hear you talking.' 'You see what I mean,' the turbaned woman said, 'I really couldn't.' So I gave her an edited version of my childhood, speaking slowly, and to do her credit she was able to pass on a fairly accurate account of it to the others. I told her so and she went pink with pleasure.

So the course went on. Margery's lecturing manner seemed to have been modelled on a Challenger tank, but at least it could be said for her that she never grew any more dislikeable than at that first meeting. She taught us about milestones, about how an infant of between six and nine months says 'Mama' and 'Dada' indiscriminately, whereas a child of eighteen months has moved on to use the words 'Me' and 'Mine'. We learned that the typical six-year-old is very active, but that the same child will, with any luck, have calmed down by seven. That eight is the expansive age, the age of driving everyone mad with riddles, and that nine-year-olds experience quick extremes of emotional shifts, but also like to plan ahead. Ten-year-olds, I was more than happy to learn, are relaxed, casual and like to participate in discussing world problems.

We learned about bonding and the lack of it. About how being separated from the birth-parents causes some children to appear old for their years, while others revert to babyhood. About the three stages of separation, first protest, then despair and finally detachment. 'Sometimes you have a child of nine or ten who's stuck emotionally at two or three, because during those first three years he may have been caught up in the Social Services' favourite game – pass the parcel – and may have been subjected to as many as six different carers. Now, most people can accept the idea of a child being emotionally stuck *as an idea*, but place before them a healthy, robust-looking ten-year-old who is wetting, soiling, crying, biting and screaming one minute and giggling manically the next – in fact reliving what happened to him at two – and they freak out.'

'It's all words really, isn't it?' the turbaned single whispered to me behind her hand at that first meeting. 'We could do with more practical help. They can talk about a disturbed child messing the bed until they're red in the face, but until it happens to you, you can't know what it'll be like, can you? You're on your owr, aren't you?'

I nodded, hoping she wouldn't persist. Margery might hear us and decide to draw blood. 'I guessed you were a single. No offence. Are you nervous? I am. It's all part of their plan you know. You don't even get to see a child until they've turned you into a nervous wreck. Then they expect you to be able to act normal while they're watching you. I've come very close to helping myself to one from a pram outside Waitrose just to avoid having to go through all of this. I think you're very brave. They'll want to know every minute detail of your sex life you know. Mine you could get on a postage stamp and still have room for the Lord's prayer. Not the world's best public speaker, is she? I'm finding it hard to concentrate. Should we be taking notes of what she says, do you think?'

'The child who doesn't express strong feelings may be easier to deal with in the short term, but in the long term, watch out! He's using the only semblance of power he has, the power to cover it all up. It's difficult for him, and he uses a tremendous amount of energy to keep anything from being revealed, energy that could be put to better use dealing with the feelings themselves.' It was 'just words' at that time, I have to confess, but they were words that came back to me later and must, I suspect, have done so to us all.

At a later meeting a couple of experienced foster parents were introduced. It was clear that the husband had not combed his hair before coming out, and he wore a sweater which had holes at the elbows. His shoes were down at heel, his face wore a world-weary expression, and he spent most of the evening biting a piece of dead skin from his thumb. Was this meant to encourage or to discourage us? The man's wife was a little more presentable, but even her facial expressions spoke of a life spent on the very edge of tears.

By contrast, the middle-management man with the low sperm count and his wife always dressed as though they were on their way to a cocktail party. Every ten minutes, this middle-aged childless couple made physical contact with each other and smiled. At one point I timed the gaps between these moments of reassurance and no gap was shorter than nine minutes or longer than eleven. Only once was this routine broken, when the alarm on the husband's expensive wrist watch went off and an extra contact was made to cover the moment of embarrassment as he excused himself to make a telephone call. Then his wife's smile subsided, her jaw-line lifting to denote the extra concentration she would give to the talk on his behalf.

Our first meeting had begun with group activity, and none of our meetings passed without some form of it. Frequently we were made to role-play. How would we introduce our newly acquired child to some old friend who was surprised to see us out walking together, hand in hand? I did particularly badly at this one, though I had been instructed, as we all had, that a child who had suffered emotional deprivation might insist on a constant touching so as to reassure itself that the new parent was still there. How would we enrol the child for a school where the headmaster had particularly strong preju- dices about children from Care? To the middle-management man this seemed to present no problem; he would just tell the bugger where to get off. How would we find out what the child really felt about being adopted? How would we know that it had been properly prepared, that it knew the true facts about its past and had come to terms with the need for adoption? I supposed that the children would be prepared as we were being prepared, but preferably not by Margery.

'The child will alternate between feeling powerless and powerful, sometimes within the space of a few minutes. It is unlikely to commit itself to you and your delightfully cosy home for some time, and will want to keep a contact with its last place of residence. A foot in both camps. If you'd been shuffled around every six months, and every time the music stopped yet another well-wisher had tried to unravel you, I expect you'd want to hedge your bets too. Some children manipulate their own reactions in order to terminate an adoption. Leaving a family is something they know, and are comfortable with. The idea of permanence is too frightening. That would be stepping into the unknown; they have never experienced it. It's hard to believe that there can be any stability to life when you've just been told at school that the ground on which you walk, the firmest thing around, on which everything rests, spins with incredible speed on an invisible axis; that in addition it rotates around the sun, all the while hurtling through space with the rest of the solar system. This is how a child thinks. How you must learn to think, if you are to be a good-enough parent.' The turbaned woman's eyes became glazed, and it was clear that she was having second thoughts, if adoption was going to require an understanding of the mechanism of the solar system, but Margery crashed on. 'Tough, isn't it, when up until now your major concern has been whether you've put enough coins in the parking meter.'

She really was a poisonous woman. I shall always be grateful to her.

Picnic

The man had brought tinned salmon and cucumber sandwiches and a flask of orange juice with lumps of ice in it. He was round as to face and body, short with short legs, and wore a light brown overcoat and brown shoes; he looked like a teddy bear. He had asked James to say if there was anything worrying him, and James, picking the cucumber out of the sandwiches, had shaken his head. The man had cleared his throat several times, had commented on the weather, the playing field where they sat, three feet away from each other on a damp wooden bench, and on the asphalt tennis court on which two fat middle-aged ladies, in thick track suits and headscarves against the cold, were playing their own version of tennis.

This man had seen an advertisement in the *Guardian* newspaper, which had stated that James (among other children) was available for adoption and that single men would be considered. So there they were together, he and James, sharing a picnic brought by the teddy-bear man and getting to know each other. The man's hands had trembled as he poured the orange juice, saying, 'If you agree, I'd like to give you a proper home, and look after you. I think it's time your life was a bit easier and a bit happier.' And James had nodded, not in agreement that the man was capable of making his life happier, but simply out of politeness, since James had decided that politeness, under these circumstances, would be his best policy.

The man had gone on to say that, if James agreed, they could consider it a kind of partnership and had then gone even further by adding, 'I want a son, James, and you need a . . .' Much, much later the man would be told that it was in his favour that he had chosen that particular moment to hesitate and to leave that particular sentence unfinished . . . 'What I mean is that you need somebody, some one person to care about you.'

In the gents' toilets, James stood at one of the broken windows, watching the man he had left on the bench fold the tea-cloth which had contained their sandwiches. The walls of the toilet were covered in graffiti – neatly written but desperate pleas for oral and anal penetration, explicit drawings, scrawled offers of comfort, excitement, companionship, guarantees of satisfaction in capital letters, offers of thrills, submissiveness or domination, love and loyalty. As the man on the bench zipped up the leather bag in which he had brought their picnic and leaned his back against the back of the bench to squint up at the watery sun, James turned away from the broken window and kicked open each of the four cubicle doors in turn. All the toilet bowls had been either cracked or broken. All were stained, and more graffiti filled the walls of the cubicles, into which small holes had been bored.

The man had said, 'A partnership will only work if it's what you want, James. During this trial period of you and me getting to know each other, I want you to remember that you have the right to say if you think it's not going to work out.' And once again James had nodded his agreement, having been told many times by many people that nothing would work unless he wanted it to, and that he, James, had the power to affect his own future. These people had reminded him that in all those foster placements which had broken down, often violently and with everyone concerned emotionally devastated, he had not always been the innocent victim. So let him watch it. 'This could be really permanent. A dad like you've always wanted. We've checked him out thoroughly, gone over him with a fine-tooth comb, and he's a real find . . . a gem, far too good for a difficult little sod like you. But we're feeling generous, so there you go. For Christ's sake, make it work!'

James looked at his wrist watch, and moved back to the window. He had experienced their 'checking out', their casual use of the fine-tooth comb before. The man on the bench sat in much the same position, only now with his eyes closed. James decided he would wait a bit more, give the man a little longer, just to be on the safe side.

He remembered shivering under a blanket because the pain in his stomach had caused him to foul his clothes, and they had been taken away to be washed, remembered lying on the floor on a cot mattress, looking at a world turned on its side. The floor had been dotted with other small mattresses which had earlier been occupied by other children. And he had watched a nursery assistant's shoes pacing back and forth between these empty mattresses while she chain-smoked. He remembered being lifted by a policewoman, remembered the words, 'I'd castrate parents who abandon their kids. I'll see you get the blanket back.' Other faces had come and gone, smiling faces mostly, but none which he had recognized. He had been found other clothes to wear and they had placed toys in front of him. He had watched many legs in black stockings and shiny black shoes coming and going and moving around him carefully, but all these shoes had flat heels and none of the legs had matched the legs he knew. Later there had been other faces. A carpeted floor on which other children had crawled around him. A bath in which he had sat while warm water was splashed over him. A bed. A room. A window. A woman, the first of many, all with either short fingernails, or hair which did not hide their faces.

When the second hand on James's watch had circled the dial three more times, he left the toilet and returned to the man who wished to become his adoptive parent.

'I was beginning to think you'd – what is it they say? "Done a runner"?' James nodded. 'But you hadn't, had you?' James

63

shook his head. 'What's it like in there? Pretty foul, I expect. I didn't think you'd want more food, so I . . .' The man gestured towards the bag under the bench. 'You didn't eat much. Is that because you're as nervous as I am?'

James turned his head, looking properly at the man for the first time, and then moved his head from side to side slowly, smiling his most charming conjurer's smile. The man looked at the smile for a long time, until James finally turned his head away. Then the man said simply, 'I see.'

Again they sat in silence, watching the two middle-aged women bounce around the court in pursuit of tennis balls coloured bright orange. Finally the man said, 'I suppose that's it really, isn't it? I've chosen you, but in order for it to be an equal partnership, I have to be the only person you would want to choose.'

As they walked back towards the Children's Home, the man said, 'I'd expect you to look after me when I'm old and decrepit. You do realize it's the only reason I'm doing this, don't you?'

Again James nodded, out of politeness.

Then the man asked, 'What kept you so long in the toilets? Have you got a bad stomach?' James shook his head. 'Why so long, then?'

'Can't you guess?'

This time it was the teddy-bear man who shook his head, and the boy ran on ahead and leaped into the air to catch an imaginary moth.

Lynn

'I have been asked to write something about my ideas of what makes a good parent, and how my own parenting skills would differ from those of my father and mother. The most important thing to my mind is that a child should be made to feel wanted, and be helped to become a person in their own right. And I venture to suggest that these things might in some ways be more easily achieved in a one-parent, one-to-one situation.'

At eight fifteen a.m., I take Edward's breakfast to him, prop him up with extra pillows and then wait while he runs through the series of facial expressions he uses every morning at this time to demonstrate his displeasure at having survived yet another night. I gaze as always at the deeply creased skin, the colour of newspaper left on the larder shelf too long, fly-blown with blackheads, now stretched to tearing point for my benefit, and wonder as always whether it would be possible to improve the quality of both our lives by giving him a good scrub with a loofah, or whether the closeness this would involve would only induce another collapse. Then I wait as always for the old man's good fingers to grasp the spoon and over-fill it with cereal, before retiring to wash, shave and finish dressing.

At eight thirty, I remove the breakfast, mostly uneaten, and shave the shaking Eddy. The ozone-friendly shaving foam blots out any late news-flash grimaces, leading articles on euthanasia, or angry letters concerning human dignity, signed, 'E.H. The Post Office. Readby'. Father's eyes don't register his son's closeness to him, even in this closest of close shaves. The old man's head lolls, sometimes forwards, sometimes to one side, as though it is about to drop off and roll away. I imagine the head descending the stairs one at a time, rolling out into the street and making its way to the church-yard to wait with vacant eyes for the rest of his body to follow.

His eyes are the main reason I guide him carefully down those narrow winding stairs every evening and place him before the fire. If they can't be lighted from inside any more, then at least I can watch the reflected flames dance about in them, and pretend for a while that his mind is still working.

'At eight thirty-nine on the dot, I unlock the shop door and take up position behind the reinforced counter screen. No one has held me at gun point as yet, or tried to smash open the safe. Pension and child benefit days are the busiest and Wednesdays, when travellers arrive to try and get me to buy things I don't want and wouldn't be able to sell. Mother was a keen knitter, and assumed that everyone else was. We still have large quantities of red, white and blue wool she bought to celebrate the Festival of Britain.

My staff consists of a pool of three or four women who live locally, who I can call on if need be, and one youngish woman, Lynn, who assists me regularly, part-time. She is separated from her husband, has four young children of her own, and happens to be a close friend. Over the past eighteen months, she has not only helped me with dad, staying with him if I needed to go out anywhere, but has also given a great deal of moral support, which it is only fair to admit was needed.'

Nine thirty-five. An amply filled coral-pink jumper suit can been seen arguing with the hand brake of a ten-year-old Ford Escort, before bouncing across the road and into the shop, waving both its arms in greeting, kissing me on the cheek and commencing to wrestle and tickle me. This morning ritual usually lasts between three and four minutes, depending on the size of the audience of customers waiting to be served. The larger the audience, the longer the performance.

'I've just been proposed to by the bread man. When you have children, Graham, you can't just sit around waiting for the ravens to feed them. Until you've sampled Wonderloaf and baked beans for Sunday lunch, you haven't lived. Sadly, I

66

didn't feel I had the energy for wedded bliss today, so I'll just stick as I am, and forgo the treat. It's amazing the way people react when they discover you're going it alone. You get offers of instant marriage from incurable recidivists, letters from unbalanced confidence tricksters – once I even got a grubby fiver wrapped inside a thumb-marked mis-spelled letter from a man who promised to send all the children to the best public schools and give me double-glazing.'

By nine forty, the giggling, coral-pink, one-parent mother-of-four is overflowing the high stool behind the counter and has begun her five-hour work shift, dispensing postal orders, Social Security benefits, TV licence stamps and advice on any topic brought to her attention.

'State bounty comes in many guises. It's just a matter of being able to map-read your way round the bureaucratic obstacles. If you don't waste away on the journey, you might reach the hidden treasure. There you go, Chucklebum, count your measly pension. I try to ignore money. It is, after all, the acknowledged root of most nastiness. Is that a hot-water bottle under your coat, Elsie Needham, or has that excuse of a husband of yours still not perfected the art of safe sex?'

Elsie Needham does not rise to the bait, other than to glance sympathetically at me from under her tow-coloured fringe as she leaves the shop. Lynn is allowed her ruderies because she is clever and confident, but Elsie has other compensations. Her husband may be out of work, but he's not absent without leave; he's at home, at 34 Bankcroft Road, the council estate on the outskirts of the village, available and eager several times a day.

I remember Colin Needham from school days as the boy whose shorts were always too short and too tight, whose nickname was 'Champion the Wonder Horse', and who, despite the holes in his vests, his badly darned socks and the dirt on the collars of his shirts, would always be saved a place on the back seat of the school bus. Colin Needham was the only boy in his class never to have spots.

While still in my late twenties, I had courted the then unmarried Elsie Bartlett for a while. It had not been love at first sight, since I'd experienced many sightings of her at school, mostly with dried sherbet round her mouth and her shoelaces undone. No, it was a matter of mutual convenience, neither of us having anyone else. Our brief courtship had consisted of many hours spent silently sitting before a small or large screen, or of going for equally silent walks together. After six weeks, Elsie finally spoke, but only to end the romance. 'We don't seem to talk much,' she said, and I'd had to agree.

Now Elsie crosses the road slowly, counting over the money she has just received in exchange for her Social Security giro, and enters the phone box, glancing at the number scrawled on the back of her hand, a phone number copied from a card in the post office window. I watch her. She is twisting the tow-coloured fringe nervously as she speaks into the mouthpiece. The conversation would be about a second-hand pram. Elsie and Colin Needham found things to talk about; they had their compensations, three and a half at the last count. And they're still young.

At the end of the day, when Lynn and I are alone, checking each other's figures, I broach the subject of adoption and receive her encouragement.

'Course you're going to fail. To grumble, to mismanage the housekeeping and forget to send the kid to school with plimsolls on PE day. It's a nine-day working week with children. You just have to get up two hours earlier than you're used to, Vim the bath out with cold water, boil eggs in the kettle, and start the day with the biggest grin your mouth will stretch to, hoping it'll last. Small chores gather in battalions either to bear you ahead of them or crush you underfoot. The choice is yours. Important to look outwards, Graham, not inwards, even though you seem to find the latter more comfortable. Important to be tranquil, which you are, presentable, which you are, and above all interesting. You've got

68

nine twenty-pound POs marked here. I make it eleven. Now, what was I talking about?'

'I've got to be tranquil, presentable and interesting.'

'Right! And, of course, the bread-winner. You've also got to get used to being emotionally lopsided. Children draw on you; if they didn't, you'd have even more problems. But who can you draw on? At least you won't have anybody coming home knackered at six o'clock to fall over the toys in the hall and disapprove of your mothering. That's one of the things I like about running my own show, that and not sharing with another female. There was this woman once, who sat cross-legged on the floor all day, serenely practising day-starvation – followed by noisy midnight fry ups. I wouldn't have minded, but she never did a stroke of washing up. Said she couldn't function in the mornings, being so guilt-ridden. Another thing I like is buying Weetabix with money I've earned myself; it's a completely different thrill from buying it with reluctantly doled out housekeeping, maintenance, or even a cashed welfare chit. Hello! – I don't agree with this either, I can only find twenty TV licence stamps, you've got twenty-one down here. Most of the fight for maintenance isn't worth the personal wear and tear. Heard in Chambers where all judges seem to speak in whispers, and you're always placed right at the other end of the room so as not to contaminate them; the poor are terribly prone to germs. Now, what else do you need to know? They wouldn't give you a baby to look after, would they? No, that'd be daft. Think yourself lucky. Babies, Graham, do not make good room-mates. They set the neighbours' teeth on edge, for one thing. And forget all that crap about them giving off a new-born smell which adults just can't resist. Forget motherly instincts; there's not a lot to choose between your own kid's waste matter and that of its peers. What is true is that it reeks the place out from sparrow-fart to breakfast time. Oh, and while we're on the subject of your motherly instincts, you do have another option with Edward, you know. I don't suppose you've ever thought of it, but it's there. Might spoil your chances of adoption though, to have just plonked your old dad in a geriatric ward or a home, like the one over at Memmerley, where they hose them down every morning and chase them around the grounds to dry off. On the other hand, it might not. Don't suppose being over-sentimental wins many credit points when it comes to rearing sprogs. And for all you know, Edward's just as sick of you as you are of him. Is that it, then? Can I go home to my little orphans now?'

'I'm not sick of him, Lynn. That's part of the problem; I'm not anything of him. It's no great hardship looking after him.'

'No great pleasure, either.'

'Wouldn't someone who gained great pleasure in spoon-feeding and changing his parent be rather suspect?'

'Absolutely. So why does it bother you that you don't feel anything?'

During the Infant Social Worker's third visit, I took her on a tour of the village amenities and the school which I had attended, and where, I supposed, any child I adopted would probably be sent.

'James Lennards? Hardly. He's ten now. He'll be eleven by the time you get him. If you get him.'

'Oh! . . . Perhaps we'd better take a look at the local comprehensive. It's five miles away. The village children go by bus.'

'Save it. My feet hurt. Actually you've given me an idea. He'll have to change schools anyway at eleven. If the adopting process lumbers on at its usual speed, he'll do a term at the comprehensive near the children's home, then get uprooted and have to start all over again at yours. Stupid! And bound to unsettle him, right?'

'Right!'

'Maybe, if things are going well, and you haven't blotted any copybooks or gone in head first at the water jump, it would be better for you to start off as his foster parent –

fostering with a view to adoption – and he comes to you some time in the summer holidays – say August – I'm thinking on my feet here – '

'You do it very well.'

'Then he starts at the local comprehensive school in September, and by the time the adoption is final he's already settled in, right?'

'Right!'

'Now, don't get your balls in an uproar, Gray. All sorts of things can go wrong. You could still fall at some fence, and there's a whole series of week-end visits to come, during which the two of you could go off each other spectacularly, but it might be something to work towards.'

'Yes, it might.'

'I'll suggest it. It'll have to go through channels. It's the common-sense way, but that's not how the Social Services usually work – or any Government department, come to that. We'll see. Anyway, that's not what I really want to talk to you about.'

What she did really want to talk to me about was what Lynn had also really wanted to talk to me about, and the course of action she felt herself bound to suggest was the course of action Lynn had already suggested.

'How do you know you're giving Edward better care than he could get somewhere else?'

'Ah, the magic "somewhere else"!'

'Does he know where he is now?'

'I've no way of telling.'

'Does he respond to you personally?'

'He responds as best he can.'

'Does he? Are you sure? Isn't it true that your friend Lynn has a little more success at getting him to do things?'

'He was never a man's man.'

'Certainly not this man's. The stroke was the ultimate rejection, wasn't it? – his final statement to you? Ever since you can remember you've been trying to get on terms with

71

him, right? Trying to form a close emotional relationship. And he blocked you at every turn, didn't he? Your parents had each other and nobody, not even you, was going to be allowed to threaten that. Then suddenly there's just him and you, and he's terrified because you're starting to get cosy with him. You were even showing every indication that you actually loved him. I mean! Your own father for God's sake! Now that called for something drastic.'

Snaps

In the Bungalow the teddy-bear man chose to sit on a large orange bean bag. It was rarely used, and reacted noisily to his weight, and, as he sank lower and lower, took its time to adjust and remould itself around him. When the process of adjustment had been completed, it was clear to James that the man's knees were closer to his chin than they were used to being, and that the man himself was already regretting his attempt at casualness.

The man had brought with him (because he had been asked to do so, James supposed) a snapshot album, three boxes of coloured slides and a small slide viewer. These were for James to look at. What the man had to look at was James's Life Story Book, handed to him by Bernie the Tank Top.

'I thought this would be the best way of your getting to know each other. While you look through what we have of James's past, he looks at what you've compiled about yourself. James, as you know, doesn't like talking about his Life Story Book, but he has agreed, after a little pressure, to your seeing it and to you and me discussing it.'

The man stared blankly at the object on his lap, which was not a book at all but a loose-leaf file with very few pages, while Bernie the Tank Top chatted on about his sense of responsibility to James as James's Key Worker. Bernie supposed that he knew James as well, if not better, than anyone, and although James couldn't see that everything being done was being done in James's best interests, Bernie had been long enough in Child Care to know that no relationship could work unless each party knew as much as there was to know about each other, the very worst as well as the very best.

The man opened the file, and began to look at its contents. The first page was blank apart from the words 'No birth certificate'. The next seven pages, one for every year of James's life in Care, contained photographs of foster families and Care Workers. Another set of pages had maps indicating where he had been born and where he had lived – nurseries, children's homes, short-term placements in foster homes and other placements which had been intended to be long term, but which had, to use the word currently in vogue, 'disrupted'.

These pages were neat, compiled almost like a school exercise, the photographs and maps captioned in capital letters, which had first been written in pencil and then the pencil letters traced over with a black felt-tipped pen. But the next page, containing what little was known of James's family tree, showed signs of individuality and strong feeling. The black pen had scrawled angrily over the neatly pencilled heading, making the words much larger, and the words themselves 'My First Family' had been underlined several times.

In the centre of the page, enclosed in what the wielder of the pencil had intended to be a neatly drawn rectangle, but which the black pen had changed to a coffin shape, were the words, 'James Lennards. Born 12/3/81?' and above that, not traced over but left in pencil, 'Mother: Mary Connolly. Born ? Father: John Lennards. Born ?' A vertical line upwards from the word 'Mother' led to the names of her parents, James's maternal grandparents, also 'Connolly', with question marks where their forenames should be. Why did these grandparents lack forenames, and why had they not taken James to live with them?

There were no snapshots of James Lennards's mother on any of the pages of his Life Story Book, and the only picture of his born-to father had been cut from a newspaper and was smudged, yellowed and torn, and the torn parts patched with Sellotape to prevent them from tearing further. Although smudged, it was clearly the picture of an extremely handsome man. Instead of a vertical line above the name of John Lennards, there was a neat circle of question marks and inside that the word 'Orphan'.

The bottom half of the page was similar to the top, except that here were written the names of foster parents and their children, either born-to, adopted, or merely others who were being fostered. These were people who had tried to make a home for James, their names, dates of birth and occupations set out in the order that he had stayed with each family, giving the date of his arrival and the date he had left.

Watched overtly by Bernie the Tank Top and covertly by James, the teddy-bear man looked carefully at each page. It seemed as if he were expected to comment, but whatever his comments might be, he kept them to himself. Finally he said, 'It's just a scrapbook, really, isn't it?' and Bernie replied, 'That's one way of describing it. For obvious reasons, we don't call what – with help from us – the children put together about themselves "scrapbooks", but that has to be the principle on which they're compiled because no Life Story Book can ever be the whole story. It depends how much one can discover, and if you're working with a reluctant subject, such as we have in Jimbo here, your hands are tied, so to speak.'

The teddy-bear man said, 'Well, mine's just a photograph album. That's not even a scrapbook,' and, thus prompted, James began to manifest an interest in it.

The album contained glued-in snapshots of the man himself and his parents. In many of the snapshots the group of three was standing beside or peering from the windows of a lime-green Morris Minor parked in various lay-bys. The colour slides were of the same three people. James looked first at the snapshots and then at the slides, and found no other human beings depicted. Neatly printed at the bottom of each snapshot and slide were the names of the people and the places where the photographs had been taken. 'Mother, Father, Me aged 7. Bibery Trout Farm.' The elderly couple were almost always holding hands or had their arms around each other, and the child was almost always standing a little apart. Who had taken the pictures? James knew that he should attempt to appear interested in the man and his past life, so he decided to ask, 'Who took this one?'

The man rose with some difficulty from the bean bag, took the viewer and looked at the slide. 'That one was done with a timer, I think. Or sometimes we'd just ask a passer-by to click it. My father had a thing about all three of us being in every photo, not leaving anyone out. He said he was superstitious about it.'

James nodded and said, 'Like wishing somebody's death.'

'Yes. A bit like that, I suppose.' Having shown an interest and engaged in con ersation, James returned his attention to the viewer and the slides.

'They're rather boring and badly taken. You don't have to look at them all.'

James smiled and said, 'This one's over-exposed. You look like three ghosts.'

Reassured by James's smile, the teddy-bear man also smiled and Bernie the Tank Top smiled to see them smiling. It was all going swimmingly. The man said, 'We were, and still are, a very ordinary family, Jamie. I think it probably takes some flair and initiative to be a ghost.'

There was silence for several minutes while James continued to occupy himself with the viewer. Then he said, 'You might have been an ordinary family once, but you're not now.'

Was this loaded in some way? The man looked towards Bernie the Tank Top, who gave him no clue as to how he should reply. 'No. You're right. If I were to succeed in fostering you with a view to adoption, then we'd be a most unusual family.'

'And even if you don't succeed, just to have tried makes you unusual. Not many single men try to adopt, do they?'

'No, they don't.'

'Have you always lived in this same house?'

'Afraid so.'

'And gone to the same school?'

'Two schools, primary and secondary.'

'I've been to six schools so far. I'd have thought you'd have won a scholarship to a private school or something.'

'No. I told you – no flair.'

'What sort of things did you do when you were my age?'

The man seemed at a loss. Perhaps he never had been ten years old. Teddy bears were notoriously ageless. Finally he said, 'Kept my head down, I suppose, and kept out of trouble. Nothing very exciting.'

'Is what you've read about in there exciting?'

James was pointing to the Life Story Book. The man thought for a moment. It seemed to be one of his characteristics to think before he spoke. Then he said, 'More disturbing than exciting.'

'That's what they say I am, isn't it? Disturbed.'

'And what do you say?'

James did not answer this. Instead he placed in the viewer a colour slide which he had earlier put to one side and held the viewer out for the man to take. 'That's you when you were my age. You're on a beach, and you look a right tearaway.'

The man lifted the viewer to his eye and kept it there for a very long time. James and Bernard waited for him to say something, but for too long, much too long, the man remained in the same position, looking at the colour slide in the viewer. Eventually Bernard coughed, held out his hand and asked if he might see the picture of the man, aged ten, on a beach somewhere.

When the man did take the viewer away from his eye, tears were flooding down his face.

77

'It was a holiday alone with my father. The only time he and I were ever alone for any length of time. The only time he and I were ever really close. I'm sorry. I'd forgotten about the picture . . . I really am very sorry.'

Younger Chaps

There was another colour slide, a companion to the one of me as a tearaway on the beach at Westward Ho. This one was of Edward in baggy shorts and funny hat and I had taken it. There had been no nonsense with a timer; we had taken pictures of each other. On the evening I returned from my visit to the Bungalow, after I had thanked Lynn for looking after him, I brought him downstairs to sit before the fire as usual. I placed the slide in the viewer, and held it up to his right eye, which is stronger, I think, than his left. I gave him a little time to take in that first slide, then I showed him the one of me.

I'm not sure what I expected, or if I expected anything at all. Just as well really, since what I got were the words 'Blue Grass' several times, and a gesture indicating that he was thirsty. After I'd made him a milky drink, I tried to explain to him why I'd shown him the colour slides.

'Mother was in Scotland, do you remember, looking after a sick great-aunt, who, it was thought, might bequeath her a few hundred pounds. In the end she got a silver-plated tea service with thistles all over it.' Then I waited, watching him use the good side of his mouth to sip at the drinking chocolate.

I lied a moment ago. I had expected something. I'd expected him either to look at me properly or to turn his head completely away from me. But neither happened. Instead he continued to look into the fire and sip his drink. I waited for this turn of the head for about three minutes before going on. What's an extra three minutes after almost thirty years?

'You were never happy behind the counter, were you? Panicked by mental arithmetic, always forgetting what people had asked for. When mother was there, your role was to fetch and carry, chat to the customers, and see off any unwelcome travellers. You always used to say that mother was the brains and you the brawn, with a modicum of public relations thrown in. What happened to personal relations, dad?'

From where I was sitting, I could just see his eyes, see the fire reflected in them, could, if I'd wanted to, have imagined a reaction and made of it whatever I wanted to make. Only somehow I didn't feel like playing both parts any more.

'Ten-year-olds aren't supposed to sell stamps, fill out official forms, or stand behind a counter all day paying out large sums of money, but no one reported us to the NSPCC or reminded us of the Child Labour Laws. Then, one morning, you woke me up at the usual time, only you hadn't taken in the post or swept out the shop, because a Miss Johnson had arrived to take over as our holiday relief.

'When I got downstairs, you were reading a road map, and our suitcases were packed. The idea of us taking a holiday without mother had never occurred to me. Nor to you, until that morning. But I'd noticed how uncomfortable you'd looked standing beside me behind the counter, watching the customers watch me do all the adding and subtracting, while the jokes about my possible future as a Chancellor of the Exchequer wore thinner and thinner.

'Nothing had been booked, and it was high summer. You didn't care, you said; if we had to, we could always sleep in the car. And you didn't telephone mother to let her know what we were up to until we reached Barnstaple. When you came off the phone, you were all smiles. You said, "We were in luck. She was busy, so we got away with just leaving a message."

'For a whole week, it was as if you were a different person, almost as though you were happy for the first time in your life, and you have no idea how good that made me feel. We sang all the way in the car, driving down. We'd sit in pub gardens, with you wearing a handkerchief on your head tied with knots at the corners, and you'd talk to me, telling me things about your own childhood I'd never heard, and using phrases I've never forgotten. "Innocent as a new-laid egg, and no more chance of escape than a sheep being driven to the butcher's back premises" – that was you being dragged to school on your first day.

'You told me about your travels to find work between the wars, cycling from one job prospect to another, with your only suit rolled up in your saddle-bag. The common lodging houses you stayed in, where fleas came up from the bottom of the bed and everyone had to get threepennyworth of Blue Unction, a strong ointment of mercury, to smear around their ankles, to hold back the mid-night invasion – lodging houses where, to save on heating, they only opened the windows once a year in Marcn to let out those staggering and bloated fleas.

'You told me about the time you were a drug pusher in Bilston, working as an assistant in a chemist's shop, selling people four ha'porth of laudanum to tide them over the Bank Holiday. About the regulars, old women who looked like pollarded oaks, you said, old women who claimed to have everything wrong with them but who lingered year after year and finally fell from sheer decay. You told me about the grubby pencilled notes handed over the counter by urchin children – 2d Grossmith Face powder, 2d Parma Violets (in a bottle) and 1d Carmine. "Somebody's going out tonight to earn next week's rent."

'I remember the names of the people you talked about, the "characters" who were your customers, some of them opium addicts, others just heavily constipated drudges. The cobbler, Mr Bullworthy; Ira Bodfish, the tinker; Shem Allit, the wheelwright; Noah Cooknell, Myrtle Amos, Ronald Blyth-man. You told me how many hundredweight of Epsom Salts you sold in a year, how much jalap, aloes, and hiera picra (called 'hirapike' by the customers), all in penny and two-penny packets. How on market day they stood along the counter three deep, waiting for their purgatives. You would sell Epsom or Glauber Salts, bicarbonate of soda, cream of tartar, tartaric acid, linseed oil, turpentine, pickle spice, turmeric, vinegar and methylated spirits, all to the one customer. You were lucky if you got ten minutes to grab a sandwich or dash to the toilet yourself. You said, "Best purgative in the world is a war. Nothing like it to unblock the system."

'You'd strike up conversations with complete strangers on that holiday, and then, with an arm over my shoulders and hugging me to you, you'd tell them, "This is my son. We're on the loose," and you'd giggle. We laughed a lot that week. I suppose it was the feeling that we were doing something secret and slightly wicked. Hence my tearaway expression in the slide I just showed you. I felt important, wanted, almost needed. You'd ask my opinion about things, and really listen to my answers.

'Every ride I went on at the fun fair, you came on it with me. By then you'd won a cowboy hat on a side stall, and you wore that. "You younger chaps" became your new favourite phrase. "In my day, younger chaps like yourself would always have run out of funds by now. The bank's open, if you'd like to apply for a non-returnable, interest-free loan."

'We'd found a twin-bedded room overlooking the sea in a small hotel. We got up early and, tired and sunburned, we went to bed early and just lay there talking until we fell asleep. Every night I was given a goodnight kiss, and then you'd lie on your back, looking up at the ceiling and just talk, while I listened and watched you.

'You told me about the men you'd known in the army, described them in detail so that I could visualize them. Before that holiday, I'd never known you describe people so vividly. "Len came from Tyneside. Short feller, red haired – that blond red – had a funny-shaped mole on his hip, just here," and you pointed to where the mole had been, remembering Len and involving me. That was what I had always wanted, to be involved with you. "If he did anything wrong, he'd claim he'd been so poor in Civvy Street that his brains had leaked through a hole in his boots. Or he'd say he'd been born stupid, and had greatly increased his birthright, and then he'd just stand there, grinning at you like something from the Funny Farm." You remembered so much of what it had been like – the closeness of the other men, the friendships and grievances, the skiving off and the fear. You said, "Then there was Bill, hell of a big man, six foot four, covered from head to toe in thick glossy hair like a Grizzly, and stammered something chronic whenever the Sergeant went near him. It was another world, the only world as far as we were concerned. If we thought about home, it upset us, and being upset brought everyone else down, so what would have been the point of that? We had to try to live as though that was our home, a different kind of home, as though we were a large family – brothers, cousins – husbands and wives sometimes. We were thrown together too close in some ways. That's what happens when you don't know if your time on earth is going to be limited or not. You take what you can get to make some kind, any kind, of contact. Human beings adapt in the most extraordinary ways, you know, to crisis. And if that crisis goes on for years, it's hard for them to recollect what they were like before. I would have done almost anything then to improve my chances of staying alive."

'I wanted to ask why you never wrote to the men you'd known in the army, why you never tried to see any of them, but for some reason I didn't ask. Perhaps I sensed that the reason was there in what you'd told me, and that some day I'd know what that reason was.

'Every morning I was asked, "What shall we younger chaps do today? Come on! I didn't spend four years fighting Corporal Turner's smelly feet so you could lie in bed like Lady Muck."

'We found a conch shell in a junk shop. "Probably from the West Indies," you said, "never been near a British beach. Never mind, we'll take it to remind us of the fun we had getting to know each other." And we sat side by side on the shingle of the beach at Westward Ho, passing that conch from one to the other, trying to hear in its depths the far-away West Indian sea, while the real sea was just in front of us, sucking up the pebbles and spewing them out again, drowning the sound in the conch shell altogether.

'It was the best time of my life. I was the happiest I've ever been.

'When the week ended, we came back here, but almost before we'd reached home the closeness we'd achieved on holiday had gone, as though it would have been embarrassing and out of place in front of your wife, my mother; she'd not been pleased at our going off without her. And a few days later I overheard you telling her that it hadn't been much fun. Poor food and lumpy beds, you told her. "Not much of a holiday for me," you said, "having to keep the lad occupied. You know how difficult it is to amuse him. But he'd worked hard in the shop, and I felt I had to do something."

'I was ten years old then. It was another ten years before I realized why you'd found it necessary to say that about our holiday, ten years of very mixed feelings. Silly really, when you think about it. Such a small thing, for such a large grievance. It was, after all, only seven days we'd spent together.

'Now it's been suggested that I should get rid of you, father – put you in a home. They say that, if I'm right about what you feel for me, you'd probably prefer to be somewhere else. If you can feel emotions – and I don't know, dad, you see, I just don't know – but if you can, the sense of being beholden to me must be very painful for you. I can't be sure about any of this, can I? Nothing's as simple as adding the cost of ten first-class stamps to that of a packet of envelopes and deducting that sum from an invalidity pension. But I have done the arithmetic about the home. Assuming that the State won't take care of you, your pension and mother's three building society accounts would just cover it for about three years. After that, who knows? Lynn would, I expect. But don't worry. Nobody of your age has to sleep on the back seat of a Morris Minor, unless of course they feel like it.

'It's been suggested that it would be money well spent for both of us, and I dearly wish you had some way of giving me your opinion on the subject. I want my own life now, you see – with my own son. I made a mess of it today and I'll probably have to start again, but I'm discovering that I really am a patient and persistent person. It was Jamie showing me that colour slide, seeing it again after all these years. And him pointing out to me the expression on my face. "Like a tearaway."

'I haven't told you much about Jamie, have I? It wasn't a case of my taking what I could get to make some kind of contact. We weren't thrown together in crisis. I did choose him. He's very bright, I think. And if I hadn't been taken by surprise today, I think it might have worked. Sad really. Very sad. I would have liked to have taken him on holidays, would have liked to watch him enjoying himself, liked to have made plans with him, or just to take off with him and go "on the loose", not because he'd worked hard, you understand, but because I loved him. Because I wanted to look after and protect him. Particularly from grievances and from loneliness. Do you understand anything of what I'm saying, father?'

'We have something to talk about.'
  'I thought we might have.'
  'What did you make of the boy's Life Story Book?'
  'Hadn't we better talk about what you've really come to talk about?'
  'If that's what you want. I thought we'd start with your reaction to the meeting. Have you had a chance to write something down about it?'

85

I handed the Infant Social Worker a couple of sheets of paper to read. We had agreed that, in addition to writing about myself for the Adoption Panel, I should also keep a diary of my day-to-day thoughts and feelings as things progressed, or didn't.

'Have you edited this, or is it as you wrote it when you got home?'

'Just as I wrote it.'

'Not much here about the poor kid's Life Story Book. I've seen it. I'd have thought it would have sparked off all sorts of questions.'

'I thought that would be irrelevant, under the circumstances.'

'What circumstances? You've changed your mind? You want to pull out? Back off? Is that what you mean? Say the word and I'll disappear in a puff of unleaded smoke.'

Finally we reached the point at which we both knew the interview should really have started.

'I cried.'

'Yes. I know.'

'I know you know. You know everything. You know that I blubbed uncontrollably in front of the child I was hoping to adopt.'

'Right.'

'So would you please – instead of coming here to play verbal games – could I please ask you to apologize to Jamie and to his Key Worker?'

'Bernard.'

'Yes, Bernard. And explain whatever it is you explain when the prospective adopter falls at the first fence.'

'Hardly the first. And before you get too comfortably engrossed in self-pity, it wasn't a fall, more a meaningful and extremely useful stumble.'

The Infant Social Worker was already moving around my kitchen as though she owned it, and preparing us both tea

86

which hadn't been offered, and, as she saw me watching her select only chocolate biscuits and leave the others, she paused in her domestic preparations to wiggle her bottom excitedly and pull a face to match.

'Guess what.'

'I'm all ears.'

'I've noticed. Bit like Clark Gable without the tache. Well, your tired and emotional few moments on seeing yourself again, aged ten, wearing swimming trunks and a Just William expression, had two effects – or rather, a similar effect on two very key persons in this real-life drama in which we are all struggling to get the moves right. One, James has gone a bundle on you, and is telling everyone that he's going to live with you. Two, sleepy-eyed Bernard has done a complete valse farce – '

'I think it's "volte-face".'

' – and is now one hundred per cent behind us. I quote, "Graham's own needs appear to match those of James almost exactly." So go on, celebrate. See if you can waggle those ears a bit, for a start.'

I stared at her. I didn't know what to say. I had already discovered that it was a mistake to allow the Infant Social Worker any kind of verbal advantage, but I was, for the moment, gobstruck. Meanwhile she devoured two large biscuits as a preliminary to beginning her tea in earnest, and then said, 'You didn't really think that a good old sob about your dad not loving you enough was going to scratch you from the race, did you, Gray?'

Three weeks later my father suffered another stroke, luckily at breakfast time while I was with him, so that I was able to summon help at once. He had been blowing on his tea, and fell sideways, but, as I've remarked, the tea is never too hot, so he was not scalded: it was only the stroke itself which damaged him. If he had been alone, I suppose he might have lain helpless on the floor for some considerable time and died there, but as matters were the ambulance arrived within forty minutes, the doctor within twenty, so he was saved, though the prognosis was not good, and I was told that I must expect him to remain in hospital for the foreseeable future.

A Lack of Light

It had been agreed that Sunday would be the best day. He was to arrive mid-morning for lunch, and return to the Children's Home after tea. There had been jokes about the need for him to sample the man's cooking before anything was finalized. Bernie the Tank Top, would deliver and collect him and use the intervening time to visit some old friends in Leamington Spa.

James had been allowed to assist in the washing of Bernard's car, and with the checking of oil, battery fluid, windscreen wash, and tyre pressures, and had been shown Bernard's AA road atlas. 'That's where we're going,' Bernard had said, pointing a finger to the name of a village. 'It's the Cotswolds. The unfashionable end.' And James, wearing his interested expression, had said, 'Vale of the Red Horse', at which Bernard had looked surprised and asked how he knew, and James had casually placed his own index finger next to that of Bernard's, showing him the words on the map.

The man-made wood of overgrown Christmas trees, where tents had been pitched at the end of an old runway, was not important enough to be included by the AA in its atlas. It was just another wood, roughly in the centre of England, and nowhere near the sea, but James remembered it. He knew where Bernie the Tank Top was taking him and what he would find, remembered following Leggo, Fang and Pimple down the hill and through the village, remembered the window of the village post office with the postcards advertising second-hand record-players, clothes, bicycles, prams, remembered the faded strips of red and green crêpe paper stretched and coiled between drawing pins, the knitting patterns with their glossy pictures of men, women, children, sometimes separate, sometimes together as families, all posing, all sticking their chests out, all wearing pastel-coloured woollies and smug expressions. He had guessed that the post office and its adjoining house, with its tiny lace-curtained windows, would be occupied by some old woman with an army of cats, who walked with the aid of a walking frame.

Bernard told him that he was to stop thinking of Mr Holt as 'the man'. 'You can't go on calling somebody who's going through hell and high water in order to adopt you "the man", not unless you say it in an Irish accent, and that might get a little wearing. He's too old to be an elder brother to you, and "uncle" sounds as if you expect to find his hand on your knee at any moment. So if you can't get your tongue round "Dad", you'd better think of something else quick, and whatever you come up with, don't forget to do one of those smiles of yours when you ask him if he's prepared to answer to it. Now are you with me? It's most important that you two get off on the right foot. Try to think of it as a three-legged race.'

As the car stopped at the other side of the road beside a phone box, Bernie the Tank Top looked at the frontage of the post office and the house next to it and said, 'Very Dickensian. Great Expectations at The Old Curiosity Shop. You should give Mutant Turtles a rest and read Dickens some time.' The car remained where it was until James had crossed the road, knocked at the door of the house with the tiny windows, been welcomed by the man (who had then waved towards the car), and been ushered inside. Then Bernie the Tank Top sighed, said, 'They wouldn't call it Care if we didn't care,' and drove away to his friends in Leamington Spa.

The first thing James noticed was the lack of light, and the fact that part of the house seemed to be a little below ground, as though either the foundations had sunk or the road outside had been built up. A tall person would find it difficult to live here, the ceilings being so low, the rooms so small.

As he moved about these rooms, twisting and turning his body to avoid the furniture, as though progressing through a maze built for dolls, the look, sound and smells of other homes in which he had lived came back to him very strongly. For a short time there had been a house which had smelt of rose-scented furniture polish, a sickly sweet waxy smell, matched by the colour of the wallpapers and curtains, one room peach, another tangerine, another apricot. At another house, where the strongest smell had been that of stale tobacco smoke, the furniture, carpets and walls were beige. Even the bathroom fittings had been various shades of beige, and the foster parents had worn mostly beige, so that often only their faces and hands were visible. That was the house where Jimmy had taken up interior decorating, using his own shit to make the walls a darker colour, so that at least he would know who was who and what was what. In the larger children's homes, where the smells were always those of cooking, disinfectant and stale sweat, there was rarely any uniformity of colours.

Here the walls were white, or had once been white. In the living-room fireplace, you could light a real fire if you wanted, and clearly fires had been lighted in it, which would explain the colour of the walls. There were many pictures and clocks, some of the pictures being the kind you could buy at Boots, others being blown-up copies of some of the photographs he had seen in the man's apology for a Life Story Book of the man's father and mother standing by a Morris Minor in lay-bys. There were also many clocks, most of which didn't go. He had never stayed in a house like this one.

The furniture looked solid and heavy, like the kind seen in junk shops; none of it was modern. The upholstery was either chocolate brown or the colour of the man's trousers and baggy cardigan, the colour of a teddy bear, with knitted pink things draped here and there and pink crocheted cushion covers to match. But the smell of the house in no way matched the pink of the cushion covers. The smell of this house was much more difficult to describe, being a mixture of two smells, the first of hospitals and the other James had no word for; all he had was a feeling it reminded him of, and this feeling was disappointment.

The stairs were narrow, steep, and wound round to the right from the bottom to the top, or to the left if you were coming down. Coming down was the more dangerous, since there was no banister rail on one side, and only a thick rope held against the wall with iron loops on the other.

'You'll have to be careful of the stairs until you get used to them.'

The man who was no longer to be thought of as 'the man' chatted continually as he showed James around. He opened doors and held out his arm like a cinema usher showing people to their seats He even opened drawers and cupboards and named the things inside them.

'Scissors, string, Sellotape, spare fuses, dustbin bags. And in here we have tea-cloths, rubber gloves, instructions for lighting the boiler, tapers and, for some reason best known to itself, a dead fly.'

There were other jokes. Nervous jokes and giggles. The man who had sat, first drowning in a bean bag, then weeping at the memory of a holiday with his father, was no more at ease in his own house than he had been sitting on a park bench or in the Bungalow. At first this unease irritated James, for he felt that any person who was going to take responsibility for him should be a more confident person and intelligent enough to realize that, once James had made a decision and knew where he was going, then, for a time at least, James would make sure that things worked out.

At the very top of the house, with the man watching him closely for his approval, he was shown into a room where the ceiling sloped down to meet the floor at one side. Here also the walls were white, a new brilliant white, and the bed cover

92

and curtains were also new, so new that a price tag had been inadvertently left on the underside of the bed cover, the colour of which and of all the furnishings in the room was blood red, the colour James had plucked out of the air when, weeks before, he had been asked by the man to write down his favourite.

James waited, allowing the man to state what was obvious, that the room was to be James's if the 'fostering with a view to adoption' went through. Then he performed several calculated but uncharacteristic actions. First, he moved quickly towards the man, placed his arms around the man's waist and hugged him briefly, thus getting their first moment of physical contact over with quickly, and leaving the man stunned and winded. Thereafter he moved around the room touching things, repeating the words 'Great!' and 'Terrific!' as he acted out enormous pleasure. Lastly, he kicked off his trainers and flopped backwards on to the bed, bounced up and down, smiling his most appealing, most Academy-Award-winning smile, and then waited for the man, who was now also smiling but weeping at the same time, to recover his emotions and remove the blood-red cloth, unveiling the blood-red mountain bike, which James had already recognized by its shape to be what was leaning against the wardrobe.

James sensed that his inspection of this first gift should be a quiet moment. He should keep his attention on the bike and his back to the man, allowing his stillness to indicate the emotion it would be appropriate to feel. He could then allow the man to approach him and place a hand on his shoulder, and could even, if he concentrated briefly on something else, permit the man's hand to squeeze that shoulder. All of this happened, just as he had calculated it would, for he had known what he would find here.

After a few moments of silence the man said, 'Be hell getting the bike down the stairs. I almost fell from top to bottom getting it up here. Just thought your room would be right for the presentation.'

Lunch was taken in the kitchen. What conversation there was concerned the food. The man revealed his own method of achieving roast potatoes which were crisp on the outside and soft inside. He spoke of the eccentricities of his oven, his preference for steamed rather than boiled vegetables, his use of herbs and which of these he considered helped him cut down on the consumption of salt. He asked questions about James's likes and dislikes concerning food and made notes of the answers. It was, after all, a meeting to enable them to get to know each other, and some people think that one is what one eats. After lunch James asked if he might mow the lawn, and did so while the man washed up.

There was then a walk around the village, during which he was given a potted history lesson, and told that at the end of eighteenth century the village had possessed a bakery, a parish malt house and had traded in coal. Now it had and did none of those things, but had grown in size, and was still growing. He was shown a small council estate of ugly grey pebble-dash buildings, to which private developers had added bungalows of varying shapes, sizes and materials, plate glass and concrete slabs, timber and multi-coloured bricks having been used abundantly instead of the more expensive local stone.

Later, landmarks of more significance to James were pointed out. The school Graham had attended. The church and churchyard and the tall larch trees surrounding them – the man himself did not usually go to church, except at Christmas and Easter, but would be happy to go if James were a church-goer. He was shown the playing field where, in the days when the village could boast a football team, matches had been played and very occasionally won and where the flower show was still held each year, though these days with less and less enthusiasm. Since the advent of deep freezers and drive-in supermarkets, and the sale of the allotments to make way for another bunch of retirement homes, what had once been a competitive display of the very best fruit, vegetables and flowers to be found locally, had more and more come to resemble a car boot sale.

They met few of the other village people on this walk, and the man did not introduce James to those they did meet, but waved vaguely or mumbled 'Afternoon!' James supposed that the man was hedging his bets. If the 'fostering with a view to adoption' were to fall through, it would be less embarrassing for the villagers not to have met James in the first place.

Tea was a more serious affair. The table in the front room had been laid ready as though for a party. The man who was supposed to be watching his weight sat opposite James, his head framed on one side by a three-tier cake stand, on the other by a two-tier stand on which were plates covered in clingfilm and containing triangular sandwiches. None of these sandwiches, James was assured, was filled with either cucumber or tinned salmon. There were also blood-red jelly, fruit salad and a trifle topped with a pink substance strewn with tiny multi-coloured flecks. Where, James wondered, were the paper hats?

'Now you've seen the house, can you think of any questions you'd like to ask me?'

James thought for a moment, removing a sliver of pork fat from inside his sandwich and placing it delicately on the side of his plate. 'There's still two rooms I haven't seen. Where you sleep, and where your father sleeps.' The man wiped his mouth slowly with a paper napkin, and reached across the table for the teapot. 'When can I meet your father?'

The tea was poured, milk added and a sweetener flicked into it from a plastic container taken from the man's pocket. James recognized the gestures and props adults use when they are cornered.

'He's not here, I'm afraid.'

'What's happened to him?' The man lifted and held out to James a plate containing slices of pork pie. James shook his head. 'He got iller, and needed to be somewhere where they could give him proper medical care.'

'Hospital, you mean?'

'Yes, hospital.'

'Is he bedridden?'

'Not entirely, no.'

'He can get about then?'

'With help, yes.'

'He wasn't sent to hospital because of me, was he?'

'No. No, of course not. He would have gone there anyway.' The man looked down at the tablecloth, where his thumbnail was sketching lines around a dollop of spilled chutney. It appeared that the man's appetite had deserted him. After a few moments he said, 'If I'd got rid of my invalid father in order to adopt a son, James, then it's unlikely I'd ever be approved. What happened was that he had another stroke, a very bad one. He v'as taken to hospital and it was decided that he should stay there. You're a very bright young man, Jamie, and your concern does you credit, but I refuse to let you take on any guilt about my father.'

'Would they let me come here if he hadn't been put away?'

'We don't know yet whether they'll let you come anyway, do we?'

'That's not an answer.'

'I don't know the answer. Possibly not. On the other hand, over the last few years you've demonstrated quite forcibly that mother figures aren't your cup of tea and the number of suitable single men who apply to adopt can be counted on the fingers of one foot. You only have to look across this table to see that they were already scraping the bottom of the barrel when they let me get this far.'

James nodded his agreement, and smiled at what he recognized to be a joke, and the man turned in his chair and produced two paper hats from the sideboard drawer. He held them out for James to choose one. James hesitated.

'Are these too babyish for you?' Again James nodded, and

the man draped one hat over the cake stand, and placed the other on his own head. 'They're not for me. You know, all the books and all the social workers say that the stage you and I are at now is supposed to be the honeymoon period, have you heard about that?' James nodded. 'We'd better enjoy it then, don't you think? It's said to get very difficult later on. Have you thought yet what you'd like to call me?' James shook his head. 'I think "Graham" would be rather nice. If you feel you can manage that.'

When Bernie the Tank Top arrived to collect James he was pressed to tea, sandwiches and cake, there being so much over. Smiling, he removed James's discarded paper hat from the cake stand and wore it on his own head, while the cinema usher showed him the house, the room which was to be James's room, and James's new mountain bike, at which point he wagged his finger and used the word 'Naughty!'

James cleared plates from the table and stacked them by the sink. Meanwhile Bernard asked if he might see the garden and, having commented on how well the grass had been cut, led his host slowly up the garden path to talk to him.

'Did James ask about your father?'

'Yes.'

'I thought he might. Told you, did he, that he couldn't bring himself to step into a dead man's shoes until they'd cooled down a little?'

'Something like that. Though dad isn't dead yet.'

'Sometimes you can look at a child causing mayhem all around it, stealing, swearing, lying, systematically destroying other people's property, or dropping its trousers in the most unlikely places to gain a few bob or the chance of a bit of a cuddle. And you think to yourself, "What a thoroughly disturbed godless little animal that is!" But I lay you a hundred to one, that child has its own most elaborately complex moral code over issues you or I might not even consider.'

James, who had begun to wash the dishes, watched

through the window, as the two men continued to walk in circles at the bottom of the garden.

'We've managed to discover where his maternal grand-parents live. I've written to them. No reply yet. They may not reply at all, of course. They may not want to know.'

'Hard to believe.'

'Harder for you than for me.'

'If they object to the adoption? If they want to make a home for him themselves?'

'Cross that bridge when we come to it.'

'You think I've jumped the gun, getting him that mountain bike?'

'Maybe a bit. Debbie told you my attitude had . . .?'

'Changed, she said.'

'Crystallized. Become more positive. I don't want to raise any hopes, but I think you ought to be ready for an Adoption Panel. That means working on your support system and lining up your referees.'

Family Matters

'What about my support system?' I said to the Infant Social Worker.

'What indeed? I've been worrying about that. Who are you going to let off steam to when our laddo's playing up and you decide the whole thing's a ghastly mistake?'

'He may. I shan't.'

'Who's going to look after him if you're sick or away?'

'I never am.'

'If, Gray, if. The question's going to be raised.'

'Lynn.'

'Have you asked her?'

'I don't have to ask her. She looked after dad; she'll look after Jamie. We're friends. She's very giving.'

'And who besides Lynn?'

'If you've got Lynn you don't need anyone else. She'd resent anyone else, as a matter of fact.'

'OK! That's your support system. I hope it's enough. And your referees?'

'Bernard mentioned referees. Why do you need them? You know me. You know all about me. You've been assessing me long enough.'

'If we decide – that's us in the Social Services – practically speaking, Bernard and his team leader, me and mine – even more practically speaking, me and Bernie – if we decide that you and young Lennards may make a match, then you go before an Adoption Panel, which will have our recommendation, but not necessarily be bound by it. Are you with me so far? And the panel will require you to provide the names of referees.'

'Solicitors . . . clergymen . . . people like that? Doctors?' I supposed the doctor would do it. He'd found me quite trustworthy in taking care of dad.

'Christ, no! You're not applying for a passport photograph. Real people. Real ordinary people who've known you since childhood. Who's that girl you used to go out with?'

'Elsie.'

'She's married now, you said. A married woman you used to be almost intimate with – she'd make an ideal referee. Come to think of it, you're also supposed to have some experience of dealing with kids already. See if she'll let you baby-sit hers. You never know your luck.'

It wasn't the kind of matter I could raise in the shop, with other people probably present, so I decided to visit Elsie and Colin Needham in their own home on the council estate.

Colin answered the door. He was unshaven and barefooted, and wearing only a cordless shortie dressing gown over a pair of very brief underpants, on which there was a printed photo-montage of Cape Canaveral and the American Star Wars Programme.

Since I was attempting friendship, and not a donation to any political party, I had decided to knock at the back door not the front, and was led through a kitchen which smelt of stale food, burned milk and used nappies, every surface of it covered with dirty pots and pans and open packets, or piled high with washing.

'She's gone to look at a pram. Nothing the matter with the Social Security, is there?'

I watched Colin's bare feet expertly negotiate the plastic building bricks and small toys which littered the cheap and stained carpet. He moved quickly, picking things up and putting them down again in different but equally unlikely places. For a moment, I felt the pangs of guilt the royal family must feel on the rare occasions they drop in on ordinary people unannounced, or embark on an unscheduled walk-about, only to discover factory workers asleep or doing the crossword.

'No. The Social Security's fine. It's nothing official.'

Colin ceased picking things up and moving them, and stood leaning against the fireplace, one hand gripping the front of his skimpy grey towelling dressing gown to hold it together. Under the dining table, three pre-school toddlers were attempting to fit pink plastic triangles into yellow plastic ovals.

'It was both of you I really wanted to talk to.' It seemed premature to come out straight away with the request that the Needhams should be my referees. I decided to approach the matter obliquely. 'About children.'

Using his free arm, Colin gestured towards the group sitting between the table legs. 'Buy two, get one free. Plenty more where they came from. The one in green belongs next door.'

'I'm trying to adopt one. I thought perhaps you might have heard.'

Colin shook his head slowly, then, still watching me, moved a toy dumper truck from the top of a lampshade and placed it next to the cruet set on the dining table. Finally he said, 'Think I would have remembered that if I had heard. Bit of a brave thing to do, innit?' Again he gestured, indicating that I should sit in what was clearly his own special chair, a high-backed swivel-and-rock armchair.

'Why do you think it's brave?' Taking an open box of paints from the seat of the chair and closing its lid, I sat with it on my lap.

'You still being unmarried, and living around here. Looks a bit odd, doesn't it? No offence meant; I speak as I find. Didn't even know they allowed that sort of thing with single men.'

'Yes, it's been legal for some years now. You have to be checked out, of course. They're very thorough.'

'I should hope they are. Have to be. Christ, the papers are full of it these days. Can you credit what some people will do to kids? Babies, toddlers even! There's not just the rich politicians at it either. Witchcraft my eye! That's just them perverts finding excuses to bugger about. I'd castrate the lot of 'em, the sods, I would straight, and not waste anaesthetic on the bastards either.'

Oblivious to what was being discussed, the unmolested toddlers under the table had tired of the intellectuality of pattern making, and turned to cards. I looked down at the picture on the lid of the box of paints, which depicted two healthy, happy children on a see-saw. Their clothes and hair styles were of the 1940s; they might well have sat beside their parents listening to 'Dick Barton, Special Agent', which mother had never stopped hoping the BBC would resurrect. Colin said, 'Anyway, what was it you wanted to ask us?'

'It was nothing really. Just wanted to let you know what was happening, so that if I do get approved and have a child to come and live with me you won't wonder what's going on.'

I heard the words come out, and knew that they were the wrong words, and that, if I went away without saying what I had come to say, it would be more difficult to come back and say it later. For what must have been a long time I just sat, looking at the paint-box but seeing no more than a blur of primary colours, knowing that I should get up, was indeed expected to get up, to say my goodbyes and leave, rather than remain as I was, locked in time, wallowing in present disappointment and the prospect of a future filled with much of the same. I looked down through the misty colours of the box to the end of a long tunnel where, instead of the 1940s children, a tubby man in a light brown overcoat sat on a damp bench with a ten-year-old boy, eating sandwiches and watching two fat ladies playing their own kind of tennis on a public court. The man had asked the boy if there was anything worrying him and, picking the cucumber out of the sandwiches, the boy had shaken his head, which might have been

102

a comment on the sogginess of the sandwiches, or an indication that nothing troubled him, or even a gesture signifying that he was not in the habit of discussing his problems with prospective adopters on their very first visit. The man had said, 'If you agree, I'd like to give you a proper home and look after you,' but the nod the boy then gave had not meant, 'Yes, thank you, that would be very nice,' but simply, 'Carry on, I'm listening.'

'Are you all right?' I realized the words came from close to me, and, turning my head, saw a pair of muscular knees and above them the worried face of Champion the Wonder Horse as it had looked when entering the classroom to sit a half-term spelling test. Colin Needham was squatting beside me.

'She'll be back any minute. I know she'd like to talk to you. She's got a lot more confidence now than when you and she . . .'

He was squatting close to me, clearly worried about me; his cordless dressing gown had fallen open. 'She will be back. She's never away long,' he said. His skimpy underwear was inadequate to conceal what he was showing me – the reason, if any reason were needed, why Elsie had found my conversation inadequate. It looked as if Cape Canaveral was about to make its most spectacular blast off yet. Simply the anticipation of his wife's return had aroused lust in Colin Needham's body, and this must have been so frequent an occurrence in his life that he no longer even noticed it, so that his face continued to express anxiety about the health of his guest.

I diverted my eyes to the children under the table. Colin said, 'Are you sure you don't really want one of your own? This lot have changed me. Well, you know yourself how I used to be a bit wild. Your own is always the best, Graham. There's nothing like knowing you've made something like that. Look at our Jeff here.' He stood, reached under the table, lifted an infant in pale blue cotton dungarees and dangled it in mid-air for me to take. I stood also. A thick worm of mucus hung suspended between the child's nose and mouth, and the child's lower lip curled downwards and his eyes narrowed as I approached.

I took him. He was heavier than I expected, his breath noisy, being taken in large gulps through his open mouth. The tiny body wriggled and writhed inside my arms then contracted, making itself stiff in an attempt to slide from my grasp to the floor.

And I loved it. It was someone else's child, and I wanted it. Very badly. No large doe-like eyes here, no 'Help me, I'm so small and helpless' expression, no 'Hug and care for me, and I'll develop all your virtues and wipe the slate clean of your faults', just an unattractive lump of writhing humanity and all I could think about was the gut-deep aching need I had to take care of it.

'You're not used to tiddlers like our Jeffo, are you?' I shook my head, attempting as I did so to avoid being hit in the face by one of the tiddler's fists. 'What does it feel like?'

'Difficult.'

'I never used to understand why folks always want to pick up small children, but you do when you've had one. It's the life in there, isn't it? Holding a kid you've given life to, Graham. There's just nothing like it!'

The curled lip close to my ear erupted into a wail of anger so loud and so sudden that I felt my heart stop momentarily. 'Listen to that! He's a little devil when he feels like it. He's full of life. Shut it, Jeffo, will you? I'm telling this man about parenthood.'

I lowered Jeffo to the floor gently and the noise stopped as suddenly as it had begun.

'Now there you are, you see, that's number one mistake you've just made. Give in to them the moment they yell and they know what to do next time.' I suppose I must have looked rather abashed, because Colin's tone became encouraging. 'Tell you another thing I like. We could do it now, and I could show you, 'cept our two had theirs last night, and too

104

much water's not good for them. It's watching them play in the bath. Gives you a really funny feeling that. Our Tina's feet are just incredible. I've never seen anything so perfect. Doesn't work with other people's kids, though. It has to be your own.'

Six foot two and broad in proportion, muscled and sweaty with a six o'clock shadow like wire-wool! Who would have thought Champion the Wonder Horse could be so gentle? *'Did you ever play with dolls when you were a small child? A teddy bear, perhaps? Were you ever allowed a puppy?'* I remembered Margery in full flow at the community centre. *'It's all well documented. Boys as well as girls can satisfy the desire to give birth and care for a baby. It's an important stage of development. Problem starts when some cack-handed adult makes the male child aware of what he's doing before he's achieved a secure sense of identity and moved on to the next stage. Then you have infant George, faced with an almost uncontrollable desire to be tender, caring, even perhaps to suckle this helpless thing and you're telling George that in reality his uncontrollable desire can't ever be satisfied; you're telling infant George he's unnatural, a freak, a one-off, when he isn't. And by the time George is twelve years old, he's got his name down for the SAS just to prove you wrong about him being a nancy boy. He'll probably never discover that his foul-mouthed sergeant had the very same infantile desire to dress and undress dolls.'*

'Is it marriage you don't like the idea of, is that it?'

'I don't think I'm going to meet anyone now.'

'Haven't been out and about much to see, though, have you? Too late now, of course, but fifteen year or so back, if I'd known you were interested, you could have come around with me. You always seemed a bit . . . well, you know . . .' I nodded, knowing only too well what he meant. 'Sad really, when you think about it. Was it just shyness, then, do you think, what I took to be you being a bit stand-offish?'

'Mostly shyness.'

'Reckon I've been lucky. Well, you know, don't you? You being interested in her yourself . . . at one time.'

'Platonic.'

'Yes, she said. She thinks you're a proper gentleman. What age would this child you're going to adopt be then?'

'Ten, eleven maybe.'

'Christ, man, they're a mess by that age! And someone else's. You must be mad.'

'I wouldn't be considered for a younger child. And there's no guarantee I'll be approved at all, but I'd like to try. What I really came to talk about was references.' I waited. It was clear that Colin did not understand what was required. 'From people who've known me a long time, preferably people with experience of children.' I decided to go the whole hog. 'I'm also supposed to try and gain experience myself. Baby-sitting. Helping to run a group or youth club. Something like that. I mean, if you and Elsie . . .' I looked at the card school under the table, who now seemed to be playing a version of seven card stud with jacks and deuces wild. 'If you ever needed . . .'

'We don't go out much. Haven't the money. If we do, then mum-in-law likes to come round and sit with the kids. My own mum was complaining just the other day that we hardly ever ask her to do it.'

'Seems as if you've got a waiting list, then.'

'Yes, it is a bit like that.'

'And the reference?'

'Why don't I talk to Elsie? She knows you better than I do – and anyway, they'll probably want to know you're not totally uninterested in women. I'm still not all that brilliant at writing official things.'

At the back door, Colin shivered at the freshness of the air in the world outside and said, 'She'll be sorry to have missed you. I know she'd like to have talked to you. She's changed a lot too, you know.'

'Perhaps I'm trying to go too fast, I don't know.' I waited, hoping to be contradicted. Instead she stared at me through the gap between door and jamb. 'We had a bit of a row, you see. I sense he doesn't want me poking into his past, even with his supervision.'

'Supervision he's now withholding by staying around the corner in the car, right?'

'Right. It's always difficult to know what to do for the best, isn't it?'

'Always.' The woman thought for a moment before undoing the safety chain and holding the door open just wide enough for me to enter. 'Has he poked into yours?'

'Sorry?'

'Your past? Go through.' I went through, and she followed me. 'Has James had a good look at that?'

The room was dark and untidy, with clothes strewn about. It smelt of damp. 'That's one of the problems. My past is hardly worth poking about in. It's very dull compared to his, you see. Same house, same school, only child, reasonably comfortable.' The woman pointed to a chair and I sat in it. Though she was fat and had heavy streaks of grey in her hair, she could not yet be sixty, and must have retired early from the Children's Home. I wondered what she found to do with her time these days and suspected that the answer might be not very much.

'What about your wife? Can't she offer him a little diversity? A few skeletons to be rattled?'

'I'm not married.'

'Widowed, or divorced?'

'Just never married.'

There was a long silence during which the woman leaned back in her chair and looked at me. Though I was, of course, ill at ease, I did my best not to show it.

'And they've actually let you get as far as the Life Story Book stage?'

'Yes. And it's looking very hopeful. That's why I don't want to make any mistakes now.'

Her businesslike, no-nonsense expression softened a little.

She seemed genuinely pleased for me. 'Congratulations. Good for you! Things must have moved on in the last two years. James with a single-parent dad, eh? Well, yes, I suppose there's some kind of logic there, even if it is only postponing the real problem. They must have put you through hell.'

'Not really. Everyone's been very helpful.'

One of the ways in which they had been helpful was in finding me this woman – and not only the woman, of course. There had been past foster parents not all of whom bore James good will, teachers at various schools of whom the same could be said, many of the names which figured in his Life Story Book, but not the maternal grandparents, who still chose not to reply to letters. Bernie the Tank Top had told me forcefully that, however much I might be tempted to think of adoption as a new beginning, that was far from the truth. 'You can't say, "This is day one. We start from here." He comes with baggage. You can't ignore it.' I would have to talk to as many of the people of James's Life Story Book as could be found and would see me. 'Even as it is,' Bernie had said, 'you'll filter a lot of it out. You'll only take in what you want to receive.'

This woman had been James's Key Worker at a previous Home. 'What did you mean by "postponing the problem"?' I said.

'Nothing. Just my out-of-date amateur psychiatry. Surely your single status alone should give you enough bonus points in James's eyes? Single man adopting screwed-up ten-year-old boy?'

'Isn't my being single likely to make it harder for him? Taunts about me, about the sort of man I might be, from other children?'

'Rubbish. He can handle any amount of that. Water off a duck's back for that young man, unless he's changed since I knew him – developed into a shrinking violet. Stranger things have happened in Child Care.'

'He is very sensitive.'

'Course he is. When there's something in it for him. Aren't we all? No, you're worrying over nothing. If James lands himself a real home situation, with a mature male to dote over him and no woman around to complicate matters, then he'll have come up smelling of daisies. It's what he's always wanted. Fantasized about even.'

'The woman at the Children's Home said you had got quite close to him at one time.'

'I was about the only member of the female sex he'd allow within arms' length of him.'

'Why would that have been?'

'Has he ever mentioned his mother?'

'No. And I've been warned not to ask about her yet.'

'Or ever would be my advice. Women to James aren't just unnerving as they are to many pre-pubescent boys; they're also disgusting and they're evil. You may not have discovered any of this yet, but it has been known for the smell of face powder to cause him to throw up. Whenever he saw a passably attractive young woman on television, he'd start scratching his arms till they bled. Now you know what I meant by "postponing the real problem".'

I began to doubt the efficacy of Lynn as a support system. However, it was possible that the woman might be exaggerating for some purpose of her own. I said, 'Why didn't he consider you disgusting and evil?'

'He did at first. Even though I was middle-aged, fat and far removed from the dolly-bird type that used to make him itch. Good thing there was no one taking snapshots the day I sat on him for the best part of an hour. Had him pinned to the floor, screaming his head off while I dangled my boobs in his face. He spat, he bit, he wet himself, banged his head, held his breath, pulled out hanks of my hair. I think if I'd been the make-up wearing type he might well have done himself in.' She stopped, looked at me, made a decision and said, 'You have been told that he has attempted twice to do just that?' I nodded. 'Tell him I'm deeply hurt he wouldn't get out of the car to come and see me after all we went through. We had some good times together until he was moved. So he's going to allow you to be a stand-in for his real dad, is he? You must be someone very special. I assume his dad's still in prison?'

'Yes. Before everything is finalized – if it is – we'll be going to see him.'

The woman sighed heavily, leaned back in her chair and looked at me thoughtfully. 'You poor bastard! That's a condition of the adoption, I suppose. All this "open" rubbish they're so fond of these days. If born-to parents want to keep tabs on their kids, they should fucking well look after them properly in the first place, or better still not have given birth to them at all.'

'It's not like that. I very much want to meet him, and Jamie is very keen.'

'I'll bet he is. All his idea, I expect.'

'Yes, as a matter of fact, but the social worker was also in favour.'

'And how old is she? Fourteen?'

I had no intention of being disloyal to the Infant Social Worker. I said, 'No, she's very mature in her outlook.'

'Look, friend, I don't mean to be rude, but you'd better go now. We're both wasting our time and this is beginning to sicken me; it's just so bloody predictable. You're out of your depth and you're being used by a ten-year-old to get another glimpse of his dad. You'll never get to adopt him and, believe me, you're well out of it. The moment those two meet again, even through the bars of a cell, you'll be out on your ear.'

'Have you ever met the father?'

'Don't need to. All I know is he's got some kind of background in – I don't know – mercenary or something, freelance soldier or whatever, and it's landed him in clink. I'm simply going on what I know of Sunny Jim out there, if he is still out there. For Christ's sake, man, wake up! Why do you think he's not sitting in here all comfy with you and me right now?' I began to feel like an errant infant being given a pep talk by the headmistress, and could sense my lower lip beginning to curl.

'I told you, we had an argument.'

'Because you'd managed to find me?'

'Well, yes, as a matter of fact, it was. I thought he'd be pleased, you see.'

'And was he? . . . As a matter of fact?' I shook my head. Helpless, hopeless, I was to be awarded the lowest marks in my class and kept in after the bell. I was to write out a thousand times 'I must think faster.'

'What a surprise! So you said he didn't have to come inside and meet his old mucker Maureen if it was going to upset him?'

'One has to be careful.'

'Oh yes, one does. Who knows what I might come out with about him? You're just not up to this game, are you? He's many moves ahead of you, isn't he?'

'We're talking about a ten-year-old child.'

'Well, just in case that "child" isn't still waiting in the car where you left him, there's a phone box on the corner. It's usual to inform the police when a child in your care has done a runner, and they're none too happy if you delay.' The woman rose quickly to her feet and led the way to the door. I was to be dismissed, let off this time with a caution. 'Thank you for dropping by, and either get your act together, and stop believing the sun shines out of his anus, or leave him to the mercies of "Care" and the so-called professionals. He might be as bent as a snake buckle, but by God he deserves someone with a bit more grey matter between his ears.'

Standing on the doorstep, I discovered to my surprise that I was very close to tears yet again, not because the woman so clearly despised me, but because all the while I had been listening to her, snatches of conversations and arguments with James had been replaying themselves inside my head. And what they had told me was that the woman knew far

111

more about the boy who was to be my son than I did. There could be no reason for her to have made things up or to have a grudge against Jamie. Her manner might have been gruff, but the expression in her eyes had been that of someone who had been very fond of him.

'Whatever happens don't be afraid of James's past,' Bernard had said. 'It can only harm you by harming him, and that's most likely to happen if you ignore it and hope it will go away. Take it out, look at it, bring it into the present and then put it back in the past where it belongs. Until you've done that – both of you together – James can't explain himself to himself, can't know his own value, can't even be sure that he exists.'

I walked back towards the car, glancing around for a telephone box, since I had already convinced myself that the woman was right in every respect, and that Jamie would have taken off. I suddenly realized that some of what I felt was fear, fear of the responsibility I was taking on, fear that I would be neither patient nor persistent enough to make any kind of go of it. Why kid myself? A solitary life spent in a village post office, counting stamps and green giros and doing double-entry book-keeping was in no way a sufficient grounding for what lay ahead of me. Half of me actually wanted Jamie to have done his runner. Only then, I thought, only when he had been brought back, only when my mind was clearer, would I be able to know the right questions to ask.

In fact the woman was both right and wrong. Wrong in that he was still sitting in the car just as I had left him, right in that by not doing a runner he had managed to keep several moves ahead.

I set the car in motion, and drove without speaking, hoping the silence between us would eventually get to Jamie and force him to ask me what had been said. Perhaps this was the key to handling him; I must respond and not instigate, keep my pathetically mismatched set of cards held close to my chest and let him do the bidding.

Five miles later, by which time the stillness in the seat beside me had become unbearable, it was I, as always, who spoke first.

'I'd half expected you not to be waiting for me.'

'That bad, was it?'

'What?'

'What she told you about me.'

'No. Not bad. She remembers you with . . . well, she likes you. She was upset that you hadn't wanted to see her.'

'So she got the spite gun out, and blasted my good name to smithereens.'

'She tried to straighten me out on one or two things.'

'Why? Were you bent on them?' I felt the palms of my hands on the steering wheel begin to sweat. Despite his stillness and apparent casualness, this was the most verbally dangerous he had been with me.

'I'm bent on finding out all I can about you, if that's what you mean.'

I leaned forward to turn on and retune the car radio in an effort to appear unruffled and casual. Consequently I missed seeing the traffic lights change, accelerated too hard and too suddenly, and then had to brake quickly, so that the car kangarooed for several yards along the road. Jamie bounced about in the seat beside me with a self-satisfied grin on his face, and when finally I got the car back under some form of control I allowed my poker face to crack and joined him in his mirth.

It was several minutes before I returned to my meeting with the woman, and my first question coincided with a change of programme on the radio, as a pleasant string quartet gave way to a screechy soprano gambolling up and down scales. My first impulse was to switch the radio off, but I decided that this would make my questioning seem too premeditated.

'How come you used to like this woman when women generally tend not to be your cup of tea?'

'Perhaps because she's a bit of a lez.'

'Sorry?'

'Lesbian. Butch. Gay. Wasn't she wearing leather and studs and looking like she hadn't slept for a week?'

'No. She was a bit untidy I suppose, but . . .'

'There you are then, aren't you?' The tone of his voice had suddenly become sharper, higher, almost as though he were choking. And as I took my eyes from the road briefly to glance at him, the cool and composed, laid-back ten-year-old, who, until a moment before, had been reclining with his head against the head-rest smirking, was now leaning forwards, scratching at his thighs and the backs of his knees. 'Not a proper woman, that's why.'

'What constitutes a proper woman, then?' With this question, and the radio soprano's sudden and unexpected bravura attempt to shatter glass, came even more desperate and violent scratch'ng and an equally sudden and equally loud explosion of anger from James.

'Tits and silk and frills. Make-up that stinks. And legs that shoot apart the minute you touch them with your little finger!' As he shouted these words, spittle sprayed in my direction.

I turned the radio off and pulled into the side of the road. There was a thin trickle of blood on the side of his legs. He had wound the window open, and with his head turned well away from me was looking down towards a ditch into which a split refuse bag had been hurled.

'You could have turned the radio off, you know, if it was bothering you.'

'Nothing bothers me. It's your radio.'

I waited, knowing I must tread carefully, but determined that the moment shouldn't be wasted or patched over if we were ever to advance. Finally I said, 'Does that mean that, from now on, I have to know when a subject is likely to upset you and avoid it?'

Time passed. Then he answered. 'Didn't they warn you what being a substitute parent was like?'

'OK. One to you. Even if it did take a little time. And suppose I need help?'

'Who doesn't?'

'Which was worse, my questions or the woman on the radio?'

'Both.'

'So if we were to eliminate one, you could get to keep half the skin on your legs. Or perhaps have one leg with skin and tie the other up in bandages. You see there have to be questions, Jamie, because unless I know why you hurt I'm not going to be able to prevent myself from accidentally causing some of it. You do you see that, don't you?'

'Did she tell you about the time she sat on me?'

'Yes.'

'Then you don't need to know any more, do you.'

'I disagree. Minimally talented sopranos we can do without, but I have to know more, a great deal more, if you and I are to be close friends.'

'Is that what we're supposed to be?'

'Among other things.'

'Like what?'

'That's partly up to you.'

'Like lovers? They always want to know everything about each other, don't they?'

'Yes they do, but not like those kinds of lovers. You're back to playing games now. You know damn well what I'm on about.'

'Oh, you mean the jug of water game. They play it with the little kids at the Home.' He assumed a 'Nanny' voice, 'Here I have a jug full of loving and giving, children. And if I pour some into this glass here, which is Martin, I still have some left for Mr and Mrs Jenkins. But when Martin stayed with Old Mrs Pain-in-the-arse, he put clingfilm over the top of his glass so the old bag couldn't pour any of her special loving and caring into him. Wasn't that naughty? That's why he doesn't trust anyone any more. Martin is all dried up inside. That's why he plays with himself in assembly, flashes his willy down the High Street and swings the cat round his head when he's bored. It's all down to him believing this jug is filled to the brim with loving and caring. When actually it's just sodding H_2O!'

'Who's Martin?'

'Boy I know.'

I waited for the excitement of his performance to subside. The temptation to put the car into gear and leave the discussion for another day was strong, particularly as I wasn't even sure what we were discussing any more. I was rather tired and more than a little shaky, but I decided on one last attempt to spell out what I considered to be the ground rules.

'Forget the games. All I want to try and get across to you is that if our relationship is to work, we should end up feeling a kind of love for each other. That is what I expect to happen. And what I think everyone concerned with us expects. Now, what about you? What do you want?'

'Would that be the same sort of love you and your father had for each other, that week you spent on holiday? Is that the kind of thing you mean?'

Considering the scratchy soprano incident, our first full weekend together, which occurred shortly afterwards, went more smoothly than anyone had a right to expect. Jamie arrived late on Friday afternoon and spent much of Saturday morning with myself and Mrs Linford in the post office, sitting on a high stool to the side of the counter, watching the customers' expressions as they longed to know who he was but couldn't decide how to phrase the question. From twelve thirty until one, at which time we close promptly on Saturdays, he even acted as commissionaire, opening and closing the shop door for customers and smiling at them graciously. During lunch he pointed out to me that at least two of the notices in the shop were out of date, particularly the one requesting donations for the Sudan Emergency Appeal.

In the afternoon we visited a vintage car museum and spent the evening watching an exceptionally violent video, said to be popular with sub-teens. The video recorder was a recent purchase. Lynn had explained to me that the possession of a video recorder distinguishes the liberated 1990s parent from the Victorian paterfamilias.

On Sunday we slept late, worked a little in the garden and drove out to Bibery Trout Farm in the afternoon. In the evening Jamie rode his bicycle around the village several times, returning at fifteen-minute intervals to peer through the living-room window and reassure himself that I was still where he had left me.

It was, all in all, a very satisfying week-end.

Treasure

He had been collected as usual on the Friday evening, and in the car the man who wished to be called Graham had told him that the post office would be understaffed this week-end, and that the man would have to be behind the counter early and stay there all morning. Consequently, to the man's regret, James would not be woken with a cup of tea on Saturday morning and would have to prepare his own breakfast. Since preparing his own breakfast was something James enjoyed doing, and they both knew it, this was no hardship. 'If you can't find something you need, come through to the shop, and ask,' Graham had said.

He awoke on the Saturday morning in the room with the blood-red furnishings and the sloping ceiling, perfectly content not to have tea brought to him, content to enjoy something more precious, which was time to himself. After some time in bed, he got up, not because he had been exhorted or encouraged to do so, but because he, James, wished to do so. Wearing the new pyjamas which he had found the night before under his pillow, he walked about the house, soon to be his house, beginning with the floor below his own. No one would interrupt him; no one was in the house. He would prepare his own breakfast at a time of his choosing – within reason, since, if he did not make an appearance in the post office to ask the whereabouts of some object whose whereabouts he already knew perfectly well, it might be thought that he had fallen downstairs, tipped a boiling kettle over himself or suffered some other lethal accident.

First he listened at the door of what he knew to be the old man's bedroom, then slowly turned the door handle and went in.

The double bed had been stripped of its bedding. A large fitted wardrobe stood against the wall opposite the bed. James opened the doors. There were a rail and hanging space on each side and two banks of narrow drawers in between, with a shelf for bedding running right across the top. One side was empty, apart from a black lace evening glove screwed up into a ball and covered in dust, which James at first took to be a mouse cowering in one corner. The old man's clothes filled the other side. Arranged on padded hangers were two suits, three sports jackets, trousers of corduroy and of worsted, and many shirts, some with long sleeves and some with short, some white, some striped, some checked, some coloured. The narrow drawers on that side contained vests and baggy underpants, handkerchiefs with the letter 'E' embroidered on them, ties, neatly darned socks, and lavender heads confined in small bags of net. The drawers of the other side were neatly lined with a paper patterned with rosebuds, but were empty, even of lavender bags.

The dressing table was set against the same wall. There was a mirror on a stand on top of it, two photograph frames containing studio portraits of the man and woman who were otherwise usually photographed in lay-bys, and a third containing a wedding photograph of the same man and woman. There was no photograph of the man called Graham, either as a boy, or as teenager, or as a man. The top drawer on the left side was empty; the top drawer on the right contained collar studs, various tubes of ointments, pill bottles, a thermometer, a tin of foot powder and an elasticized bandage. The drawer beneath was lined with the same rosebud paper, but empty. The drawer beneath that contained neatly folded hand-knitted sweaters and cardigans and three pairs of long johns too bulky to fit into the underwear drawers of the wardrobe. The drawer beneath that was locked.

James went downstairs to the kitchen, and rummaged until he found a hammer and a screwdriver, which he used to force the drawer open. Inside, wrapped in tissue paper, were a khaki forage cap with the cap badge of the Royal Army Ordnance Corps, a battle-dress blouse and a webbing belt. James could recognize an army uniform when he saw it, though this appeared to be rather out of date. Hidden inside the blouse was a conch shell. He lifted it to his ear and could hear, deep inside it, the sound of the sea. Then he replaced the conch where he had found it and closed the drawer. His forcing it had left no marks to notice, and it was unlikely that the man who had asked to be called Graham would discover that it was no longer locked. James suspected that Graham did not even know that the drawer ever had been locked. The mother's clothes had been removed, but the father's were still in place. Therefore this must still be considered Graham's father's room, its privacy to be respected.

He sat on the bed, looking through the window at the playing field and the hill beyond it. After a while, he lowered his back on to the slightly stained mattress, lying as he imagined the old man would have lain, and looked around the room from that lying position, listening to the sounds outside and to those which the house made. Then he got up, stood on the mattress and bounced up and down, using it as a trampoline. Then he left the room to continue his investigation.

He half expected to find that Graham's bedroom was locked, though he did not know why he thought this. He was wrong. Here the wardrobe was the large ugly kind with a full-length mirror fitted to the door. James stood before it in his new pyjamas with the bed reflected behind him, taking in the reflection of the room and himself in it before examining its contents. He moved to the bed and pulled back the covers to reveal pale blue winceyette sheets. He placed his hand on the lower sheet to feel if it was still warm, and it was. He felt underneath the pillows and found a pale blue handkerchief, which he first pressed to his mouth and nose, then, kneeling on the floor beside the bed, spread the handkerchief on the sheet and lowered the right side of his face to rest against it. Finally he folded the handkerchief neatly and placed it in the pocket of his new pyjamas.

He remade the bed, then paused to look out from the window over the back garden and the lawn which he would mow again today. He returned to the wardrobe, opened the door and went through the pockets of every item of clothing in it. Fluff was removed from all the pockets of all the clothes, as well as from the pockets of those which were not hanging up, but had been left on the backs of chairs, and James studied this fluff as though he were assisting the police with their enquiries at the scene of a crime. One of the inside jacket pockets contained, besides fluff, a small key.

On top of the wardrobe were three suitcases. James climbed on a chair to take them down. Two were empty. The third contained boys' clothing – a grey school shirt and short trousers, black gym shoes, a pair of swimming trunks and a pair of Aertex underpants, which James tried on in front of the mirror, and a school cap with the name 'Graham Holt' printed in marking ink on the torn lining. He placed the cap on his head back to front. Underneath the boy's clothes, and wrapped in tissue paper, he found baby clothes – hand-knitted matinée jackets with blue ribbons, bootees the size of a matchbox and a baby's bonnet with rabbits embroidered on the earflaps. Below these were clothes for a three-year-old – a romper suit of blue and white cotton with a ship's anchor on the bib, a small overcoat and a pair of ankle socks. James added one of the ankle socks to the handkerchief in his pyjama pocket.

There was an old hairbrush on the chest of drawers, which James pressed hard against the side of his face and held there for a while, but otherwise the chest of drawers and the bedside cabinet provided little of interest. Protruding from beneath the chest of drawers, however, was a cardboard attaché case which was locked, but the small key unlocked it.

This case contained copies of letters to local authorities concerning the writer's wish to adopt a boy, together with a collection of used cheque books, a receipt from a firm of undertakers and several sheets of lined paper torn from a notebook on which the words 'My name is Graham John Holt. I am a single man, aged 36,' had been written and re-written. Among these sheets of paper was a smaller sheet, which had been screwed up into a ball. James flattened out the paper and read the words of a list:

WANTED
bread
milk
tea-bags
a son
something for lunch (ham or pork pie)
sugar
Chinese cabbage

The church clock struck the half hour. Half past nine, time to be thinking of breakfast if he was not to arouse anxiety. James replaced the key in the pocket from which he had taken it. Then he went quickly to the old man's room and took the conch shell from its hiding place inside the battle-dress blouse before returning to his own room at the top of the house, where he sat for a while with the objects he had brought with him – handkerchief, ankle sock and conch – spread out on his bed. Later he would decide where they should be hidden.

'So you're the gardener. I've never known the lawn look so trim.' The fat woman in pink kissed and hugged the man called Graham and, smiling an empty glossy-lipped smile, said, 'I'm being nosy. I've come to meet Jamie.'

Outside, staring from the windows of an old car, were four children. The woman's eyebrows looked as if they had been drawn on her face to illustrate surprise. She held out a large plump hand to be shaken, wrinkling her nose and flirting as she looked at James from beneath a curly mop of peroxide-blonde hair. 'Are you settling in all right?'

James nodded, moving away from the woman to stand by the window and get some air.

'Funny little village this. Stay twenty years and they might just realize you're not here on holiday.' She patted Graham's thigh as he lowered himself to sit beside her on the sofa. James wondered why the plump couple grinning at him from the sofa hadn't married each other and shared the children who were playing noughts and crosses in the steam on the car windows.

'This chap here is the only born-and-bred local who doesn't make me feel like a townie. Our Graham is all right, our Graham is. You look after him, Jamie. Is "Jamie" what you like being called? You look more like a rather butch Jim or a Jimmy to me.'

The man who had asked to be called Graham said, 'It has to be Jamie or James, Lynn. He doesn't answer to anything else.'

'James. That's quite classy. See that lot out there, gawping out at the world to elicit sympathy. That's Cora, Giles, Jasper and Ludo, and not one of them knows what a fish knife looks like.'

Later Graham asked James what he thought of the woman and James replied that he didn't have any thoughts about her. This was a lie. What James thought about the woman was that she would very much like to share her swankily named children with the bachelor postmaster, and that she was now jealous. James had grasped several things from the look the woman had given him. One was that she was the kind of person who always pretends to be happy, but is actually quite the opposite. Another was that she was trying to guess whether he had been sexually abused and if so in what manner. And third, that she had realized that her best friend, Graham, was being used and that she would have to be extremely careful how she told him this.

*

123

Sunday morning. From now on, it would become routine. Every morning he woke in the room with the blood-red furnishings and the sloping ceiling, he would lie with the sheet covering his head, would place his right ear close to the conch and listen to the sound of the waves hitting the rocky coastline while he studied the folds in the sheet covering him. Somewhere in these folds, with the strips of brilliance from the edges of the curtains forming light and shadow, his imagination could arrange the features of a face. A mouth with its corners turned down. A nose. Hooded eyes, waiting. Always waiting.

Testing

Children at the Home were allowed one free four-minute phone call a week to a person of their choice. Jamie and I had agreed that he should make his to me each Tuesday evening and that I would phone him on Thursday evenings to firm our plans for the week-end. These calls helped to remind us that, although we might consider we were on honeymoon, officially we were still in the process of a long-distance courtship.

During the last thirty seconds of Jamie's telephone call to me on the Tuesday following our first week-end, it became evident that I was being given a coded message and that, unless I could decode it in the remaining few seconds and also respond that I was prepared to act on it, I would lose any merit points I might have acquired.

I learned that the reason for code was that the phone calls had to be made from the office of the Children's Home, with people coming and going and sometimes with quite inconsiderate people sitting there at their desks writing long case-reports or letters of apology to persons whose property had been vandalized during the previous week, and that any words overheard from the child which might be thought to indicate acquisitiveness would be duly noted, ridicule and teasing being administered later by way of punishment.

If Jamie had not risked raillery to get his message across, I might never have known that, just as every good boy deserves favour, every good-enough substitute father should have in the boot of his car what James describes as 'a serious tent' – and for 'serious' read army surplus, and definitely not a blue, yellow and red shiny nylon fabric job with a plastic window or a picture of Snoopy and the Red Baron pinned to its side, which is exactly the kind of tent I might well have purchased had I followed my first impulse and rushed out to the nearest tent shop to load up the car.

Fortunately my natural tendency always to seek guidance, particularly when the expenditure of money is threatened, protected me. I realized that, without father to take care of, I could leave the post office in Lynn's capable hands and drive to where Jamie was, collect him after school, and take him to choose the tent he thought most serious.

It is said that, just before death, recorded highlights of one's past life are played back. I very much hope that one of mine might be that shopping expedition. I had simply no idea that spending large amounts of money could give such pleasure.

To begin with, Jamie knew exactly what was needed and where to get it. Judging by the familiarity with which the teenage shop assistant greeted him, Jamie wouldn't ever have been seen window-shopping anywhere else. 'This is Graham, Mike. He's going to adopt me.' And, smiling, Mike held out his hand to be shaken, saying, 'Great! Hope it works out.' Then, turning to Jamie, he said, 'That's good news, innit? You pleased?' James nodded his head sagely and immediately asked for a discount, which was as immediately granted, whereafter the young shopper and youngish assistant bartered and bantered and fell about laughing.

Yes, laughing. Jamie actually laughed. Several times. Full-blooded, indulgent, uninhibited, belly laughs. I had never heard him laugh fully before then. It was a most pleasing sound. Then, when I confessed what was becoming obvious, that I had neither erected nor even slept in a tent in my whole life, his face lighted up as though I had given him something he had always longed for, which in a way I had, since what I was offering was my innocence to his experience. 'I won't let the ants eat you. Will I, Mike?' he said, using his whole body again to laugh and including the assistant in our pleasure, and the flicker of a look he gave me a moment later was one I hadn't seen before. I doubt if anyone had seen that look in the previous four years. I daren't say that it was expressing anything like love, and it was very brief, but the effect it had on me was durable enough, if it is possible for something to be both durable and devastating. Jamie was showing me the possibility of a future in which I might care for someone as totally as my parents had cared for one another, and with a faint hope of some small exchange.

Up to that time, if you had asked me what I thought about tent people, I suppose I should have manifested the usual prejudices of my kind. To Jamie, as I now know, tents represented what he believed to be his father's pattern of life – soldiering and exploring and climbing mountains and all that sort of ruggedness – but to me and those like me, brain-washed by the middlebrow media, people who spent their free time in tents were probably ardent naturalists, re-claimers of rights of way, rare-bird spotters, badger protec-tors, people who protested that they could scent a meat-eater three buffet compartments away, and went barefoot in sandals through the snow: all very worthy kindly folk, no doubt, who might by their efforts save rare species of birds and animals from extinction, replant the rain forests and, in the end, protect the human race itself from suicide by global warming, but cranky, eccentric and ultimately ridiculous. To me tent living was not something one did to relax; it was a masochistic activity to be endured because one's ten-year-old friend happened to be a sadist and one wished to make him happy. What did one do for the entire day once the dawn chorus had woken one up?

In the serious tent shop Jamie had said, 'If you're not used to sleeping bags you'll need more room than you get in a single one,' and I had wondered in a mildly paranoid way if perhaps the size of my girth was what was at issue. But this had not been the reason why I was instructed to buy a double sleeping bag for myself, a single for him; any even semi-serious single sleeping bag should easily accommodate a forty-inch waist. What I now believe is that from the first it had been Jamie's intention to join me in the double sleeping bag.

It was a Bank Holiday week-end. The post office was closed on the Monday and Jamie need not be returned to the children's home until the Tuesday morning. We sang Beatles songs in the car and at lunchtime were the only customers to brave the chill of a pub garden close to Ross-on-Wye. I asked him safe non-probing questions about his likes and dislikes and we talked discursively about films, politics, religion and nuclear waste. I had, on instruction, brought simple food with me of the kind which can be cooked on an open fire – chops, chicken drumsticks, sausages, with potatoes to be baked in foil and bread, butter, cheese, salads and fruit to be eaten cold – and we shopped for milk, Diet Coke, tea-bags, in a village before finding a place to camp. Jamie chose where we should pitch the tent and patiently instructed me in my role, with none of the loss of temper I'd anticipated at my lack of dexterity, and in my relief at this I relaxed a little and grew correspondingly less clumsy. We made a fire without diffi-culty and sat by it, toasting sausages on sticks. We had exerted ourselves very little, yet both of us felt that pleasant tiredness brought on by the open air. At nine thirty we retired to sleep in our separate sleeping bags, and really it was not at all uncomfortable and I had plenty of room. I slept like a child and I suppose that Jamie, being a child, did so too.

Waking with the sun on that first day, we made and drank tea, wiped our faces with a flannel soaked in dew and squatted to defecate (in my own case rather clumsily) over a shallow pit dug behind a bush by Jamie with a garden spade brought for the purpose in the boot of the car. After defe-cation, the spoil was covered with earth and a new pit dug for the morrow. We walked, cooked, ate and walked some more. And for what must surely have been only minutes, but now

128

seems for ever, we sat side by side on a fallen tree and watched a sparrowhawk dive, swoop, glide and hover. What the bird saw from its thermal perch we could not know, but its ease, its alternating stillness and sudden movement, hypnotized us both into adoring silence.

Again the camp-fire, the smoky and partly burned chops, the hunks of bread and processed cheese, the easy companionship and talk by flickering firelight in the dark. By ten thirty we had committed ourselves once more to sleep. I don't know at what hour I woke to feel Jamie moving into the double sleeping bag beside me.

It was nothing to upset me, should have been nothing. There was no reason to feel both excitement and fear. It was probable that all he sought was comfort and reassurance. Perhaps my perturbation was due to the fact that, until that moment, he had shown no sign of either needing or wanting either from me.

My whole body stiffened as he placed one of his arms across my stomach, laid the left side of his head on my chest and pressed his meagre, delicate, scanty body against mine. Instinctively I covered my genitalia with one hand. Would this human warmth, this never before experienced closeness of another body, albeit a child's body, excite me sexually? Though sweating, I suddenly felt cold and very frightened – frightened that this emotionally damaged child's embrace might be a re-enactment of some form of seduction he had experienced in the past, frightened of how I might respond, filled as I was with such longing, such aching need, such uncertainty.

He said nothing, but just lay there, as though it were the most natural thing in the world, with his grubby face pressed into my chest, his hair smelling of wood smoke, his warm breath causing my skin to tingle. I could hear Colin Needham speaking in my head, 'It's the life there, isn't it?' Jamie's small bony arm gently tightened and relaxed around my stomach. He was hugging me, clinging to me for protection, occasionally twitching, occasionally brushing against my nipple with his lips as his breathing gradually slowed and he drifted towards sleep.

It came to me that this child who had cuddled up to me was there simply for warmth and love, that he was showing trust, liking and affection towards me in what was for him a completely natural way. I felt an almost overpowering urge to shout for joy, to wake him and return all these things, to match his hugs with cuddles and kisses, with expressions of care, fondness, tenderness, attachment, love, relief, all of which swooshed around inside me. The immediate effect of this conflict of heart-tearing emotions – the sudden surges of elation and excitement, the swell of contentment and pleasure, then the stab of awareness of my own vulnerability and a steep drop down into the fear of ridicule and rejection, all this splashing and gushing about inside the chest under Jamie's head, all swelling and merging, welling up inside me until I choked, pricking at my eyes, and tightening the muscles of my throat – was that I gagged and spluttered and could hardly breathe.

The second effect, which might have been expected but nevertheless took me by surprise, was that Jamie's head on my chest, his arm on my stomach, his right leg resting on top of mine, did elicit an erection. Had Jamie been a sexually aware child looking for excitement, I fear I might easily, and to my lasting shame and self-disgust, have been seduced – that my need and longing for love, and my belief that I had forfeited any real chance of it, would have let him take me over a line which I could not cross and hope to be his parent.

In the morning he lay there looking at me, his head no longer on my chest, but beside me, level with mine. I thought he was about to speak, to say something cryptic, challenging, dangerous, perhaps even to tell me what a child I was to allow myself to be trapped so easily, to let me know that he had noticed my erection and pretend to have been shocked by it.

I looked back at him, unable to speak, and he, without any expression on his face whatsoever, held my look, as though he was intent on staring me out, content to remain in his present position all day if necessary.

As usual it was I who broke the silence. 'Were you cold?' He nodded. Then after a long pause he said, 'I promised I wouldn't let the ants eat you.'

During that third day, whether in the tent or walking together in the woods, we talked very little. Conversation did not seem necessary and James was more relaxed when I shut up and only said what was important to say. Much of my working life had been spent in small talk, most of my life so far in saying rather than doing. This new discipline would be good for me.

In the evening, while I was arranging chicken drumsticks over an improvised barbecue, Jamie returned from wood gathering with a bruise on the side of his face, and told me a branch had swung back and struck him. He crouched down with the side of his face close to mine for me to inspect the injury. I did so, giving him words of sympathy and adding that there was a first-aid box in the car and that he should smear the bruise with antiseptic cream. He did not move to get the cream, but simply remained as he was, holding his face close to mine, until I no longer knew what to say or do.

After a few moments I was told what to do. In a voice I had not heard him use before, the voice of a three-year-old, I was told to kiss the bruise better. When, somewhat surprised, I had done this, I was instructed to do it again, only this time to do it properly. I asked what constituted 'properly' and was told that properly meant longer, much longer.

We were in the middle of fields, close to a wood, with no other human being or dwelling in sight and I was pressing my lips to a ten-year-old's cheek for approximately thirty seconds. What could have been more natural? Satisfied, he then sat on the ground beside me and rested the injured side of his face in my lap. The bruise was no more than a very small scratch.

Still using his baby voice Jamie then said, 'Do you love me?'

and I replied that I loved him very much, too much for my own good, adding that our meeting was the best thing that had ever happened to me and that I was very happy. He did not respond to any of this, but instead used a piece of wood to rearrange the fire.

I had, of course, been warned by Margery, she of the personalized cushion, about the disturbed child's regression to babyhood, but somehow I couldn't help believing that Jamie also knew about this and was play-acting. The baby voice he had used was so far removed from the one which had spoken knowingly on the subjects of lesbians, the Labour Party and nuclear waste. I suspected that he had adopted this behavioural oddity to assess my reaction to it, perhaps to tease me, and if I had replied as to a three-year-old, I should have failed the test and he would have dropped the pretence and mocked me, delaying even longer my emergence as a mature self-confide.it adult. Margery had neglected to warn her would-be substitute parents of the possibility that their adoptees might know, from personal observation and experience, just as much about the behaviour of disturbed children as they could learn from her.

As the evening light failed, the three-year-old forgot his injury and reverted to a happy sophisticated ten-year-old, his face lighted by the flickering flames of our camp-fire, enjoying barbecued drumsticks and jacket potatoes, singing dreamily to the stars about prairies and coyotes, and using my Christian name unprompted and with ease. I had, of course, been wondering what would happen that night about shared or unshared sleeping bags, but at bedtime there was no pretence, no jokes about ants or discussions of the need for extra warmth, no surreptitious embarrassment, just the simple and direct request, 'Can I share with you?' and my slightly shaky but relieved 'Why not?'

As before, his head on my chest, his arm across my stomach, his right leg resting on top of mine. My right arm this time was around his back, holding him to me, my left hand no longer clutching the front of underpants which hadn't been changed for three days, but free to scratch my nose or to stroke his hair. I even kissed his forehead. My heart beat remained regular, there was no cold sweat, just the merest watering of the bachelor postmaster's eyes, followed by the deepest, nightmare-free, most contented sleep I'd had in years, to be interrupted at daybreak by a son with wood ash smeared on his face like war-paint, some of which floated on the surface of the tea-bag tea in the tin mug he held out to me.

Thinking about the whole experience afterwards, I at first wondered whether Jamie had been testing me, trying to discover – even perhaps helping *me* to discover – whether I was in fact a secret pederast who, given the opportunity, would abuse him. But the more I thought about what had happened, the more I became convinced that, although it was deliberate, although, as I've said, he intended from the beginning that we should share the double sleeping bag, it was not his intention to test me in that way; he was more wise than that. I am convinced now in my own mind that the child I have chosen to be my son is in fact some ancient guru in kid's clothing, convinced that he knew full well that if our relation-ship was ever to move forwards, one obstacle had to be confronted and overcome, that of my sexual innocence, and that those deadly rivals, sexuality and the physicality which is not sexual but gives comfort and reassurance, had to do battle. That was what Jamie was helping me to discover.

I am led by the nose by a ten-year-old who knows more than I, who cuddled up to me because he knew that if a naturalness were ever to exist between us he had to feel able to touch me at will, and I had to know that too. After all, an erection can be achieved by merely lying on one's back and placing one's hand over one's penis. I have not only to know this, but also to believe it.

I have also to be a self-confident mature adult. And what in hell's name are we to do about that?

End of the Pier

'How is he?'

'Much the same.'

'Don't suppose he's missed me. I only have to set foot inside hospitals and I get symptoms. Is this the lad you mentioned?' The man Graham nodded in answer to his Uncle Turpin's question. 'And was that the best you could find? He looks a bit of a worrier to me. Very sad and sorry, he looks for himself. Not had him over your knee for a good thrashing on the way here, have you? Look at him, just look at the little bugger trying to stare me out and fix a curse at the same time. I'd watch that one, our Graham, he'll get thee in trouble.' Graham turned and winked at James. 'And what does my big brother Eddie say about you interesting yourself in little boys?'

James took the wink to mean 'Remember what I said.' It had been James who had insisted on this visit, James who had pointed out that Graham had seen his Life Story Book, whereas all James had been shown was a lot of snaps in lay-bys and a view of the beach at Westward Ho. If Graham was to make himself familiar with James's past then James had an equal right to poke about in Graham's. Graham must have more than a father in hospital; there must be a whole family network into which he, James, should be introduced. And Graham had said there was no network, that his mother, like himself, had been an only child, that the only living kin he had in the world was his father's brother, Turpin, and that nobody in his right mind would want to be introduced to him. And James had said, 'Well, I do,' so there they were.

He had been warned; James had been warned. Graham had said, 'Take everything he says with a pinch of salt and don't let it get to you. He's a crabby old man who thinks he's a bit of a character. He's bored unless he's playing to the gallery and being rude. Actually he's very lonely, I think, and a bit sad.'

So they were playing games and Graham, being on his metal, was keeping his end up. 'It's not a question of little boys, Uncle Turpin. There's only one, and Jamie came on the scene after dad's first stroke, so dad couldn't voice an opinion.'

'I see. You waited till he was ga-ga, then did the dirty deed. Well, you picked a right sulker there. I doubt even a pound of Everton Mints could put a smile on that fizzog. Shall I risk it with a bar of chocolate? Will he be able to control the excitement of it all, dosta think? And I hope you've had it house-trained. That cushion it's got its bum on had a new cover a week last Tuesday.'

The man spoke for effect. Nothing he said had anything to do with the truth. The cushion did not have a new cover. It seemed to James that nothing in the room had ever been new. The house was a narrow two-up two-down in a long terrace of the kind romanticized in Hovis commercials. It was old and dirty, and so were its surroundings. The room in which they were being entertained was small, with one small window, through the greasy net curtains of which one could see only the outbuildings in the back yard, which obscured most of the sky and allowed a minimum of grey light into the room.

The mention of chocolate seemed to be some kind of invitation, but James let it hang in the air, since no question had been asked of him directly. Thereafter a very small bar of chocolate was taken from a drawer, which was stuck and had to be prized open with a screwdriver, and Uncle Turpin played out at length a game of chocolate-offered chocolate-withdrawn until James, tiring of the game and annoyed with himself for having been drawn into it, stopped reaching for the gift. The chocolate bar was then slapped down into his lap by a clammy hand and held there while Uncle Turpin stared, breathing heavily, into James's face, and ruffled the hair on the top of James's head.

'Well, I don't know! I've only got one nephew, who never comes to see me, and when he does, he turns up with a sulky pipe-cleaner in tow. I'm not surprised it grabs for food; I could feel its bones sticking out.' Uncle Turpin left James, and turned his attention back to Graham. 'And while I'm on the subject of bones, I couldn't get down for your mother's funeral. I were a bit indisposed meself.'

'I never expected you.'

'Like that, was it?'

'You and she were never very close, were you?'

'Couldn't stand the woman personally, begging your presence, but I suppose I should have made a bit more of an effort.'

James decided to enter the conversation. 'What couldn't you stand about her?'

'It speaks! My God, it does an' all. It not only utters, but asks bloody cheeky questions of its elders and betters. Graham lad, get yon mongrel of yours under control before I bite its floppy little ears off. My word! I shall need a tablet any minute. I've never heard such a rude ha'porth in all me life!' Uncle Turpin's bedroom slippers were shuffling on the spot, as he attempted to execute half-pirouettes, pointing at one moment, clutching his heart the next, waving his arms and flapping his hands like a camp comedian. It was end-of-the-pier stuff on a bad night.

Graham said, 'I thought it was a fair question. I've never really understood why you and mother didn't hit it off.'

'Oh, well then, if it's you that wants to know, I'll give you chapter and verse. Not that I make a habit of speaking ill of the dead in front of tadpoles that don't eat the chocolate they've been given.' As if exhausted by his bravura performance of outrage, Uncle Turpin permitted what appeared to be the only comfortable chair in the room to receive him. Once sitting, he seemed calmer, less manic, and he combed his hair back from his face with fingers spread out, as a young man about town might do, and lowered his voice to emphasize the weight and seriousness of what he was saying as he explained his dislike of Graham's mother.

'There are women and there are women. Why you take to one and steer well clear of another is probably down to what happened to you at the breast. Either that or it's what happens the first time you try to get your leg over one of them. Your mother reminded me strongly of a lady of my own experience who, for reasons of avoiding slander, I'll call "Weeping Violet". Ever so dainty, ever so delicate and refined, and ever so much of a tease she were, but the whole shooting match were a con from start to finish, for if I hadn't shed me pelt regular every autumn for the last forty years, I could show you the scratches and scars that Weeping Violet decorated me back with when she were on heat.'

'I don't see what that's got to do with mother.'

'Same point – never judge by appearances. Your mother were as tough as old boots and your dad as soft as blancmange. Only your mother thought it politic to wobble a bit as she tried to shoehorn your dad to fit the old boot.'

'They were devoted to each other.'

'Mebbe, if you say so. But I always reckoned all that lovey-dovey stuff that used to sicken anyone who caught 'em at it were because, underneath it all, our Edward weren't all that struck, but she'd convinced him she'd go to pieces if he strayed even so far as the end of the garden to do a widdle on his own. Control, you see. That's what all marriages are about and family life the same, which is why your old uncle, refusing all offers, has remained a bachelor. You're better off without a family, Graham lad, so why you want to go and saddle yourself with a wizened orphan is more than I can tell. Does he cry?'

Graham looked sideways at James. 'Not a lot, as far as I know.'

'Pity. I like watching little boys cry. It were best thing about my schooldays, were that, making them cry, kept me attending regular as clockwork. Your Grandma used to see me to the gate with me dinner money of a Monday and she'd say, "You'll like it when you get there. See how many you can upset and don't be late home."'

James laughed out loud at this, which had an immediate effect on Uncle Turpin, proving to him that his efforts had not been wasted, so that his manner became immediately warmer. 'You know, I've always maintained boys have no character to speak of, but just for a minute there that sounded like a sense of humour slipping out. Are you keeping his weight down so he can be a jockey? They often find themselves gazing up the funny end of things, least the ones I put me money on do.' He rose slowly to his feet as though about to address a crowded meeting at the Town Hall. 'Now, the next thing I have to ask you is if you'll stay for tea and you have to say, "Thank you ever so kindly, but no, we're in a rush," because if that is not your reply, then we're all going to be mighty embarrassed when I find the key to the pantry.'

Even James could tell that this was not an invitation to go but to stay, and that the pantry would not be empty. Over tea on which you could trot a mouse, great hunks of bread and cheese and slabs of plum cake, Uncle Turpin became more serious, turning away to speak confidentially to Graham. 'It is all above board with you and the little lad, isn't it? I'd hate to read about my only nephew in the papers, not unless it were a knighthood or summat. You know what I'm on about, don't you?'

'Yes. I don't think you have any cause to worry.'

'Had to be said. Hope you'll understand. After all, if it hadn't been for me, you wouldn't be here.' There was then a long silence, during which James decided that, if Graham did not ask the meaning of this remark, he would have to do so himself. Then the old man continued speaking, 'For years our Edward reckoned that Droopy Dora, your mother, didn't want children. Kept promising and putting it off, promising and putting it off, so he told me. Folks kept asking when they were planning a family and he were getting frantic. I said, "Hop it, Eddie. Start again with someone else. If you wait, it'll be too late." But he wouldn't leave her. So it were left to muggins here to do the next best thing.'

'And what was that, Uncle Turpin?'

'Tell Droopy Dora a tale about how he'd said to me he were going to apply for a single assisted passage somewhere warm, if she didn't fall pregnant within a year. I kept writing off to travel firms to send him their brochures, anonymous like. Six months later you were giving her morning sickness. I can be very convincing, when me heart's set on something.'

'Did dad ever know what you'd said to her?'

'Not from me he didn't.'

James said, 'Why did you reckon he wasn't all that struck with her?'

Uncle Turpin paused, plum cake on its way to his mouth. 'Eh?' He allowed the cake to complete its journey and took time to chew, while James watched him silently and Graham watched James. Then Uncle Turpin said, 'Little pitchers.'

'Have big ears. So I've heard. Mine are small. You said you reckoned he wasn't all that struck, in spite of their lovey-dovey talk.'

Uncle Turpin said to Graham, 'That lad of yours should go into undertaking with an expression like that.'

'Please answer him.'

'It weren't nothing. I always enjoy stirring the pot a bit; you know me.'

'I'd like to know as well.'

Tea was swilled thoughtfully around Uncle Turpin's false teeth. 'Well, your dad followed your mum around as though she had him on an elastic band, didn't she? And she couldn't keep her fingers off him, always touching and clutching.' Further thoughtful consumption of tea. 'Stands to reason when two people work as hard as that to show each other affection at least one of them has to be play-acting. Probably because they're guilty.'

'You mean dad was guilty because she'd finally given him what he'd always wanted, only he didn't want it any more?'

'Don't give in to self-pity, Graham lad. It only leads to putting on weight. If your dad didn't show you the affection you thought he ought to when you were a lad doesn't mean he didn't feel it.'

'He didn't show me any at all. Most of the time.'

'He were guilty 'cos he didn't know what to do with you. You scared the shit out of him, and him in his own home, not even in the trenches. Play-acting with your mother could've been a way of keeping you at a distance because he just didn't know how to behave towards you.'

'Naturally might have been best.'

'Hardest thing in the world for some people, that. Your grandad were much the same. Hardly said two words to me till I were leaving home. Then it were only three, "Don't come back." Anyway, I've made a dog's breakfast of this. Time you and the lad were on your way, I reckon.'

In the hall as they were leaving Uncle Turpin clutched Graham's arm and held him back. James waited just outside the front door, leaving it open a crack so that he might continue to hear what was being said.

'Hadn't you better forgive your dad before he dies on you and it's too late?'

'Other fathers have managed to show love. To other sons.'

'Fewer than you think.'

'Well, I hope to do so.'

There was then a long silence before the old man spoke. Then Uncle Turpin said, 'I always did reckon you took after your mother . . . even though I had her worked out all wrong. It weren't her who didn't want kids; it were him, the lying devil, him who couldn't bring himself to poke the fire properly. Something to do with his time in the war . . . I dunno . . . some long emotional doo-dah with one of the other lads. Would you credit it, eh? – me own brother having me on like that for all that time! It were eight year or thereabouts before he could bring himself to put it where it ought to go naturally. All that clinging on to each other – it were play-acting awright, but nowt to do with you – couldn't tell you that in front of the lad, but you might as well know it. And it were your mother should have read my travel brochures and taken off for the tropics.'

'Won't you visit him? You could stay with me.'

'No, I'm not the sort. Couldn't stomach watching me own brother pull faces and make noises, you understand? Now crying, that'd be different. That I'd go anywhere to watch. Any road, I'll make a special all-out effort for the old pooftah's funeral; shouldn't have long to wait, should we? You didn't mind me asking you in there about the situation between you and the little lad?'

'No.'

'Felt I had to, under the circumstances. You see that now, I expect. And try to understand why your dad were a bit cool wi' you. She'd have been watching his every move with you, wouldn't she? I bloody well know I would.'

During their long drive back down the motorway James conceded to Graham that, if Uncle Turpin were a fair example of the kind of relative one might expect to discover if one began to poke around in the past, then there might, after all, be advantages in having very few of them. To this he received very little by way of a reply, far less a discussion. The man who had asked to be called Graham, who usually talked rather too much even when driving a car, did not seem on this drive to be talkative at all.

It was possible that having been informed by Uncle Turpin that his father was a pooftah was the cause of Graham's silence. If so that seemed to James be an over-reaction. The word 'pooftah' is much bandied about in children's homes, sometimes as an insult, sometimes as a term of casual affection. The fact that somebody has been called a pooftah doesn't necessarily mean that the somebody is a pooftah. Things and people, in James's experience, were often called what they were not.

Visiting

It was Sunday, the most depressing day to visit a hospital. Jamie had spent much of the morning deciding which flowers from the garden would be the best to decorate a hospital ward. It was odd to watch him standing at the kitchen sink, cutting their stems and arranging them into a bouquet. I had warned him that there was nothing to see, only the shell of an old man who no longer communicated with anyone, and he had given me the kind of long hard look that brooks no opposition. Perhaps he thought that by seeing me with my father he would gain some insight into aspects of my character which were still unfamiliar to him.

I sat on one side of the bed, holding father's hand and playing the usual game of pretending that he could hear and understand. I chatted to him about the village and the people he knew, while Jamie sat in silence at his other side. I told father who Jamie was, explained that he had been staying with me on trial week-ends, that I'd furnished the top room for him, and that he had already been stopped in the village by old Mrs Dickenson and congratulated on looking just like me.

I omitted to tell father that the previous week-end, while Jamie was being interrogated by the village's version of Reuters, I myself was discovering that he had been through all the pockets of my clothes in the wardrobe and had rummaged through all the drawers in the house, and that this had not been a search for money, since none was missing, and in any case, whenever I offered him pocket money he either politely refused it or graciously accepted exactly half the amount suggested. Nor had he taken any of the household disposables beyond a handkerchief (which he might have borrowed, and I forgotten).

As I chatted on about Mrs Simmonds, who had come collecting for Friends of the Earth, and – presumably because she was so embarrassed by village gossip about the proposed adoption – had, for the first time in living memory, refused to cross the threshold, and remained standing in the doorway while I searched for change, Edward's head moved from its eyes-front, give-nothing-away position, and slowly turned towards Jamie, almost as though he had heard and understood what I was telling him, and wanted to see for himself the young person whose presence in my house had caused Mrs Simmonds to behave in such an uncharacteristic way as to deny herself five minutes' chatter and a good look around.

Even then Jamie did not speak, but held Edward's look with what I can only describe as sympathetic understanding. Perhaps the very old and the very young do empathize more easily.

With one eye on the ward clock, I was trying to think of what else to talk about when I was approached by the staff nurse, who, standing so close to me that we could have exchanged ringworm, asked in hushed tones if she might have a word and led the way to sister's office.

Staff had been asked by sister to talk to me. It was not going to be good news and I should brace myself. Would I like a cup of tea? I explained that I would rather have the news first and then perhaps the tea to wash it down.

'Well, it concerns your father, of course. Concerns his condition, naturally. It's really about the prognosis, as a matter of fact.'

Then she took time out from playing Second Messenger to explain the meaning of the word 'prognosis'. It was a word used a great deal in the medical profession, she said, and in her experience, despite the number of hospital programmes on television, not every member of the lay public understood what it meant.

When we were both clear in our own minds what 'prognosis' meant, I was considered ready for the main part of the news bulletin. Seventy-seven, the Staff Nurse said, was seven more years of life than was allocated in the Bible, and although certain people did live to great ages these days, if one reached seventy then one wasn't being short-changed, was one? I was clearly a devoted son and what she had to say was bound to hit me very hard, but I must take pride in what I had managed to do for my father so far, which was far more than some people did for their parents and more than a great many even considered doing.

The staff nurse reached into the box of paper tissues she had placed before me and used one to blow her nose, putting the used tissue, somewhat unhygienically to my mind, in her breast pocket. The fact of the matter was that . . . it was thought by all concerned that . . . she did want me to understand that the gravest consideration had been given to the question by everyone involved, right up to the highest levels, but the unanimous opinion was that my father would never be fit enough to return home.

She waited for my emotional collapse, gently nodding her head to demonstrate sympathy. I also waited, suppressing an almost overwhelming urge to grab the staff nurse and waltz her around sister's office. Since I couldn't supply the expected collapse, I had better at least try to receive the news with stunned silence.

'He's going to have to be watched the whole time, you see, either here, or, if he improves just a little, then in a nursing home. After the injuries he sustained last time he fell it's just not safe to leave him. I knew this was going to be a real slap in the face for you after all you've done.' I nodded dumbly. 'And I can tell by your expression that you haven't really taken it all in yet, have you?' I shook my head. 'After two major strokes

. . . well, there could be another at any moment, and it's very rarely third time lucky for a man his age.'

I removed a man-sized tissue from the box in front of me and covered the lower part of my face with it for a moment, partly to hide any evidence of the enormous relief I was feeling, and partly so that the staff nurse could report back to sister that Mr Holt Junior had received the news with suitable distress.

Back in the ward Jamie was holding Edward's hand and talking to him. He fell silent as I approached and I shall probably never know what he had found to talk about.

In the car returning from the hospital Jamie asked me what had caused the faint bruising on the side of Edward's face. I suppose he may have had some idea, gleaned from a casual skimming of the Sunday papers which were making rather a feature of recent scandals about the treatment of old people in nursing homes, that the nursing staff of the hospital knocked their patients about. I explained that the skin of elderly people discolours easily and that it might have been simply because that was the side on which Edward slept.

I had been a little unnerved by the searching of my clothes. Not that it mattered. He'd made no great effort to cover up his tracks. Only my uneasiness mattered. Yet why should I feel as though I'd been burgled, when nothing had been taken? Stupid to feel defiled, used, interfered with, when the intruder is someone to whom one is trying to get closer.

Jamie's maternal grandparents did not want to meet him, nor did they want him to know their address. They would not respond to letters from him, should these be forwarded, and would prefer that he did not know of their existence. They had set out their reasons thus.

Their daughter, the boy's mother, was dead. Though there had been no report of her death, and no body found, she was dead to them. She had died for them from the moment when, aged sixteen, she had left the security of their home. True that, during the first six months of her absence, she had sent them two postcards and had telephoned three times, each time asking for money – money which had not been sent, since to have sent it might have been taken as proof of forgiveness – but she had not informed them when she had become pregnant or when she had given birth. In almost eleven years they had heard nothing from her, had assumed that she was dead and had grown used to living with the fact. They had also known nothing of the man with whom she had become involved, or of the child which had resulted from that involvement, and they did not wish to know now, since the girl who had left them eleven years ago was dead.

All this from Bernard the Tank Top by telephone, who added, 'They even claim they've kept no photos of her. Say they burned them. I'm writing back to say that I understand how they must have felt at the time, but I'm surprised they aren't at least interested in their grandson. Their only grandson, for God's sake; Mary was their only child. I've already told them about the possible adoption and that James needs to know about his mother, but I don't expect it'll affect their attitude. Grandparents! Who'd credit it? He needs a past. Needs to know where he's come from. It might be more comfortable for you just to start from here, but don't ever run away with the idea that Jimbo could be satisfied with that.'

I asked him to give me the grandparents' address.

'I don't know that I can do that. I hate all of this as much as you do, but I have to play by the rules. Everyone these days has a right to know who their born-to parents are, whether the born-to parents want it or not, but grandparents are a little different.'

I explained that I did not want the address for James but for my own use.

'Tricky. God, I hate this job sometimes. How will you explain how you came by it? And how do I know you won't let something slip to him? The poor kid's had enough rejection. Imagine what this arse-wipe of a letter would do to him.'

I pointed out to Bernard that, if he was bound by secrecy, then he had no business telling me about the letter in the first place. If he'd lied and told me he'd been unable to trace the grandparents the matter would have rested there. The fact that he'd let me know that at last they'd replied to his letters indicated that there were more important considerations at stake than a Tank Top's professional ethics. Many minutes later, and with British Telecom considerably richer, we had agreed on a somewhat farcical ritual which would, he assured me, only mildly soil his conscience.

This consisted of my visiting the Bungalow to be met by Bernard, who would just happen to be clutching to his chest a very thick file which contained everything known about Jamie. The grandparents' address would be near the top of the file. Bernard would then remember an urgent meeting he had to attend and would forget to take the file with him, returning to retrieve it, contents intact, thirty minutes later. I would then, if challenged, be able to say that, while being shown documents relating to Jamie, I had accidentally come across the address.

Such a stratagem would not have fooled the Loch Ness monster, but the consciences of social workers are easily assuaged. Meanwhile, since I had to make sure that no one else saw the file in Bernard's absence, I filled the time by reading it.

What I most wanted at that time was exactly what Bernard had suggested, for our father/son relationship to have begun from the moment that Jamie crawled into the sleeping bag beside me, without either of us being tethered to a past. No Uncle Turpin with his insights and meddling, no father in a geriatric ward, no grave by the vestry door to visit, no thirty-seven years of almost totally wasted life on my side, and certainly none of what I was to read about in those records, letters, psychiatric, social work and court reports on his.

I had been told, 'He's highly disturbed.' I'd been told, 'He's a very angry young boy who has tried to harm himself.' I'd been told, 'You'd be taking on a tremendously difficult child, who would have no conscience about harming himself, you, your property, or even anyone who you were close to, if the mood took him.' And I had looked at this ten-year-old with the challenging stare, with the slightly snub nose and the blue eyes, which are for much of the time dead but which crease and twinkle when he finally laughs, and all the Government health warnings in the world would not have stopped me from doing just one unlikely thing in my life, one uncharacteristically brave thing. Nothing had undermined my belief that I was the one person who could make all the difference and that between us, by love and patience, Jamie and I could change each other.

Yet for that half hour in the Bungalow, there was another difference to be considered: the yawning gap between verbal warnings and words on a page. Dates, times, statements of fact. 'That's what they say I am. Disturbed,' the boy with the dead eyes had volunteered. 'And what do you say?' the plump liberal, sitting with his knees up to his chin, had asked. But answer came there none.

The age of eight, according to Milestone Margery of the personalized cushion, was the expansive age, the age of jokes and riddles. Had eight-year-old James Lennards pondered conundrums during the elaborate preparations he had made to take his own life? Had the words 'What looks like vegetable soup and is toxic?' been the first he had uttered after the medical staff of the hospital in Reading had pumped his stomach clean?

Three months earlier, during a chilly October, he had 'gone missing' and been found after four days, lying in a wood near Chippenham. 'Though the weather was extremely cold, when found, James was naked, and his body smeared from head to foot with his own excrement.'

In that same year he had stolen from seven different shops and assisted others in breaking into a school and causing damage costing £32,000. Also in his eighth year, he had attacked his foster parents' car with a hammer and slashed all the clothes in his foster mother's wardrobe with a razor blade. Placed back into a large children's home he had attempted what the report described as: *'Another cry for help. The cuts made on his wrists with a Stanley knife are not deep. This child will certainly go on harming himself, and may well succeed in ending his life unless someone somewhere can alleviate his grief. And do it soon!'*

Another report, written six months later: *'Profoundly depressed. Spells of catatonia. This young person has a battle raging inside him which saps all his energy and spirit. I think it not too dramatic to say it's a life-or-death struggle, and that we can only watch and hope. His medication must be closely monitored by staff. This is most imperative.'*

Was this the same child who had snuggled close to the fat man inside the sleeping bag, the child who had made such a fuss about a small scratch on his face? Could it possibly be the same boy who had held the hand of a speechless old man of incomplete understanding in a hospital ward and talked to him in sympathetic whispers?

Why am I doing it? In the middle of being assessed for adoption, at a time when the various authorities involved and the child involved are supposed to be finding out all there is to find out about me, I take on a secret existence, leaving my home at the crack of dawn to drive for two hours to a suburb of Bristol in order to become a self-conscious shadow who sits for hours inside a parked car.

I am watching a semi-detached house with a purple front door and a bijou front garden. The people who live inside this house may be able to bring me closer to the person whom I dread to find, but must find, the person in whose belly was made my many-more-than-one-owner, heavily reconditioned ten-year-old son. I wish to know something of what happened during the first nine months while he was being constructed, and how much deconstruction occurred during his first three years and why. I need to know under what circumstances he was abandoned, without log-book or number plate, in a day nursery, for the police to tow away. Both he and I need this information urgently if we are ever to understand, to find a reason for and to come to terms with the seven years of emotional torture which followed.

I am getting angry now, most unlike me. This is just one of the ways in which I am changing. I have even considered breaking into the house I am watching in order to look for some of what we need. I have no previous experience of this kind of investigative snooping, but I am convinced that one of the things I want, possibly want even more than James wants, a photograph of his mother, is to be found somewhere behind those windows with their heavily frilled drapes.

What has disconcerted me most is the age of the two people I am watching. They both appear to be only a little older than myself, yet I had imagined grey-haired geriatrics. This shock has caused me to do sums on scraps of paper and to come to the conclusion that James's mother could have been no more than sixteen, the age at which she left home, or at most seventeen when she gave birth to him, since his maternal grandparents are an extremely well-preserved couple in their mid- to late forties. This makes their lack of interest in Jamie seem even less understandable somehow. Had they themselves applied to adopt him, I've no doubt that the whole thing would have been a foregone conclusion and been rushed through on the nod. Difficult of course for an inexperienced gumshoe to assess just how fully rounded emotionally people are simply by following them to their places of work.

Both have jobs. He leaves the house at seven fifteen sharp to catch a train from Templemeads station. She leaves half an hour later, takes a ten-minute bus ride and works as the manageress of the Junior Miss department in a large store. Finding out that much has been easy. The difficulty will be to make some form of casual contact, which will require a great deal of acting on my part and a believable cover story. The longer I sit here unable to think of a suitable story, the more attractive the burglary option appears.

I seem to have been either watching and waiting or to have been acting all my life. From the shadow of the cupboard under the stairs. From behind the post office counter, pretending to tidy, to count, to read, while the customers find what they need or just make up their minds. From behind a desk at school, studying today's subject, which would never be History or English, but always some child sitting a few desks away. I watch how the subject moves his or her head, how he leans over his desk to write. I count how many times she looks at the teacher or the blackboard, how often she looks at the child next to her, assess how long each look is held, and speculate on the reason for it. I watch that same child in the playground, and I wonder what that child does when it returns home, and I compile in my head a strip cartoon of my subject's complete day. This is not real interest, you understand. Not in the child. It is the only means I have of assessing how *I* should be, the only way of knowing what *I* should be doing. The land I inhabit is a land of strangers, a foreign land, and the language spoken here means nothing to me.

'Have you taken up residence in that car, sir?'

'Sorry?'

'We've had a report about a suspicious person fitting your description. One of the householders rang the station. I expect your observant eye noted the Neighbourhood Watch posters all along the street. Am I right in thinking, sir, that you have occupied that seat in that particular car for several hours on three consecutive days?'

'I suppose that would be true, yes.'

'Any particular mechanical reason for this immobility, sir?'

'No, the car's fine. It's a personal matter, constable.'

'Something to do with one of those houses, sir?'

'In a manner of speaking, yes.'

'But you don't live around here, sir, do you?'

'No.'

'A thwarted love or something of the kind would it be, sir?'

'Something vaguely of that sort.'

'Then might I sort of vaguely glance at your licence? Warwickshire? You've driven a long way. And have you driven all the way from Warwickshire to this exact spot here on each of the last three days?'

'Yes.'

'Plus two days of last week? On Tuesday and again on Thursday?'

'That would be correct. I think those would have been the days.'

'Would you step outside the car please, sir?'

I tried to explain, tried to tell the young Constable about Jamie and the proposed adoption. I requested the utmost confidentiality from this guardian of the law. It was most important that whoever watched this neighbourhood so conscientiously, and had reported my arrival, should not know the reason for my being here since she would no doubt inform Jamie's grandparents.

I'm not sure that he took any of it in. Nodding like some Enid Blyton character, the young Constable searched my car for burglary tools or bomb-making equipment and found nothing more suspicious than a small primus stove, tent pegs and a child's comic, on which Jamie had drawn mildly pornographic doodles. He studied these, holding the comic at several angles, trying to decide whether they were indeed a child's imaginative view of adult bodily parts or whether these doodles were actually instructions for the assembly of bombs.

At the police station I told my story yet again to a blueberry-faced Desk Sergeant, who had clearly taken private tuition in sympathetic-elder-brother expressions. Was there anyone who could substantiate my story? I gave the Sergeant the phone number of the post office and hoped Lynn wouldn't be too rushed off her feet to answer, and, if and when she did answer, that on hearing the words 'This is the Avon Constabulary, madam', she would breathe deeply and think seriously before replying. She had already warned me that if the detective work became any more of an obsession, I would soon be returning to find that she and her children had taken up residence in my house in order that she could continue running the shop.

Asked to describe me, she said, 'He's fat. Tell him I said he's gross, and that sitting in a fart-filled car all day is making him even grosser. Yes, of course I know what he's doing. He's wasting his time when he should be here helping me. Tell him I've bought two hundred pairs of stainless-steel knitting needles and accepted a dud cheque. Tell him to get his fat arse back here or I'm going on strike. He's trying to pluck up courage to talk to some middle-aged yuppies who don't want to know about their grandson. I'm surprised you didn't catch him going through their drawers, with his hands in their photo album.'

The Desk Sergeant laughed until he coughed, thanked her kindly, and told her that if she ever happened to find herself in Bristol needing to know the time, she should ask him. 'She's quite a lady, isn't she? What a refreshing turn of phrase she's got. Said I should give you the shock of your life and send you home in a squad car with the siren going.'

No, he couldn't advise me on how to proceed. There were laws. And if I ignored his advice and did proceed, he'd book me on suspicion, even though he sympathized with my predicament. His duty was to act on a complaint. Unless I moved my car immediately, he'd have it moved and me with it, except that I would be going one way and the vehicle another. And no, he couldn't give me the name of the complainer.

I asked whether he'd be prepared to tell me if the complaint had been made from the house I was interested in? Although I had seen them both leave for work, it was just possible that they had phoned the police before leaving. The Desk Sergeant said it was more than his job was worth to give away such confidential information, but that I should watch his head, which he then shook.

Might I perhaps go with a Constable to apologize to the person who had made the complaint?

The Desk Sergeant looked at me for several seconds, evaluating just how serious I was, how desperate, and how much more trouble and paperwork I might cause him. 'And what would you say to them? I thought you didn't want anyone to know you were snooping.'

'I'd have to tell them the truth and risk it. It's just possible they could tell me something about the daughter, if they've lived here a while. I can't give up without a last-ditch stand.'

'I haven't the constables to send them out acting as match-makers.'

'Please. Just something, anything. One introduction.'

And he agreed. If I put a crisp ten-pound note into the charity box on the Sergeant's counter, took my car to a multi-storey car park and was in a certain pub at opening time, I would there be approached by a tall dark stranger by the name of Constable Hicks whose parents lived in the road next to the one which had caused so much discussion.

With much hilarity I was warned that my ten pounds for charity would be a mere tip of the iceberg and that the cost in alcohol might prove incalculable, Constable Hicks being large in stature even for a policeman and having another physical peculiarity not unknown in beat bobbies, that of hollow legs.

Did the good Constable Hicks already know, or had he taken the trouble to find out before he came to meet me, that Mary Connolly had left the family home just over eleven years ago? She had given no warning but had just started walking and never returned. She had left home aged sixteen and it was said that she taken up with an older man, not that much older, in his mid-twenties, a man who would now be my age. Nobody knew who he was, but a friend of the Constable's mother, who knew Mary by sight, had seen her in Chippenham, heavily pregnant and holding the arm of a man, bearded and shabby, but extremely good-looking and of athletic build and military bearing.

Mary's parents both worked (which I knew), had always worked, and were liked because they kept to themselves, as did everyone in that street, which was known locally as 'Upwardly Mobile Drive'. Constable Hicks wasn't surprised by the Connollys' attitude towards their grandson. 'A ten-year-old kid from Care wouldn't fit in with their life style one little bit. I'm not sure they'd ever really wanted Mary, but at least she was a girl. If you saw inside the house, I think you'd know what I mean. I was in there once, just the once. The smell of it . . . difficult to describe . . . certainly excludes children, male children especially. Mary was a lost child, my mother says, a latch-key child, with both of them at work. Very attractive young girl, very feminine, but anyone could see the way she was going and how she'd end up if someone she cared about didn't pay her a bit more attention. Short skirts, too much make-up, highly developed top half. That was at fourteen and you could smell her expensive perfume from one end of the street to the other; mum says she must have bathed in it.'

I'd kept to tonic water, but seven pints later Constable Hicks had an idea. 'What about this little lad's great-grand-parents? They'd know all about his mother. Might be more sympathetic. Older folks usually are, and they're often great chatters. Can't swear they're alive, but they'd only be . . . what? . . . late sixties? . . . early seventies? Tell you what, get me another pint in, and I'll make a phone call. Somebody has to know where they are.'

Blood Kindred

Again they were driving north, this time over winding roads to a village in Shropshire. It was not as far as the journey to Uncle Turpin, but would take longer. They were to visit James's great-grandparents.

The man called Graham had said, 'They've not been warned we're coming. I thought it best to take them by surprise. Of course they could be out and then we'd have wasted our time.' The time wasted would be five hours at least, there and back, which James thought odd, when the waste could easily be avoided by a single telephone call, but he did not speak his thought. There were too many oddities about this excursion. Better to brood about them silently and see where they led.

Time was added to the journey by their losing the way in Droitwich Spa. The man Graham drove in silence. His neck was red. He said, 'Might be better if you waited in the car to begin with. It could take some explaining. Probably needs a bit more than, "Hello! I'm the man who's about to adopt the great-grandson you've never seen. Thought we'd just pop in to say Whatcha." Might need rather a lot more.'

James asked whether his great-grandparents had ever known that he existed, and the man Graham replied that he thought it possible that they had not, but felt confident that they would be over the moon when they met him.

How the whereabouts of these great-grandparents had been discovered had not yet been explained and was another of the oddities. James supposed that the Social Services had discovered them, but if so why had the man Graham been told, and not him? This was his Life Story, not the man Graham's. And why great-grandparents and not grand-parents, who ought to be easier to find, since it was already known (and written in the book – with their name) that they lived in a suburb of Bristol? And if these great-grandparents had been discovered with the aid of the grandparents, why were the grandparents not being visited first, particularly since Bristol was only ninety minutes away?

James was supposed to be both reading the map and looking out for road signs, so there was plenty to occupy his mind during their long drive into Shropshire.

When they arrived the old man was standing in his cottage garden, his back to the gate by which the man who liked to be called Graham entered. From the car James could hear them talking, but not what was said. Their conversation seemed to go on for ever, until eventually the old man turned towards the gate and, shielding his eyes, looked in James's direction. Then the two men moved towards him, the man Graham leading the way. James was uncertain whether he was expected to get out of the car and go to meet them, but decided to remain where he was until directed. He was being treated like a puppet. Very well, if that was what they wanted, that was what he would be.

The man Graham called out, 'Jamie, come and meet your great-grandfather,' and James complied, taking his time about doing so.

The old man was smiling, was removing the flat cap from his head and holding out a large hand to be shaken. James took the old man's hand, with its folds of warm loose skin, into his own hand, and moved it up and down.

'Are you really Mary's little boy? I've been telling this gentleman, I asked and asked what became of you, but no one would tell; nobody seemed to know.' Who were these no ones who would not tell? Presumably they were the maternal grandparents, one of whom would be the child of this old man. Oddity was piled on oddity. 'I last saw you when you

158

were a baby; your mother brought you. Ten weeks old or thereabouts, you were, and a terrible crier.' James doubted whether this was the truth. If the old man had only seen him once, that was hardly sufficient evidence. Even if it were true, it was not important; James did not cry now. 'Had your poor mum running round in circles, you did, fetching and carrying. "He's going to be a very demanding person, if you jump like that every time he yells," I told Mary. "Leave him wait for you a little." She was too young at seventeen to know any better.'

'*Love me. Love Mary.*' And she had been too young to leave him wait for her, even a little time. The old man would have a photograph of her, and that would please all those who had tried in the past to find one and failed. It would be a photograph of a girl seven years older than James was now. Seventeen and seven made twenty-four, and that would be her age now, no age at all.

Inside the cottage the old man continued to talk. He made tea and found biscuits, and told them that he and his wife had had two daughters, Cathleen and Sarah, and that these daughters had given birth to one daughter each, Christine and Mary, and then stopped. He said to James, 'And Mary had you all those years ago, and Christine – they were giving up hope, she and Bill, for it wasn't for want of trying; they both love children – giving up hope . . . Yes . . . well . . . as I was saying . . . Just this last April, Christine gave birth to twins, both girls – girls again: they run in our family. You're the only boy in this family since me. All this time and I didn't get to see you.' And at this point, the old man surprisingly started sobbing, left the room, and could be heard going upstairs.

They waited a little for him to return. Then the man Graham said, 'I think I'd better see if he's all right,' and went off after the old man. James took another biscuit, poured himself more tea and waited.

Some time later the man Graham returned alone.

'He's very upset about what happened. You see, I'd told him how long you have been in Care, and about your father.'

Graham-the-postman, about to deliver bad news, kneeled in front of James's chair and took both James's hands into his own. 'He can't face telling you this himself, but he's pretty sure that your mother must be dead. She didn't get on with her own parents – as far as I can gather, he doesn't get on with them either: it's his other daughter he still sees and her family. But he was very fond of your mother, and she was fond of her grandparents, particularly him. They were very close, he says. Came to stay here often when she was a kid and wrote to him regularly. When you would have been almost three, the letters stopped. He wrote many times, he says, and got no answer, and after a bit the letters came back 'Not known at this address'. He's convinced that if she were still alive she'd have been in touch. He says that you look a lot like her. He never met your father. Mary only came here that one time after she left home; she brought you with her, but not him; the old man's not sure why not. I know that there's a lot more we need to know, but he is an old man and we gave him quite a shock rolling up like that. We can visit again soon. I'll telephone him first. And he's told me that you'll find photographs and one or two personal things belonging to your mother in that bureau. He said you are to take whatever you want and to look after them carefully for him. Take your time to choose what you want to take with you and then we'll just slink away. His name's Percy, by the way, but you'd probably better call him "Great-Grandpa".'

In the car the postman asked James whether he understood why the old man had been so upset.

'Shock?'

'More than that. You reminded him strongly of someone he was very fond of – your mother; that's one thing. But – I don't know if you can understand this, Jamie . . .'

'Try me.'

160

'It's guilt. He feels guilty. The time that your mother stopped writing to him was just after his wife had died. He was alone for the first time in his life. He desperately needed to talk to someone – preferably your mother, because they understood each other – but she wasn't there and she didn't reply to his letters. So he blamed her. And when I told him you'd been left in a day nursery and taken into Care, and then about your father coming back for you – first when you were four, then when you were six – and how, after that second time, you'd been shuffled from pillar to post, that was when he said he couldn't face you again.'

'When I was six, my name and dad's name were read out on the radio, and no one came forward then to say they were my great-grandparents. And we were in the newspapers. They printed my dad's picture. It's in my Life Story Book. It got torn, but I mended it.'

'I suppose . . . he may not have heard it. He may not have read that paper. Jamie . . . if your father and mother weren't married – and we don't know if they were or not because nobody's found your birth certificate – he might not have known your dad's name, and even if he'd known it once, he could easily have forgotten it after six years.'

'You said he wrote to her.'

'Maybe as Mary Connolly.'

The postman was plausible. James set his mouth against him, and his mind, and his heart.

He had not taken all there was relating to his mother from the old man's bureau drawer. He had left the diamanté brooch, the baby's dummy and teething ring, had left photographs of his mother as a baby, as a toddler, of her riding a donkey on a beach, of her enjoying an ice-cream at a fun fair with her parents standing either side of her, of her enjoying a family Christmas sing-song; he had left all those mementoes of her.

He had chosen instead to take the cigarette lighter with the words 'To John. Love. Promise. Always. Mary' engraved on

161

it. And there were some photographs which he had brought away with him. One was of a baby in a cot; he assumed this child to be himself. Another was of a child sitting in a high chair holding out a toy towards the camera and smiling, a small cake with one candle in the child's other hand; he assumed this child also to be himself. There was also a photograph of the child on its second birthday, in which it was sitting on the floor surrounded by brightly coloured wrapping paper. The expression on the child's face was of surprise, almost as though it was the child itself who had just been unwrapped.

As well as his father's lighter and the pictures of an infant who did not seem to have much in common with the three-year-old who had lain under a blanket which stank of urine, watching the world turn on its side, James had taken from the bureau three photographs of his born-to mother, which he considered to be more than enough. One was of her in school uniform aged about ten. One had been taken in a photo booth. She looked frightened, and the words, 'Leaving home pic. Ugh!' had been written on the back. In the third she sat among a group of friends, one of whom James recognized to be his father, with the words, 'For Gramps and Gran, with love, Mary and John', scrawled over the faces of the friends.

James had not found what he had hoped to find in the old man's bureau drawer, had not found the thing he had thought about often, the one thing he longed for. In none of the photographs was Jimmy being held by either of his born-to parents. In none were his parents smiling at having their picture taken with their son. Where he appeared, they did not. In all of them he was alone.

At two a.m. James was standing at the window of Edward's room, watching the advertisement for engine oil outside the garage opposite rotate and flick, flick, flick, shrugging off itself fireballs of light reflected from the street-lamp. It was the only thing in this village which moved.

He heard footsteps on the stairs and listened as the

postman opened the door of the room at the very top of the house, heard the footsteps crossing to the bed and then returning to the door and retreating down the stairs. He listened to the doors of the lower part of the house being opened and closed, and waited for the footsteps to mount the stairs again, waited for them to stop outside.

Eventually the door was opened slowly and the footsteps moved across the room towards him. An arm was placed over his shoulder and he shrugged it off. The postman said, 'OK. As long as I know where you are,' and went out again and back to the room next door.

But this man who wished to become James's substitute parent did not know where James was because James himself did not know where James was.

They had completed the usual Friday evening journey from the Children's Home and reached the little house next to the post office. In the living room the post office man said, 'I have a letter for you. It's from your father,' said the words just like that and then waited and watched to see how James would react. But James did not react in any exterior way. The post office man then said, 'I'm rather nervous, I expect you are too. He wrote to me as well. I've read mine. It's a very nice letter . . . wishing us luck. He refers to you as "Jimmy". I didn't think you liked to be called that.'

During the silence which followed, James experienced a curious sensation in which he both felt what he felt and observed himself feeling it at the same time. He felt as though everything contained within his skin had suddenly disappeared, as though his legs no longer had bones inside them. He saw the postman holding out to him the folded square of lined paper, which had also been held by his father and which would contain his father's own words to him in neatly slanted joined-up writing, secret sad words from the warm lips of an unhappy man, written on paper which his father would have pressed his fingers against to fold. He watched something he recognized to be his own right hand reaching out to take hold of the folded paper and place it carefully in the inside pocket of his jacket, and was aware that he was holding the back of a chair to keep it from moving, since all the objects in the room, particularly the clocks, appeared to be revolving around him.

These rotating objects included the postman, who wore a worried expression on his face, and from the orbiting post-man – but seeming to come from a distance – he could hear yet more words, 'You'll want to read your letter in private, I expect,' and he felt his chin move up and down in answer. He observed himself placing his right foot in front of his left very slowly, testing whether either would support his weight, and by alternating his right foot with his left he reached the staircase and then, by mounting them one at a time like an old man, he climbed three stairs before the distant voice spoke again. 'Good idea. Why not read it in your room?' He considered the words 'your room', trying to work out what they meant, as images of all the rooms he had ever slept in rushed into his mind, all getting mixed up with each other, the size of the windows changing and the colour of the walls merging to become darker, until they were all black.

He stood on the third stair, turned and looked back at the room he had just left, knowing that somewhere in that house there was another room known as 'his room', but since he couldn't at that moment remember what it looked like or where he would find it, he descended the three stairs and moved through the lower room towards the hall, touching the furniture as he did so.

The postman shouted out one of his names, 'Jamie', and crossed the room quickly in front of him to stand barring his way. More words. 'Bernard said I should be with you when you read your dad's letter. It's private, I know, but if it upsets you I want to be close by.' James stared at the man, who continued to speak, but the words made a blur, only coming back into sense as the man finished speaking, 'In that case, let me just see you across the road to the playing field. And before we do that I want something else from you. I want you to let me hug you because I suddenly feel very scared.'

The man moved slowly towards James and wrapped both his arms around him, pressing their two bodies together and resting the side of his face on the top of James's head. He was not alone. Simultaneously James could see a spider's web of arms stretched wide ready to encircle him, arms of social workers, foster parents, friends, the arms of almost everyone he had ever known while in Care, all wrapping themselves around him and squeezing. It was called 'hugging', 'cuddling', or 'cooching', and it was supposed to make you feel less lonely.

The man opened the door to the hall and stood leaning against the cupboard under the stairs until James moved past him and opened the door to the street. He followed James across the road to the entrance of the playing field, leaned on a fence, and waited, watching as James turned away from the playing field and walked along the narrow grass verge towards the garage with its rotating advertisement.

James unfolded the letter, and, by the combined lights of the street-lamp and the advertisement, read what his father had written from prison.

Dear Jimmy,
They tell me that you are all right. They didn't say 'He's well and happy' which is what I've preyed for, but I suppose 'all right' isn't too bad considering all that has happened to you.

They also say that there is someone who wishes to adopt you, and that they like and trust this man, and that you seem to get on well with him. They have explained to me why they are considering a single man and why they think the adoption would be best for you. And since I know that by the time I am able to be a proper father to you we might not even know each other, I have told them that if you are sure it is what you want, then I will agree to the adoption.

I do this only because I want what is best for you, and because I have so far failed you. In an ideal world, Jimmy, my love, we would be together and I would be able to hug you and hold your hand. In an ideal world we would be able to plan for the future, and I would be allowed to watch you grow. No one would stop me from being your father. I say this because it is most important that you understand that none of what has happened is your fault. You are in no way to blame, Jimmy. Please, please remember that. I am the one at fault, the one who has failed his most scared duty, to be a good father. And you are the one who has suffered most because of it.

I will always be the person who helped make you, and I will always love you more than anyone else. There are times when I wish I didn't still see your face so clearly. Because remembering your look when we seperated tares me apart inside. Perhaps the photograph they sent to show me how tall and handsome you look now will help me to consentrate more on the present and the future.

It's important that you study and work hard, so that you will be able to make a way for yourself. Important also to give as much as you can of yourself to those who care for you. Try not to let what has happened make you mean and bitter towards people. A lot to ask of a small boy who lost everything.

One day, when you are old enough to understand what forgiveness is, I will need all you can spare. I love you most. Always, Jimmy. Promise, always.

Your Father

Time passed. The lights in the street went out. In the darkness the man took hold of his hand and pulled him away from where he had been sitting, his back supported by the door of the garage. He did not answer any of the man's questions, or respond to the man's pleas for him to return home or even give that word parking space inside his head. Finally the man used physical force and James did not struggle or fight. The force the man used was more than was necessary, more force than James had thought him capable of. He supposed it was the man's anger which assisted him to pull James along the road with such energy and to push him inside a house which James did not at first recognize as the house he visited at week-ends.

The man now looked very old and was trembling. He offered food, suggested a bath, then turned on the television and sat before it sulking. He made a speech about understanding how James must feel, apologized for his anger, and tried to make a joke of it by saying that anger was an illness and he knew who had infected him with it. James was interested to discover that the man's words were no longer a blur and that he could understand what the man was saying, even though it was of no importance. The man continued to talk, jerkily, hesitantly, about jealousy and how it crippled people and caused them to behave badly. He apologized yet again and told James that James was seeing him at his worst, that since he had not read and did not know what was written in James's letter, his earlier statement that he understood how James felt inside ha l just been words, empty words, that he didn't know, didn't understand, but wanted to, desperately wanted to. The man looked tired, exhausted, like a teddy bear someone had dragged along a wet gravel path. He said, 'All I can say honestly, Jamie, is that unless you speak to me, unless you say something, can share something with me, I don't think I . . .' but was unable to finish this sentence. James waited and watched. The man switched the television off and then remained staring at the blank screen. He continued to watch silently as the man walked around the room, clearing things away into drawers and writing out lists, some of which he read aloud. Lists of things needed or to be done – laundry, dry-cleaning, housework, unanswered correspondence. Lists of the things which were urgent, and those which could wait. Lists of things to buy – bread, milk, tea-bags, sugar. Until finally James spoke, interrupting the list to say, 'I have a father.'

The man stopped what he was doing and looked at James, stared at him, willing him, daring him to continue.

'Just because he can't look after me doesn't make anyone else my father. His letter doesn't say anything about us going to see him.'

The man waited, watched James and waited for more.

And James said, 'You can't adopt me unless I see him first. You know that, don't you?'

The man nodded slowly, and said, 'Yes, I had realized that was part of the bargain you were prepared to make. I'll talk to my social worker and to Bernard. See whether we can't pin them down to a definite date.'

Each looked at the other silently. The man was no longer ill at ease, making lists or fiddling. He sat down, and said, 'There is something more in this adoption for you than the visit to your father, isn't there? Because, if not, I'm sure it could be arranged for you to see him without having to involve yourself with me. If you were reluctant in any way.'

James heard his own voice come out higher and sharper than he intended. 'Are *you* reluctant? In any way?'

'Only the tiniest amount and only this evening. Because I'm jealous, as I told you, and I'm behaving badly, as you've noticed. Lack of self-control, Jamie; it happens to anyone. In my case it's because I want to avoid being hurt and humiliated, and I want to avoid your being hurt.'

'How would I get hurt?'

'If you feel nothing at all for me, then you won't be. If you have no conscience at all, then you won't be. And why should someone who has lost everything else struggle to keep a conscience? On the other hand, if you have kept it, perhaps as a keepsake, and you use me only in order to see your father, then we both get hurt, don't we? You won't like yourself afterwards, and you'll dislike me even more because I'll always be there, reminding you of what you did, even when you no longer have any use for me. That's why, if it is possible for them to set up a meeting between you and your father which has nothing to do with the adoption, that would certainly seem to be the best bet.'

James took the letter from his father out of his pocket and placed it on the table for the man to read.

'Are you sure you want me to read it? Wouldn't it be best to wait and think about it for a while?'

James said, 'You have to understand something about me, something about my father and what he means to me. It's only fair you should understand why you can't ever take his place.'

Support

After that things calmed down a little, with each of us knowing where we stood. That was the theory. In practice this calmness seemed to have all the characteristics of the kind of serenity from which world wars break out.

It went on for week-end after week-end. I suppose he could have ended it by saying to Bernard that he didn't want to visit me any more. Or I could have ended it by pulling out of the attempt to adopt him. Since we both allowed it to persist, doing nothing eithe. to end it or break out of it, something in both of us must have wanted it.

Jamie had taken to shuffling like a moth in wellingtons at the periphery of my field of vision. He never looked directly at me but viewed me sideways. If he had to pass me he walked round me. Would the three yards he was keeping between us ever be reduced and, if so, how was the reduction to be achieved? He would age: I had been told I must allow him to age and not try forever to keep him at ten years and nine months old. What if, in five years' time (presuming we still shared the same living quarters), he was still maintaining this distance between us? What if, aged fifteen, he was still forcing me to observe my space? There would be more need for space at fifteen. By then loud hailers would be necessary.

Inside the house, where space was at a premium and distance was difficult to keep, he would kneel on the window-seat, his back to me, looking out at the garage across the road. Whenever I approached to stand behind him and see what he saw, I'd watch his shoulders stiffen, watch the pulse in his neck begin to flutter as the moth summoned its resources, toughened its skin, prepared itself for flight.

At mealtimes this same moth would move the place I set for him next to me and take up a position at the opposite end of the table, six feet away. I knew that we should talk about all this. We should sit down quietly, with whatever space between us he needed to feel comfortable, and discuss it. Moth to man.

There were no more visits, either to the grandparents who would not have received us or to old Percy, who may have longed for contact. The weather was unsuitable for camping trips, and it seemed unlikely that Jamie would have wanted to go. Instead we went for walks. He seemed to enjoy the walks, enjoy shuffling between the orderly lines of conifers in our hideously symmetrical man-made wood. Sometimes he would even skip, jump to catch hold of branches, pace out the measurements of a glade wrapped in some private calculation, hop on one foot holding the other behind him, dance as though he were a younger child, an infant moth emerging from its pupa and turning its wings towards the sun to dry before taking to the skies. But at these times he was not with me; he was alone, or with some other imagined person, and I followed in his wake. When he raced ahead, then stopped to wait for me, it was always with the pretence that he was not waiting but had just happened to notice something of interest. And just so did I pretend not to notice him watching my approach, eyeing me with such devious scrutiny as though weighing in his balance every hair, every pore, every eyelash, every tooth in my head and discovering that they added up to very little.

I had been told that when something about the child I was hoping to adopt puzzled me I must reverse roles, imagining that I was Jamie and he me. In that way I would be able to think his thoughts, feel his feelings. Easy for others to give advice. My father was not young, not strong, not a romantic hero unjustly imprisoned, but an incontinent old man in hospital. I could not be the moth in wellingtons, fifty yards ahead, feigning interest in a log of wood. I was the tubby person pushing through brambles on a muddy path behind.

Carrying out what I conceived to be my parental duty, I finally persuaded him to say 'Thank you'. He said it resentfully and without conviction, and never to me or to any other human. He would thank the ceiling or the floor. He thanked the chair beside him or the teapot. And when he wished something to be passed to him, he would ask an inanimate object close to my left elbow for it – 'Can I have the sugar?' to my side plate, or more often it would be 'Am I allowed more sugar?' This was because I had attempted to explain the effects of sugar on teeth, and the necessity to clean same, even bitchily remarking that if the tall handsome young man mentioned in his father's letter arrived on visiting day smiling a yellow smile, the charm of the moment would be somewhat diminished.

The amount of effort required from Jamie to maintain this lack of eye-contact must have been tremendous, almost as though he had decided to test his self-control. If I felt the strain of it, he must have been under even greater strain. There! I have just reversed roles, and no good has it done me.

'Never expect gifts from a child from Care.' That's in all the literature. Presents are for receiving. How they come to be given is not the concern of a Care child, who will have arrived in Care with nothing and may well leave with the same. Possessions are for keeping if you can, for guarding, even for fighting over. Birthday cards arrive or they don't; they are never sent, not even if a thirty-seven-year-old would-be substitute father drops a few hints, not even if the same old codger sells the bloody things in his shop next door and foists on you extra pocket money the very day before the momentous event. Kids from Care don't send cards to mark the passing of time, since by marking time they remind themselves of how slowly it moves. Kids from Care don't even have the graciousness to blush when shown the birthday cards which others have sent. *'Was it your birthday then, or something?'*

There had to be something about me which threatened him. Perhaps he sensed the tensions I was feeling and received them as something else, even as the prelude to some sort of physical assault. Surely he must have known that I wasn't in any way a physical threat to him. It wouldn't have hurt him to come to meet me a little. Even his own father had given permission for generosity. Where did he find the stamina to go on day after day acting out this violent lack of interest, this gentle hostility?

Three week-ends went by, during which he didn't smile once, or show the slightest glimpse of the real him – either the swearing, angry, self-mutilating him or the 'Kiss me better. Kiss me longer. Do it properly. Do you love me?' him. Nor did he allow me to be myself. Whatever that is. The longer he held on to me yet kept me at a distance, as though he were terrified I might somehow give his absent father cause for jealousy, the odder I felt and therefore the odder I must have appeared to him.

Did one take the hand of a ten-year-old? Or wait and see if it were offered? It wouldn't be, of course. Not now the honeymoon was over. Not while he awaited orders from HQ, waited for the strategic retreat to be finalized, surreptitiously watched me waddle about in my trench shoes, just as I watched him shuffling to and fro in his wellington dug-out. (Mixed metaphor! One can't move in a dug-out; that's the point of it.) 'No,' I kept telling myself. 'No. One certainly doesn't offer one's hand to a ten-year-old boy, not unless one happens to be the boy's natural, born-to, blood-related father.' And I kept my hands to myself.

I was like a cast-off lover who cannot bring himself to cut the knot and get the hell out, an unwanted admirer shadowing the love object, hanging on every word in the hope that one might be meant kindly. 'Happy Birthday!', had it been said, would have sufficed.

There were moments when I did feel like attacking him physically, not to hit him or shake him, just to drag him into my space and keep him there until he realized that it was not a dangerous place to be. I've never robbed a moth of its wings in my life. That's not something I would have taken up so late in the day.

Finally in desperation I took my problem to the Infant Social Worker, who said, 'What do I keep telling you? Don't keep things to yourself. Get them out. Consult.'

I said, 'I am consulting. I'm consulting you.'

'No good. Most of your life as a substitute parent, I shan't be around. This is the time your support system should be operating.'

I had forgotten the support system. I knew I had to have one in order to impress the Adoption Panel, but I hadn't anticipated actually using it. The Infant Social Worker said, 'It's Lynn, isn't it?'

'Mainly Lynn.'

'Entirely Lynn, as far as I can tell. I'd better go with you, so that I can see for myself how well you interact.'

Of course it was a mistake. I should never have allowed myself to be bullied into it. Interaction with Lynn comes in two sizes, the public sort with other people present and the private sort when we're alone together, the first being considerably larger than the second.

So we went to see Lynn and were received into her caravan, which was one of the immovable variety, thirty feet by ten, a mobile home which was mobile in name only. Had I taken the trouble to listen to the weather forecast before setting out, I should have postponed the visit. It was raining heavily, which meant that all four of Lynn's children were indoors sharing the space with us.

Usually Lynn and three of her children occupied four bunk-beds, of which the two lower bunks doubled as small sofas; the fourth and eldest child, eight-year-old Ludo, had his own

174

mattress on the floor by the door in the kitchen area, and was referred to by Lynn as her draught excluder. Now the Infant Social Worker and I shared one of the sofas, Lynn sat on the other and the mattress was used by the children. 'Used' was the right word – Lynn's children put their surroundings to use. They were not given to board games or card games: snakes and ladders, Scrabble, Monopoly never held their attention; they greatly preferred trampolining, pole-vaulting or even running on the spot.

Rain drummed on the roof and sounded like a platoon of marines in full combat gear on a five-mile run. Luckily, or perhaps unluckily, Lynn interacting publicly could be heard above most other sounds short of a nuclear explosion.

'You want to own something. No not something, another human being.' Lynn was speaking to me, but at us both. Her effect on the Infant Social Worker had so far astonished me, though a more worldly-wise person might have anticipated it. Lynn and the Infant Social Worker, in the directness of their approach, their calculated unconventionality and their readiness to shock, were two of a kind, but Lynn was older and better at it. The two women had disliked each other on sight and the Infant Social Worker had become uncharacteristically reticent.

'You want a relationship, but you want it entirely on your own terms, which means you're terrified of not being in control. But Jamie is a person in his own right. Everyone is; you've got to allow for that. And I might as well tell you here and now, if you go ahead with this you have every reason to be scared. Bloody scared! That boy is distressed, and distressed children play the sort of mind games you've never even dreamed of and make up the rules as they go along. In control is the very last thing you'll be. You'd stand more chance of that with a cuddly divorcee.'

I said, 'But you're not divorced yet.'

'Leave it out! Where would we find a bed big enough? Giles, I'll fetch you such a wallop if you do that just one more time.' Six-year-old Giles had twin brother Jasper's head engulfed under his arm like a rugby ball and was running backwards and forwards, using it as one might a battering ram against the pantry door.

'He wants food.' Jasper choked and spluttered out these words from the depth of his brother's armpit.

'He's had all he's going to get until supper. And tell him while you're at it that I happen to know that there are now only five custard creams left in a packet that had nine in it before lunch, so you can inform your brother that I would like all four missing biscuits returned to their rightful owner in some form or other, pronto.'

The idea of returning the consumed biscuits in their present form sent three of Lynn's four young persons in their own right into fits of hysterical dancing, of face pulling, of shouting all the known childish euphemisms for excreta and inventing new ones, while arms waved and faces became redder, until Cora, sensing some form of mass mania from which she was being excluded, ran screaming to her mother to be picked up.

'You're intelligent enough to know that adult relationships don't work well on the basis of ownership. You also know that neither do good relationships with children. I've seen you relish a good long bout of sulking, so why shouldn't he?'

'I never sulk.'

'Can't hear you!'

I shouted. 'I never sulk. If I go silent sometimes it's only to avoid trouble. It's a form of camouflage.'

'That's not camouflage; it's a way of turning milk.'

The Infant Social Worker decided to speak up for me. 'All relationships contain an element of ownership, surely?'

'Course they do. I'd just feel happier about all this if Graham could convince me he'd ever truly owned himself. It's not a criticism. So few of us ever have.'

Cora had stopped screaming and snuggled in to her

mother, but her roaming eye indicated a spirit still poised for action. The three boys were by now sitting quietly on the mattress, engaged in tearing to pieces a fluffy blue rabbit with one eye and an uncertain number of ears. Even the marines on the roof seemed inclined to take a breather.

Lynn ignored the Infant Social Worker's contribution to the discussion and addressed me directly. 'What did the letter you got from Jamie's father say?'

'Nothing.'

'And what did the one Jamie got say?'

'Everything.'

'So your rival flashes a brief appearance and you rush over here to mummy and sit there on my sofa with your chin on your knees.'

I felt the Infant Social Worker stiffen beside me. There could be no doubt that she was not at all taken with the concept of Lynn as my substitute mother, although she had said early on in our relationship how convenient a mother would have been in my situation. Perhaps some unacknowledged part of her had considered that she herself was filling that situation. I felt like saying to her, 'Listen to what is being said. Ignore the manner of the saying. Lynn can be wise,' but instead I spoke directly to Lynn. 'There's no rivalry, it's not a competition. It was a very fair, very honest, very loving and devastatingly moving letter.'

'And Jamie immediately goes cold on you. Whereas before this letter arrived, you were both playing Cowboys and Indians to your hearts' content. Ludo, when did your father last come to see how you were getting on?'

'Which father?'

'Don't be provocative. We have guests. You know very well who your father is. That man whose face you spat in when you were five. When was he last here?'

'Can't remember.'

'And when do you estimate he might show up again?'

'Never, I hope.'

'Jasper, if you wet yourself, you'll go to school smelly. I've nowhere to dry knickers in this weather.'

The Infant Social Worker said, 'What's the point you're making?'

'Out of sight, out of spitting distance. How the hell can you expect Jamie to form a deep and satisfying relationship with Pussycat here, if the child is getting lovey-dovey letters from his dad and being promised day-trips to a maximum security prison? That man can do nothing for Jamie where he is. You have the legal power for the adoption. He should never have been contacted.'

'That doesn't square with the current thinking on open adoption.'

'What's open about confusing the kid and making life impossible for the new parent? Surely when it's a one-to-one, single-parent adoption you've gone for in the first place, then to dig up the ghost of Hamlet's father is a tiny weeny bit perverse?'

The two women's dislike of each other had begun to come out in the open and I began to sweat. Also, it had been a mistake to consult Ludo on the matter of absent fathers because the three boys now considered themselves to be a part of the conversation and had moved between us. Giles climbed on to my knee, not to sit but to stand, wobbling. Then, first clutching my ear tightly for support, he executed a belly flop into the middle of the huddle of siblings below him. I remembered how my visit to the Needhams had been similarly bedevilled by children. Was someone trying to tell me something? But Jamie was older than any of these and infinitely more adult.

The Infant Social Worker had decided to bludgeon Lynn with jargon. 'Anyway, James is near the end of his latency years. It's important for him to learn more about himself as a baby and toddler and to incorporate this knowledge into his continually emerging self-identity. The meeting with his father will assist that.'

'So when is this all-important prison visit scheduled for?'

'We're not sure yet. These things are difficult to set up.'

'There you are, you see? Everything in a state of flux. No wonder the kid's put the shutters up.'

Giles's manoeuvre had been so much admired by the other children that Cora left her mother to copy it. She was followed by Jasper, who, careless of tomorrow's discomfiture and ignominy, had indeed wet himself. Lynn certainly knew her children.

The Infant Social Worker was on the defensive and had become stuffy. 'I'm sure that when James has seen his father and been given his father's permission to love Graham the situation will calm down.'

The idea of the situation between myself and Jamie becoming any calmer than it was already dispirited me considerably, and I set myself the task of arranging my features so that they were in no danger of souring the half bottle of milk awaiting our coffee, which would no doubt arrive when Lynn realized that the heat under the kettle had not been switched on. Fortunately there was also the distraction of Cora, who had returned to her position of standing on my left knee – having rejected my right, owing to its tendency to go into spasm – and was now examining my hair for imaginary lice.

'One bachelor postmaster in early middle age and one waif fresh from seven years of institutionalization rushing towards each other at the speed of light, both screeching "Love me!" and both secretly terrified of yet another rejection! It's intense, too bloody intense. Then add to that the sexy Saint George behind bars . . .'

'Hardly Saint George.'

'You've got to accept the fact that you've entered a contest, Graham. Find out what's so glamorous about this gaol-bird, apart from his letters, and smarten up your own act. Give him a run for his money, a bit of competition. For starters, what was his line of work? What did he do with his freedom, when he had it?'

'He was a some kind of mercenary soldier, I think.'

'You what?'

'I'm not exactly sure.'

'Find out. Make sure.' And then to the Infant Social Worker, 'What's he in for?'

The Infant Social Worker went prune-faced behind her enormous spectacles. Suddenly I had a vision of her, no longer infant. I saw her finally beaten by all that she was now fighting – worn out, disappointed, ground down by the job. I felt a rush of sympathy and wanted to put out my hand and hold hers, but of course it wouldn't have done. Meanwhile Lynn blundered on, a dinosaur among mice.

'You know, with all these Local Authorities rushing to close their Children's Homes – "Very unusual now to find a child under ten in a Home," I read somewhere – with all these teenagers from Care sleeping rough or hanging themselves in prison cells, you'd think our Graham here would be more in a buyers' market and be able to dictate terms a little more forcibly. Not that I've been able to fathom what his real needs are yet. Still, it's nice to be consulted. Just sitting here chatting like this makes a change. I never could take my own company for too long, not undiluted.'

I said, 'I'll make the coffee,' removed my hair from Cora's grasp and Cora from my knee, unclasped Jasper from my calf and Ludo from my groin, and began a slow move to the kitchen. The Infant Social Worker, realizing she was next in line, stared after me beseechingly. But she was in no danger. I was the one the children followed, drumming on my bum and the backs of my legs with the fluffy rabbit. 'That's the thing about Graham,' Lynn said comfortably, 'my kids can't get enough of him. I don't know why he wants to bother with anyone else.'

*

180

The telephone call from the hospital was short and to the point. During it I started to hiccup and had to stop myself staring at my hands, which are not unlike Edward's hands. I suppose it was one of those symbolic acts one performs without good reason, either that or I was making sure that the only family resemblance I had to him, the only reminder of where I'd come from, still worked. Conscience could make compulsive hand-starers of us all.

I was ushered into a small side room, where they had placed him for me to say my last goodbyes. He looked much as he had each morning at home when I had taken him tea and sat by the window describing what I saw, except that someone had given his hair a parting on the wrong side and had plastered it down with grease. I think they had also dabbed a little make-up on his cheeks; he wouldn't have cared for that. We are even less our own property in death than we are in life. If he had died at home, it would have been I who fussed about making him presentable. I would have been the one removing or replacing his teeth, clipping the hairs from his nostrils, arranging his parting the way he had always worn it. It would not have been a stranger doing all these things for my good-enough father who was now in heaven; it would have been, should have been, his son. A son should always be on hand at such a time, in case a few last words are found, be they 'Bugger Bognor' or 'Cremate me in Cornwall.'

(What an effect Lynn has had on me, as I now realize, undermining every important moment with flippancy and bad jokes. I am a creature entirely moulded by others, a leaf blown in the wind.)

The nurse handed me a plastic carrier bag containing his things – bedroom slippers, his watch, the purse in which he kept his loose change. It all seemed so very ordinary. No Last Post sounded as I left the little side ward and wandered along echoing corridors, where patients sat in lines on wooden benches or leaned against faulty drink dispensers. There were no flags at half-mast in the town centre, just a middle-aged man sitting in his car at the traffic lights with a plastic carrier bag beside him on the passenger seat.

What does one do with all that anger when the reason for it has been taken away, leaving the volcano still unerupted? What does all that longing turn into when the object of it has to be burned or buried quickly before it starts to offend?

Three times I picked up the phone to ring Bernard to get him to stop Jamie coming for the week-end, but each time I found myself unable to dial the number. I told myself that I was reluctant to force Jamie to re-experience a week-end in the Children's Home when he had become used to a different kind of week-end, but this was mere self-delusion; our week-ends since his father's letter had not been characterized by any great togetherness. I told myself that the words 'It's not convenient at the moment' might be taken as rejection and that Jamie had experienced rejection too often, but it was I, of course, who most feared rejection. I told myself that if I was going to adopt Jamie as a son, even though he had a father already, we would become a family, and now that my own father was dead, Jamie would be the only family I would have, and that death in a family is to be shared, and that did seem to be a good enough reason, so I did not make the call.

I said nothing about it on the Friday evening. Since it had been accepted by us both that I could never take his father's place, Jamie's need to maintain space between us had considerably diminished, but Friday evenings were still characterized by an uneasy politeness. On the Saturday morning he was standing at the kitchen sink, looking out into the back garden. It was odd how often he seemed to be either there or on the window-seat in the front room. I knew he liked washing things – not obsessive adolescent cleansing, just enjoyed his hands in warm water, enjoyed gazing down into the soap suds, watching the rainbow patterns on the bubbles pop. He would ask me to find things for him to wash and I would oblige. This kitchen-sink stance was very healthy, I had been told. Not only was it the tiniest nod towards the feminine side of his nature, the very part of my own nature at which he silently sneered, it was claiming-behaviour, the flip side of his window-seat 'I'm trapped here. Someone come and rescue me' posture. Added together, these expressed his ambivalence towards me which had to be worked through.

I said, 'My father died on Thursday night. I was at the hospital yesterday, collecting his things. I'm not going to be very good company, I'm afraid. I wasn't sure whether to ask you to give this week-end a miss. Perhaps I should have. I'm sorry.'

I was standing well back from him, by the kitchen door, allowing him his space. I had been wondering what he was thinking about, where his mind went to while his hands moved within the water. I'd been observing the nape of his neck tilted forwards, his narrow shoulders in his favourite week-end check shirt, his hipless hips in baggy shapeless jeans. I looked at his bony little ankles and feet, standing inside my size ten bedroom slippers, and I remembered taking Edward's slippers from the plastic carrier bag, remembered the number of times I'd eased his feet into them, remembered that for an hour before setting out to collect Jamie on the Friday evening, I had lain on my bed with Edward's slippers on the pillow beside me, wondering what a long involved emotional relationship with someone was like, and which of the men my father had described so vividly had enjoyed the closeness he had never given to his son.

What started as laughter at the sight of those tiny feet standing inside my slippers progressed naturally to blubbering sobs. I was mourning my father, or was it myself or perhaps both of us? for we were both dead. Tears turned to anger, to pacing, to striking the walls of the kitchen with my fist, to swearing and blaspheming, to frightening guttural howls and groans, to wailing and keening, and so to even more anger at the pointless waste of it all.

I thought about my father's loneliness, his guilt and of how much and how often I must have added to it. I thought about

183

his fear of exposure and what it had made him do, of his efforts at making the best of a bad job, to make do, always to live at second best. I remembered how he had clung to my mother at the risk of ruining both their lives, and realized that, when I had seen them walking in the garden together, it had not been as husband and wife but as a mother with her shamed and guilty son. It was no wonder that they had kept me at arms' length, while they negotiated their own very special, possibly unique relationship, with the aid of all those hugs, those touches, those leanings against each other. I tried to reconstruct the conversations they might have had, tried to imagine which words he would have chosen to explain his lack of passion for her and by which he would have described the love that dared not speak its name he harboured for a British Tommy.

He would not have told her in the bedroom; it would have been in the garden, in the open air among the flowers she had planted. I imagined her small face looking up at him, her small hand raised against the bleaching sun, those furtive frightened eyes blinking at the news that a Corporal in the Royal Artillery was the reason her marriage was not being consummated properly. And then the glance away, concentrating hard on the astilbes while her neck and shoulders reddened. I imagined the pencil-line mouth tightening and trembling as she realized exactly what soldiers physically might do with and to each other during wartime, while they waited like sheep to be driven to the butcher's back premises, while they were arbitrarily pressed together, pressed into service, pressed into long involved emotional relationships.

I looked back into my father's past, and saw him being dragged to school on his first day. *'As innocent as a new-laid egg,'* I saw him sitting at a desk with tears on his face, his whole life stretched out on a blank sheet of paper in front of him, before any lists of things wanted or needed or to do had been made, saw him behind the chemist's counter dishing out laxatives and trying to hide from the manager the threadbare

184

cuffs of his only suit. I saw him in uniform, hiding in shadows and taking what he could get, to make some kind of contact. I was out of control; my imagination was spinning, whirling; I saw my father exchanging scribbled notes, love letters full of promises and pleas, offers of comfort, excitement, companionship, vows of loyalty, all posted in the cracks of walls, in cemetery urns and even in the hollow trunks of trees. *'In my day, younger chaps like yourself . . . Lived as though you were a large family . . . husbands and wives, sometimes . . . You adapt to crisis, then can't recollect what you were like before.'*

I saw my father riding the dodgems in a cowboy hat, and shouting 'We're on the loose.' I saw him in the side ward, his hair plastered down and his parting on the wrong side – the woman's side. I saw his body, which I had washed and powdered like a baby's body, had tucked in and turned, and which had lain passive and resentful while all these manoeuvres were made for its comfort. I saw the sunken chest, rounded belly, the spindly thighs between which the loose and seemingly empty Dorothy Bag of his scrotum had either dangled or, when I was turning him in bed, had been trapped and squeezed until released carefully by me. Images of my father, imagined or remembered, flooded in on me, battering me so that I myself beat at the walls of the kitchen with hands which so resembled his, my only legacy.

I became aware of Jamie watching me. I realized that I seemed to be repeating the word 'Sorry' over and over again, presumably because it not only summed up all I felt, but was also an apology for my behaviour, I hid my face with both hands and sank into a chair, screwing myself up into a ball and covering my head with my arms as though protecting myself from the kicks of hoodlums. I continued to apologize for having loved my sad and lonely father too much and for having failed to gain more than a week of his love in return.

After some time, the child whose father I could never replace took me by the hand and pulled me up the winding stairs to my own room. He managed to get me on to the bed, cried with me and for me, wrapping his bony little arms around me, and hugged me better. Then he left me for a while, returning with a conch shell which he placed in my hands, then guided to my ear so that I might listen to the sea.

It was the summer of 1976, the year of the heat wave. I had been lying on the grass in Idlicote churchyard with my shirt off trying to get a suntan. I'd have been twenty-three, I suppose. I had the day off from the post office counter: my mother had been in one of her 'Graham, you must get out more' moods, and also a little irritable from the heat. I'd decided to go cycling, not to anywhere in particular but in a great circle round the villages and back home; that somehow seemed safer to me than committing myself to a particular destination.

So there I was, feasting in Idlicote churchyard on a packet of crisps and a bottle of lemonade, and giving my chest to the sun. And there was this voice, a girl's voice from inside the church, a high fluting lonely sound. It was a madrigal or a round or something, and she explained later that the reason it sounded so horrible was that she'd been attempting to sing all the parts, and some of them were supposed to overlap. I'd thought it the most haunting thing I'd ever heard.

I stood half in, half out of the church doorway for a long time, feeling secure that she couldn't see me, watching her move about the aisles with long strides as though she were on a stage, and listening to this eerie unforgettable sound. All of a sudden she reached into her bag, and started talking in a clipped businesslike voice into a pocket tape recorder. 'Church of St James, Idlicote, on what must be the hottest day of the year of our Lord, 1976. Norman font, Norman doorway – complete with local Peeping Tom – old windows splayed from the inside; that means Saxon or something, doesn't it? Earliest date in Register, 1556. Value of parish at Domesday, eight pounds. Thirty-eight families – a hundred and seventy souls in all – twenty six villeins, seventeen bondsmen, three labourers and a rabbit called Harvey. Sorry, is this disturbing your devotions?'

I'd edged my way into the church proper by then and was standing with my mouth open just gazing at her. I said, 'I'm sorry. I wasn't eavesdropping' – though obviously I was – 'I was just interested in what you were doing with all that information.' She told me she was a researcher, employed through an agency by someone who had more money than sense, some fat industrialist who fancied writing his memoirs, but hadn't the time to come back to the village where he'd spent his childhood and remind himself of what was there.

She asked me what I did, and I said 'post office work', which seemed to end our conversation, because she just nodded and went back to squinting at the carvings. After a while I probably said something obvious about its being hot outside, but nice and cool inside, and she asked me whether I'd noticed a gravestone with the name 'Underhill' on it, because if I had, it would save her searching in the heat. That was what she was really there for, to record what was written on it. All the rest was just top-dressing to prove she'd earned her fee.

She took her sandals off and walked up and down in her bare feet, making damp footmarks on the flagstone floor, and said, 'I don't imagine my client really wants to write about Saxon Kings or two wheeler-dealers by the names of Ordric and Anegrin in his vanity publication, do you?' She was wearing a loose cotton skirt; I think it would have been cotton – red with horses' heads printed on it. Her legs and arms looked slim and strong and were suntanned that dark nut-brown colour. She had on a white sleeveless blouse, and I don't think she wore anything underneath the blouse. She certainly didn't need to; she was the most perfect shape. Her back was straight and her neck long, with just a very thin gold chain and locket around it. Straight dark brown hair, held off her face by a slide of the same colour as her skirt. Everything perfect, except for her nose, which had peeled, and was bright pink against the dark brown of the rest of her face. Black eyebrows, long black eyelashes and greeny-blue eyes. I just kept staring at her. She was the most beautiful thing I had ever seen.

I said, 'I'm Graham, by the way,' and, smiling as if she knew what I was thinking but didn't mind, she said, 'By what way?' Then she held out a hand to be shaken. It was a slim cool hand and I found that I wanted to keep hold of it, so I let go of it quickly. She said, 'Isn't it daft the hoops everyone jumps through just to find out someone's name? I'm Alice because my mother wanted me to do ballet, but of course it's led to endless bad jokes about Wonderland or "Alice, Where Art Thou?" It's extraordinary how the name Alice seems to bring out the comedian in everyone.' I said I thought it a very honest name and th.at seemed to please her.

We found the gravestone, or rather I found it while she supervised me from the shade of a tree. Then we went back inside the church, and just sat beside each other in a pew and talked. She was almost nineteen, and lived in Birmingham, sharing a flat with a friend from school. She was counting on going to university, probably Durham, and she wanted to be a journalist. I asked if I could write to her, and she said, 'No. Come and see us,' and gave me her address.

Two weeks later, when I arrived at her flat as she'd made me promise I would, she and her friend were on their way out to a party. It was a last-minute decision, she explained, and she just knew that I'd enjoy it. It was a bottle party, and very crowded with students from art college and Birmingham University. The noise made it impossible to hear what anyone said. I stuck it for three hours, hoping she would tire of it and we could go somewhere on our own, but she kept seeing people she knew and being dragged away, until finally she disappeared altogether. I never saw her again. I didn't write.

There didn't seem to be much point in it, and anyway I didn't know what to say.

It would have never done. She was right out of my class. It never would have done.

Waiting

Still nothing had been heard about James's visit to his father. What had been heard was the magic word 'parole'. As yet it remained a word, a rumour, merely a possibility, and patience must be exercised. Meanwhile James was to live with Graham full time. He was to be fostered with a view to adoption. He had plenty of experience of being fostered. And there would be no adoption until he saw his father.

There were the usual questions. Where had he come from? What had happened to his parents? Why hadn't he been placed with a proper family, and what was the man at post office really like? So far the village children of James's age had seen him only occasionally at week-ends. A few of them had nodded in his direction, or held up a tentative hand of greeting, and two or three had exchanged the odd word, always with the feeling that his presence among them was transitory, that he was odd, foreign, rare and that further contact with him might taint them with these qualities.

But now he was to be seen every day and would soon join them at their school, perhaps even be in their class, so that those same qualities which had been odd, foreign, rare, now became new, interesting, exotic, and he was indulged for them.

It was the school holidays and they were bored. His accent was not theirs, but listening to his vowel sounds appeared to give them pleasure. The village children explained to James that his bad luck had brought him to a dump of a place where nothing happened. They sat on the playing field complaining bitterly that the parental control they suffered excluded them from doing anything of real interest, such as hitch-hiking to China or experimenting with fringe religions. Instead they rode their cycles up and down the main street, or forgathered in small groups to escort each other to the Spar Groceries to buy ice lollies. Even the seasonal activities of the soil and fields surrounding them, the activities of harvest and hay-making, which had once involved children much younger than themselves, were now the sole province of large pieces of machinery hired for the occasion.

For them, the presence of James was a light relief to the boredom of the summer holiday, and they competed with each other for his company. For James, when he could get away and have a few moments of solitude, the country lanes, brooks, footpaths and hedgerows where he wandered, lingered, lay, gently but thoroughly exposing himself to nature and absorbing the stillness and warmth, were of infinite fascination.

All in all it was a very good August, a calming healing August, both for himself and Graham.

As for the new school, when term began in September, he found it was much like any other, except that he now wore long trousers and a blazer with a motto embroidered on the top pocket. He was placed in the 'B' stream in a class of thirty-two, with every expectation that once he had found his feet there would be footholds for him on the lower reaches of the 'A' stream.

In a matter of weeks this newness and novelty value would wear off. It was the beginning of the school year; the village children of his own age were themselves new to the compre-hensive, which had a catchment area much wider than that of the village primary school. The bus in which they travelled to school stopped at every lane end and farm entrance, joining in the playground a fleet of buses which came from every direction, transporting the products of other villages, other farms, other lane ends.

In the second week of term a teacher he didn't yet know

asked to see him and told him that if he needed help or got into any trouble James was to go to him for assistance. The teacher explained that he himself had been a Barnardo's Boy, and had therefore a vested interest in James's wellbeing. This teacher said, 'Just remember I'm here if you need me. Think of me as a safety line, which with any luck you might never need. I know what it's like, you see. I'm still trying to find out who my real parents were. You'll be all right here with us. I think you'll do very well.'

It did not seem to James that their cases were at all similar. James, at the moment, had something of a surfeit of parents, or at least of fathers, and knew perfectly well who they both were, the real and the substitute.

In the Queue

It was a day like any other. Friday. Lizzie Hancox was late in collecting her pension and wanted to chat. Lizzie always wants to chat and usually manages to get the subjects under discussion confused. This time it was something to do with germ warfare and a by-election on the south coast. Lizzie was maintaining that the Conservative candidate had lost because his name was Jeremy Anthrax, 'Who'd want to get into bed with a name that sounds like a throat sweet?' Two first-class stamps, please, which she hoped hadn't gone up again since last week, and did I remember when it was threepence and they always got there the very next day? Then there was the new woman from Hill Tops – they're a retired couple, something industrial in Wolverhampton; they won't stay. She was in for some dry-cleaning that wouldn't be back until Thursday. I'd explained delivery days to her when she brought it in; we had a bit of an argument; it takes time for them to understand that you can't expect twenty-four-hour cleaning in a village post office. Then, waiting behind her in the queue, was a stranger, a man with a face like something out of the Bible, great burning brown eyes and sunken cheeks, some Zedekiah or Nehemiah who'd been living on locusts in the desert and just blown in to give King Ahab a piece of his mind before being thrown from an upstairs window.

He did look ill. 'I'm Jimmy's father,' he said.

Luckily there was no one behind him. I explained that I was on my own and couldn't leave the shop until lunchtime, and suggested that he might like to wait for me in the pub. He smiled and said that even with money he didn't always find it easy to get served, and that anyway I had to go on living in the village. He said, 'I'd offer to go for a walk and come back, but I've walked a good way already, and I don't think I'd get much further.' Then we just stood looking at each other until he asked if I minded him going through to the house and waiting for me there. And of course I didn't mind and should have thought of it. I just wasn't thinking very clearly.

I closed the shop at lunchtime, went through into the house, and found him asleep in a chair. He'd walked further than he should, and was exhausted. His wrists weren't much thicker than broom handles, and I supposed his ankles must measure about the same. He was painfully thin. I'd been told he was a handsome man and this had been confirmed by the blurred newspaper cutting I'd seen and the photograph which James had taken from old Percy's bureau drawer. And I could see that yes, he had been handsome. As I watched him sleeping, worrying that he might not wake before I had to get back to the shop, I could tell that the now fleshless, almost skull-like head had once been perfect, that the face had been almost beautiful and this shrunken stick-like body had once been well proportioned. And I remembered reading something about the problems good-looking young men encounter in prisons and realized that what I was looking at was a face and body which would have been haggled over, which would have been bought and sold and bartered for along with the tobacco.

After ten minutes he woke naturally and asked for a glass of water. He refused anything other than water, and with it he took some pills. When he'd done that, he began to ask me about myself, wanting, he said, to satisfy himself that Jimmy would be all right with me.

He didn't wish Jimmy to know that he had been released from prison or that he had visited me. Jimmy was not to see him or ever to know what his born-to father had died of. He said, 'I've managed to keep Jimmy thinking I've been in prison ever since he and I last met. Actually I've been in and out three times since then. I'd like to have seen him, of course; it just seemed fairer on him to keep well away, you know what I mean? He's got a funny idea of me; I told him a lot of funny things – like sort of fantasies: he wouldn't expect me to do just six months or a year, not a dangerous man like me. Tell you the truth, my criminal career has been farcical really. You might consider it a kindness not to tell him any of this. After all, he's not going to repeat my mistakes while he's with you, is he?'

'He thought you were a mercenary soldier.'

'I may have said that.'

'Some sort of political activist. He thought you were in prison because you'd blown things up.'

'I may have said something like that. Hinted at it – you know?'

The reason John Lennards was being honest with me was that he required me to be honest with him. He had decided that, in the time he had left, it would be best if he did one thing right and that was to reassure himself that Jimmy would be safe.

'I expect you'd like to know how long they've given me. They're not so shy about giving you a time limit with something like this as they are with the more sympathy-arousing illnesses. One of the screws even said, "You're paying for your pleasure now," which was a bit of a joke in the circumstances. I've got four or five months, just enough time for a world cruise. In a couple of months, if I'm in the right catchment area, I can apply for a hospice of some sort. Otherwise it's a rush to the casualty department and everyone grabbing for protective clothing.'

I had seen programmes on television which showed nurses, doctors and the like being both caring and considerate with the victims of Aids, but I supposed that a prison hospital might be a little different. Perhaps John Lennards's illness had been a contributing factor to his early release.

Certainly he himself thought so. 'It means they've got one less death certificate to write out. Where is Jimmy anyway?'

'At school. He'll be back at four thirty.'

'Doing well there, is he?'

'Pretty well.'

'I've been trying to think of a way I could get a look at him without him seeing me.'

He seemed to want me to suggest such a way. My first thought was, of course, to oblige, since being obliging is what I'm known for, but then it came to me that this was wrong and that Jamie had a right to know the truth, however unpleasant. I said, 'Why should I help you to deceive him? Wouldn't it be fairer to tell him the truth?'

'Fairer to who?'

'To him. Certainly to me, but it's him I'm thinking about. Him in a year's time, when you're dead and he's still wondering why he vas never allowed to see you. Him in five years' time, when he still believes it was because of something he did wrong, some badness inside him that kept you apart. It's him I'm concerned about. Are you?'

'And what am I doing here if I'm not concerned about him?'

'You're concerned about the relationship you once had with your son. I think it's the memory of that you want to save at the expense of his future wellbeing.'

I could hear myself, but found it difficult to believe what I was hearing. I really am never like this. As I've already said, it is second nature to me to look for guidance. Now there wasn't any guidance. It was a time for decision, and I had to take charge.

'So you want me not to see him?'

'There's no way I could prevent it. If you just hang around the village until the school bus gets back, you're bound to see him. But Jamie will also see you, and even if he doesn't recognize you he'll know you're a stranger around here and he'll wonder. And if Jamie does recognize you as his father, either you or I will have to explain why you've lied to him. And the village people would ask questions and might end up with answers that could make it more difficult for Jamie to live here.'

'It's not hereditary. It's not even infectious unless . . .'

'You and I know that. There's a lot of ignorance and prejudice in a village.'

'Somewhere outside the village then. If I know where you're going to be, I could wait. A public place. I promise you he'll never know who I am. Please.' I shook my head. 'Does it feel good holding all the cards?'

'Yes' would have been the honest answer, but it was not a time for that sort of honesty, so I was economical with the truth. 'It feels different – being the one making the decisions. But Jimmy has told me that I can never replace you, so I'm unlikely ever to hold the best hand.'

'Then I have to risk him recognizing me, and hang about the village.'

'If you were selfish enough to do that, then I'd tell Jamie the truth – that you'd been in and out of prison and there were plenty of times you could have come to see him and never bothered. And there'd be no danger of Jamie accidentally recognizing you in the street because it wouldn't be an accident. I'd meet the bus myself, point you out to him and tell him who you are.'

'How do I know you won't tell him anyway?'

'Because some day, when you think the time is right, you'll tell him yourself. Meanwhile, you will get your suitcase – rucksack – whatever you've got in the way of luggage from wherever you've left it and come back here. You'll move into this house and stay here as long as you want or need to. We'll tell Jamie you've been given parole because of your illness and that you immediately set out to find him. We'll tell him what your illness is, give it its proper name, because he has to know his father only has so many months to live. The village people don't have to know, though they may guess or find out. Only

197

the doctor has to know and the Hippocratic oath should take care of him. Do you agree?'

He looked at me. That ravaged face, the cheeks fallen in, the eyes enormous, looked back at me. The enormous eyes filled with tears. Then he nodded. Then he left.

I said to myself, 'He won't come back. He hasn't the guts. He'll chicken out, and die somewhere out of sight, and in time I'll have to tell Jamie.' I didn't know whether I wanted this or not. I'd found within myself the most surprising strength, but I had no way of telling whether it would last throughout the man's long illness and death.

In fact he returned that same afternoon in a taxi carrying a very small suitcase. I left the counter, put the 'Closed' notice on the shop door, and went out to meet the shrunken figure climbing out of the taxi. He paid the fare, counting out the coins carefully, since he had so few. The driver pocketed the money, looked towards me, wiped his hands on a rag and spat on the pavement before driving away.

I'd made up Edward's bed so that he would able to unpack his few things and lie down. I showed him where the bathroom was, and asked if there was anything special that he would need and if there were any extra precautions Jamie and I should take against infection. He said that he used an electric razor and that he would keep his toothbrush in the bedroom and brush his teeth there, if I could supply a bowl for him to spit into. His gums were bad, he said, and sometimes bled. These precautions would remove the risk of his toothbrush being accidentally left in the bathroom and someone else using it by mistake. He thanked me and said he needed to wash and sleep a little before meeting his son, so I ran a bath for him and gave him a pair of my own pyjamas to wear.

I watched him for a while, moving laboriously around Edward's room and holding on to furniture for support, then prepared to go, sensing that he didn't want to be observed taking off even his outer clothes and telling him that I had to return to the shop.

He said, 'How tall is he now?'

'Quite tall.'

'He was always old for his years. A little old man he was at six. Much too serious. He's had no life at all, no life, no real happiness, and now he's coming home to this.'

I said I was sure that Jamie would consider 'this' a great deal better than nothing, and left him to undress.

Knots

When the school bus drew up outside the church, Graham was there waiting. This was strictly against protocol. The parents of the primary school children met them at the end of the day, but eleven-year-olds found their own way home, since they might wish to dally with friends before returning.

Graham was wearing one of his unhappy, worried looks. He still had bouts, James knew, of feeling rotten about his dad's death, particularly at week-ends, and James had devised a plan to deal with this. James said, 'You're looking broody, like a hen with constipation. Well, don't be, 'cos I've got the remedy. Soon as you finish work tomorrow, I want us to drive to where we camped that time. I listened to the weather forecast in the bus and it's perfect. It's going to be chilly but dry. I can do my washing tonight, and it'll be aired by the time we get back. Long johns, and a log fire, steamy breath and rabbit stew. It'll be great!'

'Not this week-end.'

'Why not?'

'Because we have a visitor.'

They never had visitors. It could only be someone dreadful like Uncle Turpin. Would it be Bernard, or that social worker, Debbie, on a tour of inspection? The old man, Percy? James should have been consulted – warned anyway: this wasn't even warning. If anyone had arrived unexpectedly, they had no right and should have been turned away. Now it was James who looked like a hen with constipation, while Graham looked merely guilty, which was by no means a novelty.

Graham asked whether James wished to know who the

visitor was and James replied that he wasn't interested, flung his school books on the kitchen table and stormed up to his own room banging doors as he went.

Shortly afterwards Graham entered James's room by managing gradually to edge away the chair which had been placed against the door to form a barricade and sat on the edge of the bed where James lay with his face hidden by pillows.

'I'd got it all worked out, and you've spoiled it. We were going to do exactly what we did last time and then you'd have cheered up a bit and stopped thinking of your dad. It wasn't for me this time; it was going to be for your sake, because I was rotten about your birthday and wanted to give you something.'

'I know. And I'm grateful. It was thoughtful and I'm very moved. But this is someone you wouldn't have wanted me to turn away. He's here in Edward's room and he wants to see you. I think you'd better wash your face before we go in there.'

The curtains were closed and the room in semi-darkness. They stood just inside the door, looking towards the large double bed on which James thought he could see the figure of a child. After a few moments Graham said, 'We're here, John. Would you like the light on? The switch is to your right by the bed.'

The suddenness of the light dazzled James. Then he saw that the figure wasn't that of a child but of a man. He was a small man with no flesh on his face, just chalk-white skin pulled tight over the bones. A skeleton which was still alive lifted its arm, and reached out its long thin hand towards him. The skeleton was stretching the skin around its mouth to tearing point to form a smile before speaking. 'Hello, Jimmy! Who do you love?'

Jimmy moved forward slowly towards the bed. The man's hand remained suspended in the air for him to take. He took hold of it in both his hands. It was fragile; he was sure it could easily break if roughly grasped. He had intended to shake the hand between both his and lower it gently on to the bed cover, but it grabbed for one of the hands which were clasping it and gripped it tightly, too tightly.

James could feel every bone inside the hand. The knuckles were sharp, the fingernails too long, like a woman's and he looked down at them, half expecting to see them painted blood red. The pulse inside the man's hand pounded against the dry sandpaper skin like a small animal's heartbeat. And the huge dark brown eyes which watched him, waiting for an answer to the question, began to water.

'Last time I saw you, I said the next time we meet will be for good. Nothing is for good with you and me, is it, Jimmy? Everything's temp'ry, right?'

Jimmy did not reply. He neither spoke nor moved his head. Sweat from both sides of the man's face had gathered in the well under his adam's apple, and more sweat from the top of his almost shaven head could be seen running down his neck behind his ears and soaking into the collar of pyjamas which Jimmy recognized as belonging to Graham.

'I came to find you, to make sure you were all right. You're a credit to me, Jimmy. A grown man almost. So tall and handsome. Graham says I should be honest with you about what I've got . . . my illness . . . I've got to be honest, so's you know everything, right? He says we should spend these last few months getting to know each other.' The man's lower lip began to tremble. 'Don't be scared. Don't look at me so frightened like that.'

The man's voice had become higher. As he swallowed, the well of sweat below his adam's apple emptied itself, and the sweat trickled downwards over the protruding ribs. He turned his face away from Jimmy towards the window, swallowed again and then again, kept swallowing, large gulping swallows. His voice was absolutely unlike that of Jimmy's father – a broken high-pitched sobbing voice.

'Jesus God! Will you say you're not frightened of me? I'm so scared for myself, I can't hide it from you. Please, Jimmy, say something to me. Don't just judge me like that. I didn't want you to see this; I knew you'd hate me. I'm sorry. It wasn't my fault. I didn't do this to myself, son, I swear. Promise.'

Graham took hold of Jimmy by the shoulders and, unclasping the man's grip on Jimmy's hand, pulled him backwards towards the door, saying, 'Not now, John. He needs time. Give him a little time. Try to rest. I'll come back later.'

As James descended the stairs in front of Graham, he could hear the man shouting after them. The man was weeping and begging. In a strangled whine he was asking if James had received his letter.

The weather forecast had been right – 'Dry, with below average temperatures and a severe frost overnight.' In the moonlight he could see the frost glistening on the tops of the hedges and along the lower branches of trees. His footsteps made patterns as he walked. It was both too late and too early for traffic, so it mattered little which side of the road he walked.

The skeleton of an old man lying in another old man's bed was not the skeleton of John Lennards, whose photograph had appeared in the newspapers. This was not the man to whom he had talked inside his head all those years. This man, whoever he was, would die soon; he had said as much himself, had admitted that he was frightened and had cried and begged. This man was not his father; his father had never begged.

Soon he was off the road and climbing the hill. Things scuttled about in the ditches and hedges on either side; they were animals, he supposed. Whatever they were, he was bigger and they would move for him. The moon also moved. It moved with him, leading him to where he was going. He would manage without the torch for as long as he could; he didn't want to risk its light being seen moving along the cart track towards the wood at the top of the hill.

His father's body had been solid and muscular; he had lain against it, had watched while his father did press-ups and sit-ups. His father's upper arms had been too broad for Jimmy's fingers to encircle, and with those arms he had dug a deep hole in the ground for himself and Jimmy to sleep in. His father had dressed Jimmy in army uniform and taught him how to tie knots, had told him how important it was that he should take care of his body and keep it fit, had shown him how to do things slowly and carefully to protect himself from injury, and had demonstrated the best way to light a fire with damp wood. His father had made traps to catch animals for food. He had risen to his feet slowly and had raised his arms above his head slowly when the police had come to arrest him. Doing things slowly prevented you from getting hurt.

Now, in the blackness, with the sharp spade and the sleeping bag tied to his shoulders, with the moon hidden behind cloud and with his bare hands feeling their way along the top of a fence to find the gate, he had forgotten what his father had taught him, and had tried to move too quickly, had allowed his hands to slide sideways along a single strand of barbed wire, ripping skin from both his palms. He felt pain, but only for a short time, and decided that the reason for this was because the frost had numbed his hands.

Inside the wood, everything was either shapes or sounds. The noises his footfalls made were like a fire taking hold. The shapes were mainly black against grey, sometimes dark grey against a lighter grey, with larger shapes towering above him. At times the lower shapes, outside the beam of the torch and at the very edge of his field of vision, seemed to move. These were never quick movements, always slow skirting movements, as though a bush or dead tree, already leaning in his direction, were attempting to edge round behind him. All his concentration was needed to keep looking forwards, all his will power required not to look back.

Digging a hole between tree roots by the light of the small torch had to be done slowly and took time, a lot of time. The hole should have been wider and much deeper, but the spade would go no further down and was not the correct spade for removing the earth it had broken, so that he had to remove the earth with his hands. Breaking off branches from the spruce trees also took more time than it should because, his hands being numb, he found it difficult to grip hard enough. Some dead and fallen branches were found to add to them and slowly with the aid of the torch, these branches and dead leaves were spread to add warmth and to camouflage where he had dug. 'Going to earth' his father had called it.

Inside the sleeping bag, with the dead branches and leaves pulled over him, holding the largest piece of the now broken conch shell to his ear and listening to the sea, he would fall asleep. The digging and collecting branches had tired him, but he had remembered enough to be able to create somewhere safe for himself and Jimmy to sleep.

He slithered lower into the sleeping bag. His father had called this 'going deeper to earth'. At his feet now was the coil of washing line and for a moment he couldn't remember why he had brought it. His mind moved backwards, turning pages and pictures, turning pages without pictures, until it reached the diagrams of knots pinned to the walls of the attic room he had shared with his father. There he saw the reef and the bos'n, the running bowline with two half hitches and the slip knot or hangman's knot. There was a knot for every occasion. If he practised them regularly, he would remember what each of them was for and would never go wrong. It was all to do with self-reliance, self-sufficiency and self-preservation. He was on his own in this world. Everyone looked out for number one. He had to know what was important and which were the lies. He must never show weakness, or they would take advantage of him. They would treat him just how they liked, would use him until they had bled him dry and then they would spit him out. He was never to show weakness, never to trust them, never to turn his back. They would tempt him with flattery and friendship, try to make him believe he was important to them, and when they had got what they wanted from him they would disappear and he'd be on his own.

The knots were important; they were his life-line, the symbol that he could manage alone.

He was where he wished to be. He did not wish to wake up; there was now no reason for him to wake up. If he wanted anything it was warmth and sleep, but he was not even sure he wanted those things. Nothing was what he wanted. Nothing inside him, nothing outside him. To have nothing, be nothing and most of all to feel nothing. He pressed the broken conch shell hard into the side of his face, but he could no longer hear the sea.

Best

The louder I shouted his name, the more the word became a blur of sound. Leaving me, his name contained all the longing, all the pleading, all the love I was capable of, but by the time my voice reached the wooded hillside all it sounded like was the cry of an inadequate and careless animal, unable to express its pain.

If I tried a whole sentence, the trees threw the words into the air, allowing them to fall back in any order. Also, to shout more than that one word, his name, I had to stop running and take in more breath, losing valuable time. This was time to be added to that I'd already spent lying awake before opening the door of his room to find he'd gone. Then there was the time lost in panic, in dither, not knowing what to do for the best, then more in looking for clues as to where he might have gone, searching drawers and cupboards, running upstairs and downstairs like a rat in a cage, checking rooms a second and a third time, even looking in the garden and the tool-shed, counting kitchen knives, finding the good torch gone and the one which works only intermittently left behind, and cursing him for his organization, his efficiency, his calculating bloody-mindedness even in this.

And so I had come to the wood, bringing nothing with me but fear and anger and the torch which worked only inter-mittently, stumbling over roots, pushing through nettle and elder, wishing him cold and tired and as frightened as I was, and praying that he was unhurt, was still alive, that what I was afraid of hadn't happened.

What in daylight was a man-made wood of conifers planted

in straight lines had become in the dark a tangle of bramble and blackthorn. There were arches of creepers, tunnels of branches and giant ferns; trees leaned in every direction, and some had fallen, to be climbed over or a way found round them – all with a torch which blinked on and off like the indicator light of a car. At times the carpet of leaves and twigs slid from beneath me suddenly and sent me sliding backwards. Elsewhere they were so deep that I had to wade through them.

When had he left? How long ago? Another ten minutes and it would be four o'clock. I shouted as I ran, screaming and bellowing his name in the hope that he could hear me, would know I was searching for him and would wait a little longer, would delay, would give me a chance. Just a chance, a little more time. Please!

Every few yards, wood pigeons, frightened by the blinking light, took off from the tops of trees, making a noise like tarpaulin flapping in a high wind. I had heard that there was something called night vision, but it seemed that I didn't have it, except inasmuch as I could perceive a darkness within the dark, shadows within shadows, which moved all around me as I ran, or tried to run. I went this way and then that, seeing things then not seeing them. Once I travelled twenty yards through undergrowth to look more closely at a piece of white cardboard. I made detours for a shiny strip of black plastic and a crunched-up beer can.

I reached the very top of the hill and the asphalt turning circle at the end of the old runway, and, among the cardboard boxes and other refuse scattered around, the beam of the torch picked out the shape of a sleeping bag, just to one side of the asphalt under some bushes. I was sure I had found him. I rushed forwards, weeping tears of joy; I could feel them on my cheeks, dried by the wind and the cold almost as soon as they were released. I knelt by the bushes, then lay on my stomach to reach under and pull at the roll of sleeping bag, shook one end of it, feeling the weight of something inside, calling his name, telling him to come out with his hands up because he was about to be carried home. But the something inside didn't move, didn't react. I froze, then forced myself to drag what I'd thought to be a sleeping bag slowly, carefully from under the bushes, unrolled it and saw that it was not a sleeping bag at all, but a small eiderdown which had been wrapped around a dead dog.

'Jamie!' *'I knew you'd do that – change my name. It's what everyone does, when they take you into their home. "You're ours now. We're going to call you Fido."'* I was shaking, trembling from head to foot. I hugged myself against the cold, pacing and stamping my feet on the asphalt to try and control the shakes, knowing that it wasn't cold that was causing me to shiver. If he wasn't here, where the hell was he? I was talking to myself, apologizing for having wasted more time, swearing at myself for thinking he would have gone there, to a place that was even colder than inside the wood itself, where the east wind could be heard skimming the top of the hill. What a fool I was. I could hear myself – fool! stupid fool! – telling Jamie I would find him, shouting incoherent sentences, telling him to wait for me, begging him to slow down, to stop, to take shelter, to keep himself warm. 'Warmth, Jamie, warmth! Please!'

I tried to imagine the wood as a whole, to construct an aerial view of it in daylight, and to place Jamie in it somewhere. But where? We had walked through it together many times. Which parts of it had he particularly liked? Where had he rushed ahead, then spent time waiting for me to catch up?

What if I'd guessed wrong and he hadn't come to the wood at all, but had gone off along the road to be picked up by some motorist? There was something missing, some clue that I'd overlooked; there had to be. I must stop, concentrate and plan, before wasting any more time. I stood absolutely still, closed my eyes to the shadows and the shadows within shadows, and my ears to the howling of the east wind as it attempted to slice the top off the hill, cleansed my mind of useless fear and anger, and sent it deliberately back to the point at which I had opened the door of Jamie's room and found his bed empty. I watched myself, observed the hurried dressing, the searching, the running back and forth, discovering that the sleeping bag was missing and one of the torches, checking the garden and the tool-shed where the tent was still neatly folded. What else? What had I missed? Suddenly I saw the line of hooks my father had put up in the tool-shed after mother's death, each with a name tag for the particular tool to be placed there so that one always knew where to look for what might be needed. Two of the hooks had been empty. Which two? A spade had been taken, a small edging spade, and something else. I struggled to read that neatly printed label. Two words. What were they?

He had taken a spade to dig a hole for the sleeping bag. Like the hole his father had dug for them both, it would need to be in a clearing big enough for him to be able to dig without being hampered by too many tree roots. I was already moving away from the asphalt turning circle when I remembered him sitting astride the lower branch of a tree, saw him jump down as I got closer, saw him stand for a moment with his back against the tree, then pace out yards by taking long exaggerated strides to the centre of the clearing. Later he had complained that books concentrated on the height a tree might grow but rarely gave any information about its roots, and I had replied with one of those odd pieces of information which hang about in the memory without any obvious purpose, to the effect that the roots of a poplar stretched underground exactly as far as the height of the tree, which was why house insurers increased their premiums if there were poplars in the garden.

I was racing back down the hill towards the middle of the wood, losing my balance and falling, sometimes rolling, sometimes being carried along on the carpet of moving leaves. I forced my way through brambles, which lashed and tore at my face and hands. I could feel the sting as the skin opened and my flesh below met the cold air. Thinking I heard something move behind me, I turned quickly, smashing the side of my face against a low branch and spiking my left eye on a barb of blackthorn.

Still calling his name, I reached the clearing, but there was no sign of him, no answer and no movement. I directed the intermittent beam of the torch along the ground, but it only covered a small area at a time. I walked around the edge of the glade, shining the torch into the middle, the point where he had stood to measure out the ground. If he wished, he could hide from me for ever; he was so small, even in daylight, this eleven-year-old child whom his real father had called tall and handsome. Keeping behind me, he would watch me, moving only when I moved. On our good walks together we had often played the game of 'Now you see me, now you don't', and he was expert at it, jumping out suddenly with his face contorted to scare me.

Two words. I had them now. 'WASHING LINE'. He had taken a rope with him as well as a spade. I was already sweating from my exertions and now broke into the most profuse sweat of fear. I tried to say his name again, but nothing came out except a kind of hoarse cawing sound. Hardly daring to do so, I turned the flashlight upwards to blink into the trees. I closed my left eye, which was watering and might be bleeding. The branches all round the clearing overlapped and fused into one other, as if there were just one enormous tree surrounding me and closing in. I could not see a rope, I could not see a body; he would not have taken the sleeping bag and spade if he had intended to use the washing line in that manner, not immediately, not as a first resort. I swallowed, summoned up a mouthful of spit and spoke as clearly and as loud as I could. I told him, wherever he might be hiding, that I was cold, but that I wasn't going back without him, told him that quite frankly I was scared and I didn't want to play this game any more.

I tried to move dead branches with one hand, while holding

the torch with the other. I talked on as I pulled and dragged at the wood and leaves, stopping from time to time to listen for any sound, any movement. I said that partners were supposed to help each other when one of them was injured and could hardly see. I told him I needed him to look at my eye and tell me how bad the damage was, that if I ended up unable to read I would lose our livelihood. I asked him what the hell he was playing at when I needed him.

Then I found a small branch which had been recently broken from a tree; the point of the break was white and new. The next branch I picked up had blood on it, the blood stuck to the palm of my hand, and I shone the torch on my hand and stared at it, seeing two hands with a smear of pale blood on each.

I sank to my knees, dropping the torch, which went out and stayed out, as I moved even faster, groping and grabbing with both hands. Again J shouted, asking him what it would take to prove to him we needed each other. What with the damage to my eye and the general darkness, I could see nothing now but shapes. My fingers touched the fabric of the sleeping bag. My hands clasped his shoulders through the fabric, shaking them and calling, but they were heavy, rigid and wouldn't move.

The man rocked backwards, howling at the moon, then crawled about, feeling for a torch he couldn't find. Instead his fingers found the zip of the sleeping bag and undid it. Murmuring and babbling incoherent baby talk, he felt for the boy's wrists, felt for the pulse inside them, and lifted the boy's hands to his own face, pressing his mouth against the wounds on the boy's palms, pressing his tongue to the wrists and finding the pulse again, then moving the tip of his tongue along the boy's veins to assure himself that they were not injured.

There was no movement, no reaction, no scorn, no laughter. The boy's body was warmer than the man's, but when the man found the torch and shone it, blinking on and off like the indicator of a car, into the boy's face, the eyes were dead – open but dead. The torch blinked; the eyes did not, giving no indication that the boy could hear the man talking to him. The person deep inside the boy knew that torch, knew that it was no good and had left it behind.

'Why him and not me? I'm your father more than he is. I've earned that by being your friend. He's just someone who's sick, and needs our help. When he dies, we can start from day one. We could go from good to better, Jamie, if there was just you and me. We could move away and live near the sea.'

The man had found the spade and now began digging to widen the trench in which the boy lay, holding both the torch and the handle of the spade in his right hand so that the blinking beam of light moved back and forth across the boy's face with each spadeful of earth, yet the face remained expressionless.

When the trench was wide enough, the man got down into it, and crawled inside the sleeping bag next to the boy, hugging him, then placing his head on the boy's chest to listen to his breathing. In this position they lay until it became light.

At six a.m. the church clock in the village below them played the first four lines of a child's hymn before sounding six clear single notes.

Apart from his breathing, which was no longer the slow, hardly discernible rhythm of two hours earlier, the only change in the boy's appearance was that there were the marks of dried tears on the side of his face. The man's left eyelid was swollen and his eye completely closed.

The man opened his good eye. Most of the dead leaves and branches had already been removed from above the trench. He climbed carefully out of the sleeping bag and cleared the rest away. Then he removed the sleeping bag gently from the boy, rolled it up, secured it with the rope he had found and swung it on to his back.

He bent, picked up the spade, then stood waiting for the boy to stand. Slowly, still seeming to be in a trance, the boy got to his feet, wiping the sides of his face with the back of his hand.

The man moved forward, waiting at the edge of the clearing for the boy to follow him, before moving on and picking his way carefully towards the edge of the wood, the boy still following.

They reached the cart track which ran up from the village. The mist was clearing from the fields at either side, and much of the night's frost had already melted in the peach-tinted morning light, its whiteness lingering only on the thistles, giving them the appearance of Christmas decorations.

Close to the village, the man stopped again and waited for the boy. As the boy approached him slowly, the man spoke in a quiet tone, telling the boy that he refused to be second best, that he wouldn't repeat the mistakes he had made with his own father, and that if his and the boy's relationship as father and son were to succeed, then it was to be all or nothing, and that the boy should decide soon either to take it or leave it.

The man waited and watched while the child thought for a moment before taking the man's hand into his own.

Coda

Surprisingly the only opposition so far to John's staying here has come from the local doctor, who freaked out when I told him he had a new patient and what his illness was. This was the same doctor who had known me for over twenty years and whose glowing report about me had already been forwarded to the Adoption Panel. We were standing in the hall, on the same spot where I had vomited after Edward's collapse, but this time it was the doctor's turn to look a little queasy. He went red in the face, shouting that I was inconsiderate and irresponsible, and calling my guest somewhat more colourful names. He's apologized since, and explained that it was pure funk and that he'd never seen an Aids patient until that day and was frightened. He wears his rubber gloves even to take a temperature, but I expect that one day he may thank us when he realizes that his character has been built a little.

John is usually awake when Jamie and I take him a mug of tea and his first pills of the day at seven thirty a.m. We take turns to sit by the window and describe what we can see. After ten minutes or so, I leave them together until it's time for Jamie to catch the school bus at eight thirty. They have grown to understand each other, and Jamie has begun to respect his father and to accept that, although John was never a mercenary and his only period of political imprisonment was a night in a police cell after a sit-down protest when he was eighteen in support of the Angry Brigade, his fantasies were based on an ideal, and Jamie has always approved of ideals.

I take my lunch with John in his room, and in the evenings

we help him down the stairs and he sits before the fire. He has talked to me a great deal and I am only now realizing what a pale shadow of a life I've led.

To begin with, whenever Jamie asked about his mother, John would just cover his face with his hands and shake his head. Now Jamie doesn't ask. John has told me what happened and made me promise that after his death I will find the best moment to tell his son. I use the word 'best' since I cannot imagine that there will ever be a moment which is right for such a bedtime story.

She had been very depressed. Post-natal depression, they had said at first. And they had kept her in this awful place, a mother-and-baby unit, which was just women and babies, all screaming and crying and living on cigarettes, coffee and junk food. She had smoked a lot and Jamie had been underweight at birth. After some time they had allowed her home and she had seemed all right for about a year. Then the depression returned and continued to return. She was taking all sorts of pills, was living on them, John said.

He had a job at that time, working on a building site. He was trying to go straight at least for a while, he said, because he dared not get sent down for a stretch, and leave the boy with his mother not right. One day he got back from work to find her lying on the floor, out cold. Jamie was in the bedroom with the door locked and screaming to be let out. John called the ambulance and waited. He didn't know what else to do.

The ambulance men got a heartbeat, but it was very weak – 'Touch and go,' they said. Jamie was standing clutching at John's leg, and as the ambulance men lifted up the stretcher to carry it out John had placed a hand over Jamie's eyes, and Jamie had screamed, 'Can't see! Can't see!' and had struggled and bitten the hand.

John had told the ambulance men that he would follow, but instead had put Jamie in the car and had driven in the opposite direction, knowing that, with his police record and the state Mary was in, Jamie would be taken away from him. He had looked after Jamie for as long as he could, about three weeks, he supposed, and then, with no work and no food, he had left him at a day nursery, giving a false address.

He had meant to phone the hospital but never did. He couldn't cope with Mary as she was, with her endless crying, the violent rows, her accusing him of things he hadn't done. She had been very immature, very young for twenty, and had hardly lived at all.

He had assumed that she had died; otherwise she would have gone looking for them when she recovered. He asked if I thought what he had done was selfish; this was something that had worried him a great deal. But I had to remember, he said, that the way she was and how she behaved wasn't having a good effect on his son.

The Adoption Panel has given the go-ahead for the adoption and now the legal process starts. Jamie and I both know that a legal piece of paper won't solve all our problems. We know that the hunger we have both had for a close emotional relationship has led us to be unrealistic in our expectations. We understand now that there are limits to every human relationship and that the need to own, control, to be con-stantly reassured – not only that each of us is loved, but loved massively more than anyone else – that all these needs are as dangerous as the fear of being hurt that leads to a lack of commitment. There is a lot still to be learned and a lot more to be worked at. We still have to find a technique for being a father and son. Musicians may play beautifully from time to time, but unless they have mastered a technique they could never perform twice nightly – a hard lesson for two people who would rather believe they could move seamlessly from Chopsticks to Beethoven's Fifth without ever having to re-tune.

I went into this, having discovered a need but knowing nothing, a single man without experience and without a support system. Now that I have read the pamphlets and the books, attended Milestone Margery's course, been assessed and instructed by various social workers, I have learned enough to know that this adoption couldn't ever work.

Up to now it has.